his pretty little queen

his pretty little queen

NICCI HARRIS

also by nicci harris

The Kids of The District

Facing Us

Our Thing

Cosa Nostra

Her Way

His Pretty Little Burden

His Pretty Little Queen

Their Broken Legend

Black Label Nicci Harris

CurVy 13

CurVy Forever

ISBN ebook: 978-1-922492-15-9

ISBN print: 978-1-922492-16-6

ISBN Hardback: 978-1-922492-21-0

Edited by Writing Evolution. @writingevolution.

www.writingevolution.co.uk

Edited by Mostert-Seed Editing

www.mostertseedediting.com

Internal graphics by Nicci Harris

Paperback cover design by Ashes & Vellichor

his pretty little queen

this is for you...

The girl who is both.

The girl who is opinionated, brave, resilient, and will survive whatever the world spits at her...

But would much rather curl up at Sir's feet while he plays with her hair and swears, she'll never have to survive again, because he's there to help her live instead.

song list

His Pretty Little Burden/Queen

1. Take me home - Jess Glynne
2. You should know where I am coming from – BANKS
3. Mad world – Michale Andrew
4. Deer in headlights – Sia
5. Take me to church – Hozier
6. Heaven – Julia Michaels
7. Come as you are – Imaginary Future
8. Human – Christina Perri
9. Demons – Boyce Avenue
10. The sound of silence – Simon & Garfunkel
11. Here comes revenge – Metallica
12. Feeling good – Muse
13. Control – Halsey
14. Knocking on heavens door –Raign
15. Dear Society –Madison Beer
16. Happiness is a butterfly –Lana Del Rey
17. Whispers in the dark –Skillet

Go to Spotify to listen.
His Pretty Little Burden/Queen

darkness

is just the absence of light.

CHAPTER ONE

Eighteen years old.

DUSTIN OBSERVES FROM THE DOORWAY. Even though his reputation is impeccable and the nursing staff and every other fucker in this city are enamoured by him, I still peer over my shoulder to see if we have been noticed.

My hands shake, but I ball my fingers in tight to control them. The beeping of a machine draws me back to the little blonde girl on the hospital bed.

She looks like a doll.

Her face is like porcelain. Below the thin veil of skin, her malnourished body barely thrives, the blue of her veins like soft pen lines down each white cheek.

"Get it over with." Dustin's hoarse utterance cuts through the room, and I react immediately, cramming down my innocence and youth in order to take hers.

I sit on the edge of the mattress, my eighteen-year-old frame shadowing the tiny person already barely clutching at the seams of her existence. And while the perpetual beeping indicates she *is* still alive, her white, lifeless features contradict the mechanical echo of her heartbeat. She could be dead. She looks almost dead. Peaceful. I find solace in those thoughts, accepting the cold, heartless part of me that I need to finish this.

Finish her.

For my Family.

For Jimmy.

She knows too much, but that is all he told me.

And what better way to initiate me, to test my utter loyalty to the Family, than by having me kill a helpless child for him. A child who was involved in things her naïve mind could never understand. And yet, she saw too much, knows too much—that is the bottom line.

Do I understand it?

Yes.

They don't need to tell me what she knows. It doesn't matter. The *'bottom line'* is my loyalty to them and my faith in Jimmy despite her potential innocence.

The girl doesn't move. The clock ticks. The machine reminds me she has a heartbeat, and I grit my teeth. Lifting the pillow, I place it over the sleeping girl's face, pressing lightly at first, feeling my heart spike as I try to stop hers.

I press down harder, my mind retracting absently to keep myself—

She responds.

Christ. My arms nearly buckle as ice moves through my veins because *it* is awake—*she* is awake.

Alive.

Alive, Clay.

I fist the pillow, my fingers rushing with acid, the hot rage and guilt moving down the length of each digit. Rage for the fucked-up hand she was dealt that led her to be below the weight of mine. I press harder, and her shoulders start to lift off the mattress.

She moans.

She is alive.

Her arms fly up and swing, slicing through the air, frantic in their attempt to fend me off, but they are so small and weak, flailing around a faceless girl below a white pillow. And although I can't see her expression or whether her eyes are open or shut, I remember her face.

Without removing the killer weight of my hand, I lean back, then to the side, narrowly avoiding the swinging limbs as they convulse with desperation.

She is alive.

Her hand is suddenly behind her head, below the pillow, and for a moment, I think she is trying to yank the lower pillow away to give her space to escape, but her hand comes back clasping something shiny and solid.

She slashes at me with the object.

Roaring through my head, my brain barks, 'It's her or them.' The words drilled into me since before I could understand the weight of them. *"You're above them all."*

"You protect your own."

"This is your legacy."

"Your birthright."

The chanting continues while my heart races with every bullshit emotion I wish didn't dwell inside me. Didn't feed off the last slithers of my soul. My innocence.

This is the beginning of my legacy. Cold. Controlled. Unemotional. The catalyst that will keep me locked and theirs —the *Cosa Nostra's*—forever.

"Hurry up!"

Sweat slides down my face.

No. Not sweat.

Fucking tears.

I lose sight as they flood my vision, the room quickly blurring, just as something sharp drags along my collarbone. She got me. The seeping of blood wets my shoulder, reminding me how little time we have. The blood will drop to the sheets. I'll leave evidence—

I lunge forward into her face, so close now I can smell her shampoo and the sheets. So close I can hear her dying whimpers. So close I can feel the heat from her body.

She's alive.

I apply all my weight.

My heart breaks.

Hers slows.

Her body dwindles in strength. Careless arms flop and flail with the remnants of her young life. I hear a groan rumble in my throat as my eyes refuse to stop crying like a bitch. Just like my hands refuse to allow her to breathe. Everything bubbling to the surface. Rage. Loyalty. Pain. Guilt.

Then she is still.

And I'm so close.

No more whimpering.

She isn't alive.

Panic surges through me, but I don't have time for it. Jumping to my feet, I follow Dustin from the hospital room, wiping at my cheeks and forcing myself to feign a casual manner while the new echoing of her pulse runs a straight line across the monitor. A droning tone that follows us down the hallway and around the corner.

The sound is her death song.

And mine too.

DON'T FEEL.

After I remove my soiled shirt, I stand bare-chested in the bathroom of my family home and take a white-knuckled grip on the stone vanity.

I stare at the square ceramic sink, counting the drops of blood dripping from the thick, jagged wound in my collarbone.

One.

A girl is dead.

Two.

She couldn't have been much older than nine.

Three.

She fought back.

Four. Five. That overwhelms me with pain. She wanted to live. But also... a kind of pride. No one else will give her that sentiment. No one else was there to see her fight back.

Six.

Don't feel.

"Clay?" my younger brother Max mutters from behind me, a hint of surprise at my presence circling his tone.

I'm not often here.

I twist my face, finding him in the door jamb, once again covered in bruises from rugby or boxing or simply experiencing his young dumb thug life. *A life I don't know.*

His grey eyes dart to the blood gushing from the wound along my collarbone to the ceramic, to my pained stare as I hide my emotions from him, but the sinking concern in his gaze wrings them from me. My body wrestles with my mind, seeking a kind of comfort that has always eluded me.

A world of empathy and anger darkens his expression. That hint of wisdom fractures something in my chest, making me want to grasp at it.

Does he know what this is?

Does he give a shit?

Nah. Not him. Not Max.

As feelings crest, my throat tightens to restrict them, so I bark, "Fuck off," needing him gone before they overcome me.

Max's brow furrows, but he leaves, and I exhale hard with relief and loneliness—

I face the ceramic bowl again, struggling to remove the memory of the girl as my blood blotches the basin in evidence.

"You're so handsome. You look just like my father." My mother's voice startles me, and I look up to see her standing behind me in the reflection of the mirror. "I thought your brother was bothering you. I should have known you would handle him yourself."

Dammit.

She moves towards me, her lips forming a straight line across her flawless face as she assesses me.

She sees me, sees the regret. I can't hide it as it crawls inside my eyes, finding a home.

Don't feel!

Our matching blue eyes meet, mine instantly stinging with the onset of tears.

Maybe she'll let me...

Maybe *she'll* understan—

"Don't!" she states but recovers quickly, schooling her

disdain for my sensibilities and smiling tightly. "Butchers don't cry, Clay. We have nothing to cry about. Nothing is worthy of our tears."

She grabs a cloth, and I clench my jaw until my teeth ache. It's a pleasant sensation. It overthrows the need to burst with common sadness for the girl. And, pathetically, self-indulgently, for the eighteen-year-old boy within me who wanted to shake that girl back to life and protect her from her own past, her own knowledge, from being dragged into the dirtiest, coldest corners of this world.

Like some kind of hero.

But I'm not that.

I'm the villain.

I stand frozen as my mum cleans the gash on my collarbone. It seems so motherly—It confuses me.

But her expression, if described in words, would still be meticulous. Elegant. Smooth. "What you did today was only the start," she says, and I listen to her. I always listen. "You are not like everyone else. You are better. One day, it will be your job to weed out betrayals. To finalise loose ends. To make the tough calls."

I wish I knew my mother better.

I don't. Watching her work on my wound, I lose focus on her hand. Blood seeps into the sponge. The pink water snaking down her fingers taints her perfect white skin.

My temples flare. I don't like the marks on her. Protective over her, I snatch her slender wrist when I see the crimson streams draw lines across her flesh.

She stills with my hand cuffing her. "You don't want my help then?" she asks gently. "Good boy. That's very good, Clay. You're so strong."

My heart burns for reasons I don't understand. *That is*

strength, Clay. I am strong. I didn't want to see blood on her while she wanted me to be strong; whatever brought her in here in the first place, I can't say.

I'm alone in this.

That is what strength looks like.

A leader is always alone.

I stare at her blue eyes and delicate features, confused as to what she wants me to do. She is standing closer than I remember her ever standing, and my body twitches with discomfort. Wanting to recoil. Push her away. Wanting to wrap my arms around her—

Would she let me if I tried?

Would she hold me if I needed it?

What do I know about her?

Only that she is still young. Powerful. Graceful. That much is true. She's in her thirties, having had me young and could easily pass for my older sister, who could easily be in her twenties. Stunning too.

Stunning like a white and grey marble sculpture you admire but never have the courage to embrace.

I continue to stare, and she smiles, her red lips a slight curve on her face. She pulls her wrist free from my grasp, saying, "I'm very proud of you."

Then she leaves the room.

Leaves my hand hovering in the air, still wanting her close. To clean the blood from her fingers. To have her clean the blood from me... For a moment, for just one fucking moment—I cast my eyes to the ceramic vanity covered in my blood—I think I really needed to be vulnerable with someone.

CHAPTER TWO

A FRIEND of mine told me that good things come in threes.

Him: number one.

Him...

Clay Butcher—the man sitting at his desk across from our bed with the glacier look of importance, of power portrayed through pursed lips and two pinched dark brows. Blue eyes focus on his laptop screen. His chair is an iron sword and shield away from a throne.

Through the large full-length window, the morning sun sets a soft glow to the room, accenting the curves of muscles across his bare torso with light and shadows.

I'm glad he is still here.

This man is breathtaking. I've always believed in auras; my mum swore she could see colours around living things.

I wonder what colour she would've seen around Clay Butcher.

One thing is for sure, whatever the hue, it exists as

thick, tangible supremacy that even a blind person can appreciate. So, when he is gone—at work or the warehouse—his absence makes my entire world cavernous.

My entire world... Well, that's him... This house. The maids. Jasmine. The pillow stacks. The new sofa lounge by the poolside and the old wrought-iron one that now sits as an ornament in the garden. As it should be.

My whole life... *this.*

I'm not allowed to leave it or expand it. Not until he finds my dad and... *kills him.* Of this, I'm sure. Death is what awaits the man I share blood with, the one I don't know.

I tuck my hands beneath my cheek and shuffle my legs along the sheets, settling in further. Unable to tear my gaze away from Clay Butcher's level of perfection, I simply watch him work. And while he hasn't acknowledged I'm awake, he doesn't have to.

He knows.

He always knows.

"Come here," he says to the screen, and my lips quirk into a little smile. I roll my shoulders, and the silk of his bedding slides down my naked body as I stand.

I'm always naked in this room.

That's how he likes me.

My bare feet pad over the floor towards him, and just when I'm within arm's length, he shuts his laptop, slides it to the side, and leans back slightly, making space on the desk in front of him.

An action that speaks volumes.

Smiling softly at his silent order, I perch in front of him on the polished wood with my feet swinging, my knees pressed together, my hair dangling in long straight ribbons down each breast. He considers me with a knowing gleam that forces both nerves and excitement to the tips of my toes.

I wiggle them. His gaze darts down to watch my toes and then back up to settle on my face.

"You slept well, little deer," he says in a husky purr that assists the gleam in igniting my pulse. "You didn't even move when I came to bed. That's very good. Did you dream?"

"Of burning Maggie's chicken pie." I chuckle, remembering when our lovely cook had to use the fire extinguisher. Then, blushing, I lay my hands on my bare thighs to hide the way my knees inadvertently squeeze together as I say, "And of you, Sir."

He reclines further into his big wingback chair, saying, "Show me what dreaming of me looks like."

My heart does a double tap, but outwardly, I only worry my bottom lip while I hike my thighs up and let my knees fall apart. His eyes are unwavering from mine, but his intent blazes within them. After a few seconds, he drops his gaze to between my legs.

I blush immediately.

He drags his thumb along his lower lip, his eyes trained on my pussy and the underside of my backside pressed to the desk. The heat from his gaze prickles the little blonde hairs I have newly grown for him.

A smirk tugs at the corner of his lips, and he raises his hot gaze to meet my apprehensive one. "I said, *show me,* little deer."

He watches my throat roll, noting everything. He's always made me nervous, always set butterflies to flight within me, but now this part of our relationship is both absolute intimacy and a test for me to pass.

Can I touch myself and be present?

Am I comfortable in my own skin?

Have I moved on from what I saw—what I know—happened to me?

No. It's an easy answer.

No.

He knows this, too, but I try to please him, lifting my hand and touching the lips between my legs that are already slick in my desire for him. The wetness is a point of embarrassment as my finger slides through the thin slick result of my deep arousal.

I open my mouth, ignore the echo of grunting in my head—the blood-curdling sounds of my foster brothers' pleasure the day they all took turns with this body—and part the flesh at my core for the man who lies to keep me safe, who protects me with unwavering focus.

Even from myself.

The man whose touch can drown the voices, the discomfort while everyone else's, including my own, still scorches like a fire.

I touch the inner bud, and my backside pulses off the table when sensation zaps through me. A reaction of both phantom pain and real pleasure. I groan from my throat, hating the feel of my body as it responds without my consent, but I mask the sound. Mix it with a moan that is visceral because I'm torn in two wanting closure, to please him, to play and show him how comfortable I am in my body but also wanting no one to lay a finger on my skin but him...

Not even myself.

Not my untrustworthy hands. The same ones that gripped Jake's shoulders when he thrust into me. That convinced him I enjoyed it... *Did I? Did I convince him? Did he honestly believe I consented with my hands that night?*

If not with that, then with my pussy. I consented with that.

Didn't I?

When I touch myself, the muscles inside me consent when they pulse. And I hate it.

My finger trembles on my slit as these thoughts flood me. I don't want to feel what Jake felt. *"A few minutes ago, you were hugging me so tight with your pussy you didn't want me to leave."*

It wasn't me.

I did want him to leave.

"So pretty," Clay says, a hoarse timbre wrapped around his voice. "You still don't trust yourself, sweet girl. Don't be fake with me."

I stop touching myself and deflate on a little sigh. "Is it trust?" I ask softly. "I just want *you* to touch me. That's all."

"You don't trust your body anymore. Your pussy. Your fingers. *Yes.* You still trust me, but I need you to show me what's mine. Open yourself up in front of me and show me what your pretty young pussy looks like, but you're not ready. " He rolls the chair an inch closer to me, reaching out to grip the wood either side of my thighs. Enveloping me is the scent I love more than cookies and bread and melting chocolate and all the mouth-watering luxuries I now enjoy daily because of him—the scent of his cologne, of sweet cigars, and warm male flesh. "Do you want me to play with your body, sweet girl?"

I nod. "Yes, please, Sir."

"Such lovely manners... But you have to do something for me first."

I smirk, thinking about taking his cock into my

mouth, sucking him until he is the one who is raw with me. "I'll do anything for you, Sir."

A soft smile settles on his lips as he knows this to be true. I mean those words to my core. I'd do anything for this man. I've forgiven him for lying. For using me as bait to try to lure my father out of hiding. For hiding the truth from me.

Because he is my thorns.

The only person in this entire world to believe me, to care for me, to hold me accountable, to *want* me.

His smile flattens. "You covered the mirrors yesterday, sweet girl," he says, and I cast my eyes down to hide my shame. "You forgot to take the sheet in the dressing room down before you left the room. How long have you been doing that?"

Fuck. Henchman Jeeves—my personal henchman/butler/*rat*. I know he's meant to watch me, keep me safe, but he doesn't have to share all my fucking secrets.

I mumble, "HJ is such a dobber."

"*Bolton* is paid to be... *a dobber*." His finger goes to my chin, and he lifts it until I'm anchored in his crystal-clear blue gaze. "And you know this." He suddenly stands up, a wall of muscles erected before me and so close, so perfect, I struggle not to reach out and roll my fingertips down the rippling plane. I crane my neck to keep eye contact. "Come," he orders, offering me his hand to take.

"That was the whole idea, Sir, but I'm still waiting," I say, my teasing cadence laced with false strength.

His lips tick in a corner, but he says nothing, turning to guide my defiant feet towards the dressing room.

What does he want?

For me to look at myself in the mirror?

I can do that.

I only covered the mirrors because there are so many, too many, and I'm stuck in this house, and they are like shadows following me around every room, and I'm constantly glancing over my shoulder and—

He sits me on the ottoman in front of the mirror, that entire bullshit spiel halting on my tongue as I stare at the girl from the incident reflected at me.

My brows pinch into a scowl.

She's like a train wreck—I force a smile at the reflection of the breathtaking man towering over me in nothing but his black cotton pants because I can't trust myself to speak to him right away.

He drops down—the deadliest man in the city on his knees for me—blocking the mirror for a moment with his head. His eyes heat. "Now lean back on your hands, spread your pretty white thighs, and watch me worship you."

He slings my legs over his shoulders and dips his head. The mirror comes into view, the girl in the reflection already painted in the crimson glow of arousal just as his mouth sucks at my flesh.

Instantly, I mewl around, assaulted by my reflection and by the eating motion of his lips.

His touch soothes.

And I'm whole. *His.*

His tongue presses in through the walls clinging with needy desperation to the steady penetration. I want to squeeze my eyes shut so I can focus on him. Avoid the sight of me. I want to grab his head, but I can't stay upright if I don't brace on both hands.

My backside rocks and lifts, so he slides his hands

beneath each cheek to control me as he relentlessly fucks between my folds with his tongue, as he mouths me, as his lips rhythm crash sensation with sensation. Plunging through and out. Then massaging the supple soft lips as he withdraws only to spear me again.

My nails dig into the ottoman.

I do as he commanded, watching myself in the mirror with Clay Butcher on his knees between my thighs.

My eyes grow heavy when he slows down, flattening his tongue and licking up and down, then dipping in, only to lap over that quivering flesh again.

It's meticulous.

Like everything he does. As soon as a part of my pussy wants attention he is there, reading the pulsing muscles like I'm connected to him through tangible waves of sensory information. Like I'm an extension of... *him.*

I'm so wet; I still shiver with shame for that fact—my response to him will be smeared and dripping from his lips and chin.

He growls into my pussy, his feral enjoyment vibrating for a moment through me as though he is ready to actually bite down and rip off flesh. He's dirty and carnal. This regal man is completely at odds with every-thing he shows the world.

My mouth goes wide, moans soaring through the dressing room as the sensitivity that has me weeping into his mouth turns into severe heat. My backside clenches in his palms, so he grips the plump globes, spreading them to deepen his kiss further.

I buck again.

He laps his tongue up from my opening to my clit, where he sucks the bundle of nerves between his teeth, clamping on and flicking, igniting fireworks within me.

I whimper.

My legs jolt up.

My body convulses. But his grip on my arse is unyielding, holding me to him.

"Oh. Sir." My eyes roll with dizzying pleasure. "I can't. It's, it's too—" A long moan rolls up from deep inside me as I'm hit with a bat of pleasure, blackening my vision for a dreamy moment.

I tense up as my orgasm continues.

My arms shake under my weight.

I pant his name like I'm conditioned to do, watching my reflection as I begin to come, my hips grinding shamelessly on his face to increase the pressure, to intensify each perfect lap of his tongue.

I bat my eyes until they close under the weight of arousal. The rough bristles around his jaw graze, easing the needy skin as he refuses to relinquish the suction on my clit.

"*Oh* God!" I cry out, my arms buckling. My back meets the ottoman while my hands fist his crown, my fingers desperately knotting his dark hair for control.

I arch my back as the final waves of sensation swim through me, and he keenly changes his pace to suit the flow of my orgasm.

Slowing down, he mouths me between the legs as if he were kissing me better after a bruising make-out session. And it is a ridiculous thought, but I instantly wish he would kiss my lips like he is kissing my pussy. It is something that still seems rare between us—a simple kiss.

I run my fingers through his dark hair adoringly, the light above us highlighting the sparse greys that drive me crazy. Flattening my body to the ottoman, I hum my enjoyment to the chaste motion of his reverent mouth.

My body warms as he worshipfully moves up, skating his lips between my hips, along the plane of my stomach and between my ribs as I arch into him.

His tongue slides out to taste the sweat between my breasts, and then I lift further, desperate to meet him.

Our lips connect.

He's kissing me...

My world explodes into stars as we kiss with his possessive groans mingling with my exhausted, sated moans that are wrapped in deep everlasting sentiment.

For this man.

I feel *everything* for this powerful man. There is no one else. Not a friend, siblings. *Nothing*. Only him.

My number one good thing.

Hitching my legs around the back of his, my naked body slick with perspiration slides along him. His hand moves up to grip the column of my throat, his thumb lifting my chin to direct and control our lips.

Cupping his jaw to deepen our kiss, I feel his arousal brazenly hard between my legs, bruising and teasing.

I wriggle until his erection is thrumming along the sensitive flesh between my folds. I begin to grind on him, needy and desperate for more. To pleasure him. To plea-sure me. I rub along him. Back and forth with my hips.

His mouth becomes fiercer on mine. I keep kissing him even as it hurts, even as his teeth flare and his fist tightens, hissing air from me.

He locks his jaw.

Stops.

Stilling his movement, our kiss becomes one-sided as he says, "You want more? That's very pleasing."

I have come to learn he enjoys watching and feeling me as I move on his body. He could toss me aside if he didn't like it, but he doesn't. He likes me rubbing on him like a cat. Perhaps, he likes my desperation. Lifting my hips off the ottoman, I slide along his shaft, spoiled for more pleasure.

"Good girl," he growls, the twisted timbre revealing his arousal and restraint. "You try so hard, little deer. Can you have an orgasm all by yourself for me?"

I roll my hips shamelessly, chasing the sensation.

God, I'm tight all over, desperate for—*something*. Something is missing.

I become feverish.

After his mouth's assault on me. And now this. I need to prove I can, but I can't. I need him to finish it for me. "*Please*—" I let out the words through a tight moan. "Please, help me."

Clay's lips slide into a smirk against my mouth as I continue to kiss him clumsily. The taunting sensation burns in my ears. My pussy leaks all over his pants in anticipation.

"*God,*" I growl, reaching for my climax while it eludes me, feeling as though I will combust if I don't get off again.

Using his body to get there—

"Don't cover the mirrors again, little deer," he orders, lowering one hand to slide a finger inside me so easily a second joins almost immediately. "Oh, you're so wet. So tight. My sweet, sweet girl."

I close my eyes and clench around him, but when he thrusts in, he draws back out in quick succession. I buck to chase the deep penetration. "That's it. You're doing very good." He pushes in again. "Do you want another finger?"

"*Yes*..." I barely manage to speak, laboured breath beating hard against his mouth.

"You're so greedy."

"You make me feel this way."

There is amusement in his voice as he says, "I know."

"What about you, Sir?"

"Your pleasure is for me." He adds a third finger and it's unbearably snug inside me, so when he starts to move all three with the talent of a well-oiled machine, I'm blanketed in stars. "I need to stretch you. You're tiny. You have a little hole and a small frame. Every time I fuck you, you end up sore, and I need your body ready to accept mine. I need you weeping the moment you feel me, hear me, see me. I need you ready to take me. You will be shaped to fit my cock, walking around with my cum filling your knickers—"

My orgasm rips through me with a husky cry. "*Oh*." I pulse around his fingers as he rubs and wrings my climax from me. "Sir, *so* good."

His cock bucks with bruising need between us, but he is the master of control, ignoring his obvious arousal. With the gentle massaging motion of his fingers sliding leisurely in and out of me, he brings me down from my second orgasm instead of thrusting into me like I know he wants. He hasn't taken me in such a way in weeks. Not since I saw the recording and watched my body being used like a toy by my foster brothers.

I squeeze my eyes at the thought. Focus on him. He peppers kisses over my face as he says, "You haven't had many pleasures in your life, sweet girl. I promised to spoil you. I'll spoil your sweet pussy for attention."

I roll my head on the ottoman, groaning.

His kisses gently bring me down from the wave of pleasure I'm riding. They simmer with sentiment as my muscles unfurl and relax to the reverent affection.

Looking at him again, I tilt my head to see his are now closed, his dark brows pinched, his lips a tender rushing stream over my skin.

Then they are gone, and he is standing with me in his arms. A weightless extension of him. He walks me over to the bed and lays me down on the mattress, placing a hand either side of my head. And I know this routine.

"What will you do today?" he asks, and I deflate, knowing he'll be gone all day and I'll wait for him. "Don't look so sad, sweet girl."

I break our gaze, looking absently into a corner of the room. "What can I do?"

"Anything you want."

"You won't let me leave the house."

He grips my jaw gently, moving my face until my eyes relent and meet his—crystal-clear blue orbs bordered by dark lashes. Breathtaking. Commanding. "We have been over this."

"I know," I say, disappointment coiled around my tone. "I know. *It's not safe.* I guess I'll have more clothes brought up, or perhaps I'll cook that pork belly again or watch another movie or hang out with Jas—"

His brows weave. "This doesn't please you?"

"I should be grateful," I mutter honestly, although the humility is seemingly a tatted echo in my mind. I want to want things. I want to demand them. Yet, there is this voice, the same outdated voice, a small and breathy resonance, that reminds me to accept, to shrink myself, to fit in.

He steels. Then pushes off the bed, striding over to the dressing room, the lights growing at his presence. "I'm taking care of you, little deer." He speaks to the room as he dresses. "What do you want? Use your voice. Tell me."

I sit up and watch him. "I don't know."

His phone comes to life, cutting through the air like a knife severing our conversation. I frown as he stares at it. "Whatever you desire, I will do. Think about what you want." He grabs his suit jacket and the phone as it rings perpetually.

Then he approaches the bed, leaning down on his hands, his shoulders rolling, his chin dipping so his lips can take mine. His intent is a quick, firm, breathtaking kiss, but I know this, so I cup his strong jaw to demand more than a moment of goodbye. Deepening the motion of his lips, I channel all my want into them until a groan moves through his throat.

He breaks our kiss, his lips hovering close, commanding mine to stay still as he talks against them. "I want a list. Think on it. You will tell me what you want, sweet girl, and I promise to give it to you."

He vanishes through the door, and I'm left confused. I don't know what I want. Does he think I'm withholding something? Is that a thing? Like the charades of my intentions?

I don't know who I am.

How am I supposed to know what I want?

THE WATER of the swimming pool ripples as I swing my legs through it and watch distractedly as the substance twinkles and moves below the sun.

What do I want?

I'm learning to cook, which sings to my maternal side, and I know I won't be locked in this resort-like gilded cage forever, just until he finds my dad... And *kills him*. I swallow thickly, clearing my throat as heavy footsteps pour down the path.

"*Fucksake*," Henchman Jeeves pants, dropping forward with his hands to his knees.

My henchman/butler/rat...

Not happy with you.

He breathes through a kind of panic, having exerted himself to the point he's vibrating to get air.

Three guards are now halting from their run behind him, sighing with relief when they see me sitting unfazed by the poolside.

I blink at the dishevelled men. "What?"

Henchman Jeeves catches his breath before saying, "For the love of God, how did you get down here?"

And I know it was stupid and that Clay won't approve, but I don't lie when I answer, "I climbed down the fire escape on my balcony."

"She's going to get us killed," one of the henchmen hisses, spinning and sauntering off, curses soaring around him.

Henchman Jeeves slowly shakes his head. "*Why?* Why would you do something so dangerous and—"

I shrug, interrupting petulantly. "Looked like fun? The ladder is perfectly safe. It isn't like I climbed down a fucking drainpipe. I wasn't escaping. The ladder is right there on the side of the balcony. I just had to climb over the railing."

The remaining henchman grumbles behind him, wiping his rigidly set brow. "Don't tell the boss, Fawn, or..." His voice continues to run, but the words are mumbled through annoyed breath.

Henchman Jeeves frowns at him, scolding him with one snap of his gaze. "Miss Harlow." He turns back to me and offers me a faux smile. "It would be best if you don't tell the boss that you were by the poolside alone."

Fawn. I don't correct him and ask him to call me by my given name. He slips up often, but I know he must call me Miss Harlow now. I don't even know who Miss Harlow is, really. It doesn't seem like my name; I never felt like a Harlow. I was hoping to find my identity as a Nerrock. And I'll probably never be a Butcher... I sigh. "Would you get fired?"

Shaking his head slowly, he laughs without mirth. "I *wish* the answer was yes."

"He'd kill you?" I whisper as the other guards wander back inside the house, clearly annoyed, leaving HJ and his fixed gaze that delivers an undeniable answer to that question. "I see." I nod towards the retreating backs of the other men. "They don't like me very much."

He sighs, pity tumbling through his voice. "You do talk to your food more than you talk to them."

"Clay told me not to talk to them."

"I'll have words with them. Don't worry."

My hero. "They don't treat me like they treat Aurora. They treat me like a ward. Like they are babysitting... So do you now. We used to joke."

He looks regretful. "Fawn. It's respect."

And it isn't his fault or theirs. I'm an eighteen-year-old unrequited daughter of a mob boss and the lover of his enemy. Bound in inadequacies and eighteen years of an orphan identity to boot. No idea what to do from one moment to the next or how this half of society lives.

Privilege is kind of boring...

So, I get it—they don't know how to treat me.

Just like I don't know how to behave.

CHAPTER THREE

THIS IS Aurora's concept of happiness—clothes shopping with a bottomless account.

A spare room has been transformed into a pop-up boutique. I pull another pencil skirt off the rack, wondering how it varies from the previous one.

I peer down my body, at my Bambi print shirt—the one that made Clay smile—and the white flowy skirt that bares a lot of my legs, liking them far more than the piece in my hand—

"That's a lovely choice," a voice says from behind me.

I smile stiffly, and hook the pencil skirt on the 'maybe rack' even though it's a *no*.

They are all so same-same. Black. Red. Mauve. Dusty... *everything*. Dusty pink, blue, green. Why do we want to look dusty? Why is worn and tattered the new... *new*? The entire concept confuses my poverty-constructed brain.

But then... "It's better to stand out, than fit in," I mutter to myself, as my mother's entire philosophy in life tumbles into my mind while the simple, yet stunning garments around me guarantee I will do far more fitting in than standing out.

The middle-aged woman who is pretending to search for something *I* may like keeps glancing my way as though she has more words working their way around her tongue.

I pull out a cute white flowy shirt that might look elegant as a dress with a tan belt. If I get a size too large... I might like that. I present it to her, saying, "I quite like this... as a dress, though."

The woman shakes her head, and I frown, not surprised by her attitude. I kind of want to look the part so they'll respect me, so I go along with this. "That's a Valentino," she says. "It isn't supposed to be worn as a dress."

Right...

I keep looking. I've always liked op-shopping because there are trends and styles from every era. I enjoy mixing and matching and wondering what life the garment has already lived... It is one of the few things I remember doing with my mum.

She used to say we were different. I'm not sure I was anything really... an extension of her, maybe. Looking back on what I recall, *she* was *different.* Her opinions: wild. Her theories: conspiracies she probably never honestly believed. She just... wanted something to say. Even if she was absurd. At the very least, she was interesting. *Enchanting.*

Memorable, even.

She felt the same way about her appearance and mine. While other girls wore jeans and tee-shirts, I was dressed in flowing dresses, denim jackets, and cowboy boots. She hid in her boldness, in her bullshit.

"Be like the moon, Fawn. Light up the dark."

Then she put a bullet in her brain.

"I've been dressing Mrs Butcher since she was nine," the woman says, drawing me from my thoughts. She clutches at her red shawl as she approaches a rear rack of clothes. "And her style is flawless." She spins to face me with an expression of feigned politeness. She gazes at me like a project. A quiet cringe crosses her face before she recovers her retail smile. "*Why* don't we try something new? Huh? You know, there is a certain image that Mr and Mrs Butcher uphold and—" She gives me another once over. "You're stunning, young lady, but maybe we could change your style a tad."

"Fawn,"—Aurora's voice sails through the room, although I can't seem to place her, the racks creating partitions in the vast space—"has her own style."

She appears beside me, her long dark hair pinned up perfectly, her chin tilted higher than straight, a pleasant smile set into her lips. She places her hand on my shoulder; her support can be sensed in the weighted touch. My chest tightens with jealousy, with happiness, too, because I like her. *Gah*, it's a *sucky* situation. "Mr Butcher is quite fond of her style. Don't change her."

That makes me smile.

"Oh, of course," the woman says through a nervous laugh, backpedalling like crazy in the presence of this impressive woman. "It was only a suggestion."

"And best refer to Fawn as Miss Harlow." She looks at me questioningly, and I suddenly straighten under her gaze. "Fawn, you don't need to pick anything. If there is nothing here you want, Prada has a white poplin dress and pleated tulle skirt that I think you'll love. We can bring you others." She studies me as I nod compliantly. "You don't want anything, do you?"

I worry my bottom lip, working the skin as I contemplate how to avoid offending her. I do want to be more like her... "It's just not my *thing*." I squirm, my need to please twisting coils of reluctance through me. "But I understand that I live here now, and I need clothes, so..." I trail off because she laughs softly, her eyes crinkling at each edge.

"I find cooking tedious," she admits, sliding her hand from my shoulder to smooth my blonde hair down my crown. Her touch makes me sigh. "You find clothes shopping so. You don't have to be like me, Fawn. You can finally be whomever you want. I know Clay has told you to use your voice. Say what you want here."

She rubs my shoulder with gentle pressure as she turns to leave, and I follow her with my gaze until she is out of the room. The protective dominance she carries with effortless grace vanishes, leaving me with a little pout.

I realise I like her around a lot more than I like her absence. Having her close is a direct line to Clay. Having her close is like being close to *him*.

I turn to the lady, squaring my shoulders. "I'm actually going to pass..." I glance around. "On *everything*— Thank you."

***

"MR BUTCHER?" I question, squinting at a muscular, suited back. Clay's dad moves towards the double front doors.

At least I think it's Luca Butcher.

Dude looks super scary...

Just like I remember him.

It's edging 5 p.m., and Clay still isn't home, so I'm not sure why his father is wandering the halls. Not that it's any of my business what the comings and goings of a man like him are, or—

He turns to acknowledge me; blue eyes not unlike Clay's settle on me. Matching chilling orbs of power and indifference like a fallen angel might have. Beautiful, yet heart shattering.

His muscles are larger than Clay's, his form monstrous even within a black suit, and there wouldn't be much left of the person who decided this suited man was gentlemanly in nature.

The last time I saw him, he was watching my ultrasound with entitled interest in the baby in my belly. An interest I didn't quite understand like I do now. He is my dad's enemy. Just like Clay.

The baby—me—we were bait.

I wonder what I am to him now...

"Fawn," he says my name without emotion. A polite acknowledgement of sorts. "I was looking for my wife." I expect him to ask if I have seen her, but he doesn't.

"*Oh.*" I glance around the empty corridors, which is ridiculous because it's as though I must prove I haven't seen her by indicating her absence around us. I shuffle awkwardly, saying, "I haven't seen her."

Ugh. Clever girl, Fawn.

He smiles tightly and nods his response and his farewell in that gesture, but before he can turn to leave, I step towards him, my mouth rushing as my mind struggles to catch its heel. "Mr Butcher?" He stops, and I take a step closer to him. "Tell me about my dad."

"Luca," he insists, casually turning to face me as though I didn't just drop a bomb of a statement on his arse.

"Okay. Luca. Can you tell me about my dad?"

"You should ask my son."

"I'm asking *you*," I press, unsure at what point I became so ballsy that I'm ready to stand my ground while literally standing on his. Maybe it was Aurora... I can still feel her hand on my shoulder. A humming reminder to be myself. That, of course, doesn't stop my hands from shaking, so I reach for my hair, twirling a golden ribbon around my finger to avoid the idling tremors. "You said that you have known my father for many years—"

"My son will decide what you—"

"But you didn't tell me that you meant to use me and my baby to lure him out for your revenge, which might have worked if he cared enough about me, but he doesn't, does he?" I take a big breath and say, "I'd like to know why?" I hold that breath when the last word leaves my lips. Realisation settles. I interrupted him and poked at him without any knowledge of the kind of man he is or how he would respond to my surfacing contempt. I don't hate him. I don't think I like him though. Which only lumps him in with almost everyone else I've met.

They lie.

They use.

He did both.

He remains neutral, eyeing me with scepticism shifting over his rough, hard features. Then a hint of approval taps at a corner of his mouth—a tick of a grin. "Okay. Let's discuss your father. But if you are set on talking business with an old man then it would be customary to offer him a whiskey."

I breathe out my relief, nodding at him in agreement. "Okey dokey. I can do that. Clay keeps his whiskey in the office."

His grin slides a hint further, and his arms widen, indicating that the next move is mine. That I should lead the way. It's a kind of act because, I am certain, he knows exactly where the whiskey is kept.

Even though I know the way to Clay's office, I second guess myself at a few corners in the hallway, but Luca pretends not to notice.

When we enter the rich navy-blue office space with the delicate wooden trimming around the recessed ceiling, I rush towards the glowing cabinet and cringe as I try the glass door, hoping it's unlocked.

It is.

I pour into a short glass, stopping at about halfway up the globe, but as I go to screw the cap back on the bottle of whiskey, Luca says, "And one for yourself, my girl."

I look at the carpet and notice the cream-coloured fibres entwined with slightly darker ones, the image of me on my knees as I tried to rip the miss-coloured fibres out flashes behind my eyes.

I clear my throat.

Pouring myself a glass that matches his, I ignore the memory. I sit down on the sofa opposite him, setting his glass down on the table between us. And his silence is so powerful; I bet men and women spill all their secrets and show all their cards as he assesses the scene in effortless pensive silence. "I don't know what to ask because I don't know anything about him. All I know is that he is my

blood, and everyone hates him, and I can't help but feel—
Were you ever... *friends*?"

He grabs the glass. "No." He leans back and hangs his
thick arm over the back of the leather sofa, rocking the
amber liquid in his glass with his thumb and forefinger.
"I despised him from the moment we met."

I swallow hard, those words moving deep into my
heart as though he were talking about me. I lift my chin
to hide the vicarious hurt. "Why did you despise him?"

"You are not your father."

"I didn't say—"

"Bad blood within the Families isn't uncommon, but
made men take an oath and we keep the peace. There is a
lot of bad blood when it comes to your father and the
people I care about. A lot of pain. Deceit. A lot of disappointments. You—" He pauses, measuring me up, and my
chest tightens under his scrutiny. "Your existence, my
girl... is not part of those disappointments or that bad
blood."

I exhale hard over the sentiment laced through that
statement. Despite the fact I can't read him for the life of
me, he clearly has a view of my very visceral thoughts. I'm
as transparent as a glass castle. Behind that thin sheath,
I'm testing my place within his family, dipping my toe in
to see if he'll accept me.

He nods at the whiskey I have clutched in my lap, and
I smile, bringing it to my lips. The smoky scent that
reminds me of Clay caresses my nostrils, then my mouth
as I take a small sip. It is like drinking a bushfire that tore
through vines of overly ripe fruits and berries. It is sweet
and chaotic, delicate yet masculine; I hum around the
flavours.

I fucking *love* it.

I'm a whiskey girl now.

"You like whiskey. Good girl. Now, what do you want from this new world you find yourself in, Fawn? It is a part of who you are, so what part of it do you want to accept?"

I swallow the woody fire and clear the scorched aftermath before saying, "I just want to be with Clay, be what he needs, but he's..."

Married.

The word drops into my mind quietly, my mouth parting to say it aloud. *He has a wife.* And I like her. Which makes this whole arrangement even stranger. It would be easier to hate her. The rational parts of me know that she is just his business partner, that they don't share a bed, have never shown any sexual affection, just mutual respect, but a part of me wants to be greedy.

A big part of me.

I want *all* of him.

A white dress.

To walk down the aisle.

To be his everything, like he is mine.

Happily-ever-after for Fawn ~~Harlow~~ Butcher.

"Aurora will not give my son children," Luca interrupts my thoughts, another contemplation that must have played out across my face.

I slowly shake my head, saying, "I don't think he wants children, Luca. He was only willing to care for me because—"

"I wouldn't be so sure of that. Neither did I until later in life, but I found myself with them before I was ready. My son is smarter than me. He doesn't do things in halves. If he's a father... Well, he won't be like me. I made mistakes with them all. All my boys suffered, but with Clay—Clay was basically an orphan, like you, my girl."

"You did give him family. His brothers. There is so much love between them. I—"

"They created that bond all by themselves. They could have been at each other's throats, but they weren't. I don't know who that bond is accounted to... but it sure as hell is not me."

"You are too hard on yourself—"

"None of that. Don't soften the situation for my benefit, girl. Listen and understand," he states, and I hold my breath along with my innate need to comfort him. In that way, he's just like Clay. He's discussing his mistakes, showing a sense of guilt, but that's only half of what he's saying.

What he's really saying is: 'I fucked up. I want you to know that I fucked up, and I'm accountable for it, but you may not make me feel better about it or console me.'

Are all men like this?

I wouldn't know. If I'd had a dad or even an uncle, maybe I would have a point of reference.

I think Luca and Clay would prefer me to stone them for their mistakes rather than forgive them. As though neither of them has a person to show them forgiveness, to allow them to wallow in their mistakes, to *grieve them.*

He goes on, "The fact is, I saw Clay exactly thirty-six times from the day he was born until he turned twenty-four. I loved another woman and the pain of seeing her with your father was more than I could bare to witness, so I spent every damn moment I could away from the District. Away from my family. I was a shitty, selfish father, and I did what I wanted. I boxed. I ran boxing gyms and the competitions for the Family all over the world. That is where I lived my life. I did it because I refused to see her in his arms. So, I don't need my failings forgiven or softened, Fawn. I need the right woman in my sons' lives moving forward because I neglected to give them the right one at the beginning. So are you prepared for the part you need to play?"

He doesn't love his wife; he loved *my dad's* wife... My heart pounds in my throat. "Is that why you hated him? Because you loved her?"

"I was right to... " His gaze loses focus as he stares at the glass of whiskey rocking back and forth in his fingers. Then he says, "Madeline and I had a son together, and... *dammit...* I knew if he thought the boy was his, he would love him, so I stepped aside. And I proved to be the worst kind of father as it stood, but he knew, *somehow.* Or someone told him. He tried to have the boy killed—my boy with his mother's green eyes. *Konnor.* Everything changed from there. The bad blood was rancid. There was no going back. Are you prepared for what that means for your father?"

I take another sip of my whiskey, using the delicious liquid to bide me some time while I contemplate.

My father tried to have a child killed simply because he was not his own blood.

Who does that?

A smile hits the corner of my lips at the memory of Clay swearing to care for my baby and me, asserting that the baby is his despite the blood father.

My heart steadies.

And I know I want to be the *right* woman for him because he chose me when no one else did. I'll choose him now. I'll choose him forever. "What part do I need to play?"

"You're very young—"

"I'm not weak—"

"No." He nods slowly, his blue eyes panning my resolute face as though he can measure my strength like he's the authority on the subject. "No, you're not."

CHAPTER FOUR

MY YOUNGER BROTHER, Xander, lands a hit on the side of Eddie's jaw—a heavy-weight champion twice his size—snapping his head to the side, splitting his lip open, and spraying the ringside table and the white dress shirts of the *Cosa Nostra* associates.

They revel in it. But I despise watching my youngest brother bouncing between those ropes, receiving and delivering the violence. It shouldn't be him. He wasn't meant to be part of this corruption.

He was meant to get out. Be better.

I bite down on the cigar in my mouth as the room booms and shakes with barks and calls, the youngest Butcher brother invoking chants from the crowd.

"The Butcher."

The origin of our last name. A name they used when my father lived in Sicily as Paul Lucchese before he moved to Australia and recreated himself as Luca 'The Butcher' Butcher. And now, his youngest and brightest breathes life back into that legendary boxing name.

"The Legend." The room echoes the term, provoking

melancholy to settle inside me. I've watched my father fight on the television more often than I've had a meal with him. I've heard the chanting of "The Legend" more times than I've heard him greet me.

It's a pity my brother wants the same life instead of using his massive brain to finally take the bar. I never wanted this for my baby brother, the gentlest of us, even as he spills crimson fluid to their chanting.

Yet, as I gaze across the arena, landing on the Irish as they bet with counterfeits, and the tellers as they clean their money with the real prints from the public, a slow smile settles on my lips.

It's an idealistic setting.

A poetic one, even, when a Butcher spills a pint of fresh blood in this space while the workings of our corrupt empire play out seamlessly.

Boxing is a Butcher space.

We may have bought abattoirs under the ex-Don's— Jimmy Storm's—regime and used them to manage the Family's dealing and rid us of waste. We may run diamonds across the borders for the Family and control the fisheries and the meat industry, but *boxing*—I stare at my young brother once more. *Boxing is a Butcher's world.*

My world.

And this is my new order.

My father sits on the far side of the knotted blue ropes, his fists set in tight balls in front of him as he watches the match. His eyes cut lines around the ring, following the motion of Xan's jabs as though he holds a string to each thrust.

Across his sharp features, the ghost of concern fights with pride. We can't keep the kid out of the ring. The world can't keep the ring out of a Butcher's soul.

at me for a moment, and I smile. "You've got it," he growls.

He thunders away, shouldering his passage through the disorderly audience that is now on its feet, the chanting like tangible waves of intimidation my associate seems desperate to escape.

"Butcher! The Legend."

I watch him leave.

Turning back, now alone, I tower over the arena. *My space.* I gaze past the ring at my brothers as they pat each other on the back, celebrating Xander's win. And at my father, who accepts Bronson's commentary and understands Max's nod of approval...

I now stare at the Irish. The Capos. The sharks.

Perhaps devotion and utter loyalty are unrealistic expectations at this early stage in my reign. In the meantime, I will, of course, settle *for fear.*

CHAPTER FIVE

"SHE'S BEEN in the bathroom for over an hour," Bolton calls after me, hesitation and uncertainty tightening his vocal cords, not unlike my palms will be to his jugular should she be in any discomfort.

When I push the bathroom door open, the steam blankets me, curling around my body as I stride over to where she sits. A tiny figure amidst thick humid air. She's huddled on the tiles, her knees held to her chest by her slender arms.

The faucet is pivoted to the wall, creating a stream down the white porcelain tiles, a mild spray misting the air. I wonder for a moment how she reached the head in order to twist it. Quickly noting the small step in the corner, I frown at the image of her carelessly bracing herself on top of it.

I walk straight into the shower when I hear her little sigh. My heart shatters at the vision of her so tiny. The need to wrap my body around hers, to visually give her mass, muscles that shield her, is consuming.

She stares ahead, lost in the white marble until I slide

down beside her. Scooping her up, I position her between my outstretched legs. She rests her head on my dress shirt which is slowly absorbing the spray of water from the faucet above.

When I tilt her chin, two big apologetic eyes lock on me. "I'm not sad. I just sat down, and it was nice."

Lies.

"We don't lie to one other, sweet girl." I push the wet blonde strands from her pinkening cheek. "It'll get better." Light streams of water trail down her face, a coat of mist collecting on her, settling in tiny beads. "I'm not a soft man. I won't always say or do the right things. You're a young woman and you need a mother. Or a sister. But all you have is me. Forgive me if I don't comfort you the way you need."

She sighs, batting her blonde lashes, opaque watery orbs collected between the bristles bursting on her skin with each slow flutter. "This works, Sir." She rolls her head on my shirt, nudging me gently. "You're all I need."

"Look at me," I order, bringing my hands up to cup both of her wet cheeks. She lifts her head obediently and then crawls around my lap until she straddles my thighs.

Her body is completely exposed, open. Pert breasts— sloping perfection to her delicate ribcage. Her nipples— bullets that twitch my cock.

Her nervous habit kicks in; absentmindedly, her fingers make work of her wet hair, twirling thick wet ringlets around each digit.

She peers up at me and her eyes hold my breath in my throat—brilliant green and silvery-blue. Unparalleled in their beauty but also in such vivid pain.

My forehead tightens.

I want to see those enchanting orbs shine, bordered

in crinkles of glee, clear from ghosts and memories, steady with pride and determination. With happiness. Hope. Love... for *herself.* "I know you don't see what I see, little deer."

She looks away, her lower lip vibrating as she tries to fight the pull of her emotions. "I see the girl in the recording. The one who didn't fight for herself but travelled all over the city to fight for her brother, to find his killer."

Her jaw wrestles with tremors within my cradling palms. And dammit, if I could trade my life to change hers, I would. "Sweet girl," I say, encouraging her to look at me again with the gentle tilt of her face. She does. "The girl in the footage is a survivor... Do I seem like the kind of man who loves easily?" Her breath hitches at the word— love. I don't say it often, but I say it enough. Perhaps she needs to hear it more. "I love you, little deer, and I will love you even when you won't, even when you can't. So you don't need to right now."

"And you say you're not a soft man," she says, her brows pulling with, her gaze filling with tears.

"You have the most enchanting eyes; I blame them."

"You can talk." She looks adoringly at me. "You are the single most beautiful person alive, Sir."

I sigh roughly; she is damn blind. "If only you looked in the mirror more. Now, sweet girl, give me a smile."

She offers me a sad smile for my order, so I kiss it firmly, feeling her relax into the kiss. Her backside shifts along the taut muscles in my thighs, her pelvis making a rolling motion that stiffens my cock.

Allowing her bare pussy to grind along the fabric-covered bulge of my shaft, I eat at her mouth as she fumbles in her need for pleasure.

I stifle the growl fraught within my throat as her little

dance right now and the enduring discomfort from this morning has the man in me barking to sink into her. To fill my girl with cum, to fill her with—

I shake the thought. My hands slide into her wet crown, fisting the strands tightly so I can tilt and kiss along her face, her jaw, her throat. The roll of her nervousness massages along my tongue when she swallows.

She moans with her chin to the ceiling, her pussy grounding down on my shaft to its husky tempo, her mind disappearing again in the pleasure.

I won't take her. *Dammit,* I want to. I will not allow myself to take her until she forgives herself. Until she sees what I see when I look at her. I won't allow her to hide behind my arousal, to love herself through *my* desire.

My lips skate along her collarbone before I bite the ridge gently and then drag my tongue down. Sliding my hand to her back, my palm spanning out, I push her spine towards me. She bows beneath the pressure, her chest rising, her nipples meeting my eager mouth. I lick at the pebbled bullet—one of my favourite parts of her impeccable body.

They are a contradiction to her classic, soft femininity. While her every curve is smooth and subtle, her nipples scream she's made to be fucked like an animal. They engorge and flush with rich blood, lengthen and expand, creating a sinful little bullet that makes my cock leak.

Her moans become throaty as I give my sweet girl the attention she needs. Sucking, mouthing, licking the malleable, pulsing little tubes.

Her hands move into my hair, and my body vibrates with the need to fuck her, so I need to do something I crave just as much as my own release. Something I have become rather addicted to, and she deserves. She deserves her pleasure. All the pleasures I can give.

Her nipple pops from my mouth as I demand, "Stand up, sweet girl." I grip her hips and aid her as she climbs to her feet. I gaze at her pretty pussy, newly dusted in short blonde hairs that harden my cock to the point of pain. "Put one of your knees on my shoulder and grind on my face like you do my thigh when I play with your tight body on my lap."

A whimper escapes her.

Panning my fingertips up the back of her thighs until I get to the creases of her backside, I enjoy the way her skin prickles beneath my touch.

I cover each cheek and lean into her while she lifts her knee and rests it on my shoulder. Her pussy becomes a slightly open slit. "You have changed me. Very few things affect me. Less change me."

I push her into my mouth, and her hips don't shy away from grinding on my jaw and lips. Flicking my tongue out and tilting it up to the bundle of nerves above, I massage around her plump little clit.

I hear her arms meet the tiles, hear a sigh leave her. Glancing up, I catch her rubbing her brow on her forearms. Her hair falls in a curtain around her face. I take a moment to appreciate the way her breasts hang full and pert, how her flat stomach tenses, and her lips purse into a heart shape.

Stunning.

My sweet girl.

I smirk against her, possessive and proud I'm the only man alive to have touched her. *Alive...* Those dead fuckers who touched her still haunt her...

Mine.

I drop my attention to her glistening little pussy, the scent of her sweet womanly flesh steadying my world. "This pussy," I say, licking slowly and speaking into her warm supple skin, "lingers in my mind all day."

I concentrate on her plump pink clit. Like her nipples, it's made to drive a man out of his goddamn mind. Not shy and elusive. No, not my sweet girl. Her little clit is fucking erect and hard, begging me to eat it. Her flavour is rich, salty, sugary, and feminine in every damn way.

The spray of the shower has completely soaked my trousers, the fabric sticking to my thighs. I thrust up into the material, groaning as I eat her out, eager to get her juices on my tongue.

She weeps in my mouth—such a wet girl. Her hips meet the motion of my tongue, working her pelvis in circles to the meticulous rhythm.

I thrust in deeper. Her sweet, pussy clenches and clings and it takes my entire focus to not grip her backside, flip her to her spine and stretch that rippling little cunt open around my cock until she can't breathe from being so full of me.

Growling, I fist her arse cheeks as the tension spreads through my muscles, scorching a path around my limbs. It's hot and agitating, provoking me to act on that impulse.

I flatten my tongue to her clit, work two fingers inside her pussy from behind, scoop them to hit the wall of her arsehole, and knead the tissue hard.

"*Ahh!*" she cries out, her throaty moans rolling into groans and whimpers as she comes on my tongue. "Sir. Yes. Yes." She acknowledges her screams belong to me, using her name for me in the throes of her pleasure.

My good girl.

I begin to kiss the swelling flesh, sucking all the feminine juices pooling around my fingers. Lapping around them, I tease her sensitive skin, and she bucks and writhes as the last few shocks of sensation twitch through her.

She drops, her knees hitting the tiles on either side of my body, her head seeking sanctuary in the curve of my neck. She pants against me. "Let's get out of this shower, little deer. And from now on, I want you naked and warm in my bed when I get home. Now say, yes, Sir."

She lifts her head, her dual-coloured eyes hazy from her orgasm. "Yes, Sir."

I stand with her legs wrapped around my waist and walk her through the bathroom before setting her on her feet by the heater. I flick the vent fan on. Feeling an intense sense of importance being her caretaker, I wrap a white Egyptian cotton towel around her narrow shoulders, before beginning to undress myself.

After pulling on a pair of jeans, fatigue hits me but my mind drifts to the range. I need to fuck or shoot. My cock is rock hard, and my little deer can't keep her eyes off me, watching my crotch as I tuck her in.

"Why—" She falters, as I slide the silky sheets up her naked, sated body. *Is it enough? What I'm offering her?* She's a goddamn young girl who has crawled her way from one place to the next, never finding a sense of home, and *dammit*, I thought taking care of her was simple. Routine. A sequence of necessities. Warmth. Pleasure. Sweet food bursting from between her lips. A moist pussy. Those things, I can do. Looking after her isn't like running a *damn* organisation. I have no fucking clue what to do with this girl to stop the pain... to give her meaning each morning now that she is no longer striving to just survive—

She watches me watch her, her eyes growing heavy. Her relaxed state plays out with the steady rise and fall of her breasts.

I sigh roughly. I do know what her body needs. Despite how little I manage her mind and temperament. As I brush the blonde hair from her cheek, my knuckles sweep it over her soft skin. A fan of pearly-blonde hair creates wings around her. "I need you to trust me," I whisper to her, scrolling my eyes over hers, watching as her beautiful blonde lashes bat slowly, peace and comfort at my affections weighing them down. "I know what your body needs, little deer. I know when you need my tongue and lips buried between your legs, worshipping your sweet pussy until you shred the sheets by your hips. And I know when you need me to muffle your screams and bend you to take my drives like it's the last minutes of life. I know when you need a deep, steady fuck with my nose sliding on yours and our eyes locked. I know what your body needs. But you're still a teenage girl—" I touch her temple, tapping lightly. "I don't know what *you* need... I will fix this."

I only need to understand your mind better... Numbers, I understand. *Logical* explanations. Patterns of behaviour —If only there was a way—I frown.

Reaching into the bedside table, I retrieve a finger prick blood test. Staring at it, I flip it over in my hand. It's been in here since she tried to drown herself a few weeks ago. And tonight, she sat in a shower for hours, staring at a wall. *Eccentric,* emotional behaviour.

I don't like it.

I look at the sweet girl in my bed as she drops heavily

into slumber, the ghosts of her past dissolving from her eyes with each slow accepting bat of her long dense blonde lashes. I gently take her small hand in the large grip of mine and prick the tip of her index finger.

Her eyes fly open.

My good girl doesn't pull her hand from my grip, only glances down at the small bubble of crimson fluid pooling at the tiny puncture site. "It's okay, sweet girl. I'm just testing your LH hormone."

I put her finger between my lips, sucking the small bead of blood into my mouth and then kiss the pinprick softly. A hint of concern washes over her, so I add, "I need to know everything about you. I know nothing about the inner workings of a young girl's mind, and I want to understand your moods. *Rather*, I want to *anticipate* them."

"I want," she murmurs, unable to fight the pull of sleep, willing to trust me, her eyes close during a slow nod of acceptance, "a kitten."

Fuck me. A kitten? This is not the house for a kitten. It would be just as lost as my little deer in this cavernous estate. I imagine this request will elapse tomorrow.

I breathe out hard as I watch over her, from her slender neck to the small divot between her collarbone, her shoulders and arms, her hair thick and blonde like a Barbie doll.

I clench my teeth, wincing through the pain in my chest. I rub at the ache, never having felt anything vaguely this intense or... volatile. Like I could go from calm to feral in a second for her, and—that's dangerously out of character.

Just as lost as her...

Darting my eyes to the implement fisted in my hand,

45 mlU/ml displays at me in blue on the viewing panel. According to the blood tests taken during her stay in hospital a few weeks ago, that is well above what it was. She'll be ovulating soon. Perhaps now. Perhaps tomorrow...

The baby. The cooking. The pillow stacks. It all gave her meaning. A reason to get up in the morning.

Maybe a cat then...

I look back at her slumber-settled complexion. Sliding my palm down until I'm pressing it to the concave between her hipbones, my chest tightens. *Empty.*

Christ.

I rise to my feet. Walking from the room, I make sure to shut the door, holding the handle for a moment of hesitation. Leaving her again is utterly unnatural now, not unlike severing a limb.

In my mind, for only a second, I quickly remove any flitter of sentiment that may be active across my face as I notice Bolton. He's stationed a few metres away. I nod at him, saying, "Whenever you don't have eyes on her, when she goes to our room or the bathroom, I want you to page me immediately so I'm aware no one has eyes on her."

"No privacy for the girl, then, Boss?"

I glare at him, and he swallows, seemingly wishing the fucking question back down his throat. "I mean—"

I stride down the hallway, and his explanation halts at my dismissal. He cares about her, so I let it slide, but he best not misplace his concern, his sense of responsibility, for some kind of rights to her. No one has a right to her. She is mine. In every damn sense. There isn't a fucker alive I need to share her with—not a father or mother or sibling, and I'm insatiable with her, so this pleases me to no end.

The halls are quiet, so when my phone rings from within my pocket, I scowl, the sound loud enough to have followed my trail back to our bedroom. Loud enough to wake her.

I dig it out, noting the name *John* and fisting it tightly, barking down the receiver, "Butcher."

My new solider—recruited from the boxing gym—at the warehouse answers frantically, "The fuckin' warehouse was just broken into, Boss! I tried to see the men, but there is still fucking smoke everywhere. They smashed the windows, came through the sides, but I couldn't see 'em. I shot at someone. Think I hit 'em. But now the jacks are on their way here. I can hear the sirens. The road in is still black with smoke, so I can't see a damn thing comin',"

Heat builds through my head. "Who called the police?"

"Neighbours. The boat yard, maybe?"

"I doubt it," I muse more to myself than to him. "Are you alone?"

"Yeah. But all the guns, all the weapons are still here. They didn't take nothin'. I've been tryin' to stash them—"

"Don't stash them. The fire is still burning through the North national forest, so light the entire warehouse up and get out of there. They'll presume the fire jumped."

He pauses. "What?"

I rub my forehead, repeating myself, "Check the area. Check no one is inside. Then light it up. I'll talk to the Forensic Fire Marshal tomorrow; just don't be seen leaving."

"The weapons—"

"Will be unsalvageable," I confirm.

"There is somethin' else, Boss. There is... *are*..." He

falters and I have no tolerance for that right now.

"Spit it out," I command.

"They left you somethin'."

I still, dropping my tone, "*What?*"

"*Photos,* Boss... Of... of the girl. Lots of 'em..." He obviously wasn't prepared to have this conversation over the phone as trampling his steady voice are bursts of unease. "Some are dated, Boss. From *today*. From above. Like from a drone or somethin'. She's sittin' by the pool, with her legs in the water—"

I'm not calm.

The heat that scorches through this Butcher's blood boils to the fast beat of my thunderous pulse.

A blatant threat.

Dustin...

Or perhaps old Joe grew some Butcher balls.

Fucker.

He continues, "I'll take photos of 'em with my phone, send 'em to you so—"

"No," I state, outwardly staying still, controlling my breath, to not abandon the smallest twitch in case it's the catalyst for my temper. I need them in my hands. I need my girl's image in *my* hands... And he can't come here in case he's followed from the docks. "Grab them all. Light it up. Get out of there before the police arrive. Take the burnt off-road. The fire won't jump it. Go home. Que will meet you there and collect my possessions."

"Yes, Boss."

"And John—" I state his name with severity smothering my voice over—a warning of my own. "Don't look too closely at those photos. They are not for you."

He exhales hard. "Yes, Boss."

Good boy.

CHAPTER SIX

ABOVE AND BEHIND me the only window in the boxing gym allows for a thin slice of rectangular light to permeate the otherwise neon lit area, giving off a sinister glow.

Even during the day, without lighting, it's near pitch black in here. Being a solid concrete walled construction, set below the ground, it's also uniquely soundproofed— scream proof. I tested such a theory an hour ago when I watched a 120kg heavy-weight champion crush the life from the two morons who broke into my warehouse, but not before recovering the identity of the man calling the shots.

Now awaiting my words are two Capos and an Underboss from the District's *Cosa Nostra*.

Behind me in the ring, John shadow boxes, his hands high, his head constantly moving as he beats a phantom opponent. He's from a low-level gang with quick fists and an even quicker draw to compensate for his lack of... *Sicilian* refinement. But I don't need another business partner—I have my brothers and father—I need unquestioning loyalty.

Lucky Louis, the Capo across from me, anxious in his boss's absence, moves his feet with a rightfully hesitant shuffle. His brown eyes dart from the men I have scattered around the gym to the blood stain in the centre of the training mat.

"We haven't managed to clean it yet," I mention to him, my voice steady and ripe with mocking indifference.

He feigns a neutral gaze. "Should we wait for Joe?"

"He's here," I advise straightaway but give no further explanation as I take a step towards Vincenzo—an elderly Underboss near due for retirement and his Capo, Michael, who knows it. "Last night, two men broke into our warehouse, only to smash a few windows, and"—I omit the mention of my little deer—"called the police. Does anyone know anything about this?"

Vincenzo puffs out disapprovingly. "This is the Irish. I knew they'd turn on us eventually." He is a predictable bore; every discussion with him quickly finds its way to curse the Irish, the Japanese, the bikers. We have treaties with them, however rocky at times, but he's an old Sicilian man set in his ways. But not ballsy enough to ever go against the hierarchy.

"They wouldn't risk losing our agreements, Boss. Where would they wash all that damn cash?" His Capo, Michael, shakes his head in disagreement.

"They are no better than thugs, young Mikey." Vincenzo throws his shaky arms in the air, spitting out, "I never trusted them."

The arguing continues, intensifies, and I watch them throw the blame around like a grenade that may detonate in their unwitting fists.

"That's enough," I say, my voice not wavering, calm and direct. Silence descends at my smooth utterance.

Nodding at John, I wordlessly signal for him to retrieve our guest from the rear change room. It takes a few moments for my Family's gaze to drift to the man being dragged out for them to view.

Joe is gagged and flailing around but otherwise unharmed. I lock eyes with his Capo, Louis, who starts to pant in anger and shock.

"What the fuck is this, Butcher?" Louis spits out, his face glowing red with fury. "What the fuck are you doing?"

I smooth my hands down my tie while John pushes Joe to his knees at my feet and removes his gag. Spittle flies around the space between us as he gasps for air. "You're out of control. You're—"

I kick him in the face. Throwing him backwards to his spine. I provoke a grunt through his lips. He lays still. Hovering over him, I smoothly insist, "*Boss*. Say it."

He glowers up at me, his dark eyes flaring in defiance. "Not on your life, *boy*."

Sighing tightly with displeasure, I grit my teeth on the word 'boy,' wearing only bitter derision as my expression.

Turning from him, I head towards the seating, hearing a scuffling and the calamity of voices as John drags Joe to his feet. Forcing him to follow me, John does as he was previously instructed.

I speak as I prepare. "The two men who broke into my warehouse last night said you were responsible for the hit." I drag the knot in my tie down my shirt and remove the silk, folding it, and laying it over a seat. "What did you hope to achieve?" I kick my shoes off, listening to the sound of Joe arguing with John. "Did you want the police to find my stock? *Our* stock, Joe. Your Family's stock... Are you not with us anymore?"

I turn to face him.

I don't often get my hands dirty; as the Don, I don't need to. Which is why this is further significant. I choose to. Choose to handle this like the son of a boxer—the fucking proud son of Luca Butcher.

I walk to the ring, ducking between the boundary ropes, and step onto the mat. Silence thickens until I say to the men standing in wait, "He is not with me. I understand that Jimmy allowed you to take a peacekeeping stance when it came to Dustin. It was a Butcher issue." I chuckle contemptuously. "I know you were allowed to maintain your relationship with him and his operations. I am not that generous. You must pick a side... Joe already has."

I bounce from foot to foot, the familiar texture of the padding filling me with both pride for the Butcher blood coursing through my veins and with rage that its rule was ever questioned. *Boy.*

"Don't forget to knuckle him," I remind John, rolling up the sleeves of my dress shirt to each elbow, revealing the ink lacing the muscles in each coiled forearm. The knuckles are to offer him a final favour, for this isn't a match; it's an execution.

"Yes, Boss."

I stare at Joe, his eyes fixed on the brass now snug within the web of each of his fingers. The weight of that metal often washes over a man like artificial—borrowed—power. I won't be knuckled. I plan on beating him the same way my father would, the same way my younger brother Bronson took down the man Joe fondly called "*Boss*" for most of his life.

"Let's do this then, boy," he snarls, curling his lips and bracing both shiny fists before his face. "Don't pretend this is just about Dustin. This is about the young pussy you are now playing with each night. Dustin's trashy daughter. Do all our associates know that you have her captive in your house?"

I let him talk.

He glares at me over the glistening brass as he continues, "You can kill me, boy, but this is bigger than you are. He will get the girl and the baby.

He thinks she's still pregnant...

"Dustin is the only man the blue collars will work for, the only man who the bikers will work for... Jimmy knew this; Dustin grew up with half of those thugs. He was the man in these parts well before *Cosa Nostra* ever landed in the District. They don't like Sicilians. You're never going to win. You really are just the dumb fucking son of a boxer, *boy*."

He's working with the bikers.

Dammit.

Madonna Mia; I know where to find Dustin.

Hiding in the Stockyard Motorcycle Club compound out beyond Morrup.

Fucker.

He is completely untouchable there, within their solid brick walls and barbed wire fencing. Protected from the press. From civilians. Protected by petty outlaws... Dustin wants a damn blood bath. It'll be the biggest gang war ever recorded in the District, and as the mayor, I'll be forced into appearing transparent when the streets bleed.

I'll have to give the media some kind of propaganda, a kind of constructed truth and still manage to hide my part, my family—*my little deer*. This is where, previously, I would have bid Lorna control the leaks of information... but after breaking our relationship to be loyal to my little deer, well, I doubt she is eager to aid me. My only hope is that she has maintained a healthy and intimate relationship with my *wife*.

Can I buy the bikers out?

They are like fucking animals.

The casualties will be immense.

Dustin knows this, too.

Joe's impatient, his growl ripping me from my thoughts. They are all edgy the first time they are knuckled. Eager to see what a thick piece of metal can do to the skull of a man. He thrusts forward towards my face. I duck to the side, and when his shiny brass fingers slice past my ear, I drive my bare fist into his nose bone.

His head snaps backwards.

Louis barks something from behind me while Joe's groans fill the empty boxing gym. The old man squeezes his eyes shut, trying to find purchase.

I wait for him to regain his vision, and when he does, he roars, rushing me, so I jab him again, sending him backwards into the rope. He bounces on the bungee like a sack of meat, folding down the centre.

He's old...

It's not a fair fight.

But no less fair than slicing his throat open with a wire from the backseat of a car or shooting him on the sidewalk, or slinging him up and cutting pieces from his bones.

Her life hasn't been fair.

Dustin's trashy daughter—

And he took pictures of my property, of the most beautiful fucking images of a sad girl who has been through too much. None of it is *fair*, but this life will be more than that to her from now on. The life I give her...

My body creates a shadow over him, a creeping blanket that covers the light cast from overhead. I drop to my knees, hearing the word *"boy"* echoing in my mind.

"Hit me," I hiss at him, lowering my arms, unguarded, and welcoming, "hit me, my friend."

He lifts up with a throaty growl. Charged, he implants the brass below my right eye, opening my flesh. Blood pours down my face and into my mouth. I smile around the hot, thick fluid.

Then I lay into him.

It is an eye for an eye, a tooth for a tooth, but— *Dustin's trashy daughter*—I want all his fucking teeth!

I slam my fist into his mouth, ramming several shards of white teeth down his throat, provoking him to raise his hands to protect his face. I break the bone in his forearm.

Crack!

Another hit to the mouth.

I deliver punch after punch.

The next one harder than the last, hearing his disrespectful tone talking about my father, and thinking about the warehouse. The bullshit. The disloyalty.

Fucker.

His blood begins to spray my face as I slowly cave the bones into the soft tissue within, but I keep jabbing. Even as the blood gushes from him like a fountain, as it drenches my shirt, my face.

My knuckles shift around under the pressure, once broken and having never completely healed. I ignore it.

And I keep jabbing even as he stops moving, as the silence hangs ominously between each time my fist deepens the cavity now in his skull.

I keep jabbing.

Then I stop, lean back on my heels, and pant.

Still staring down at him, the unseeing glaze of death creeps across his wide eyes.

Boy.

I spit at him, the crimson fluid landing on the bludgeoned mass of his body. "Much better." I regain my resolve through deep breaths.

Slowly and calmly, I climb to my feet and turn to face the rest of my guests, knowing the sight of their colleague's blood seeping into my clothes will churn their stomachs.

I open my arms wide, smiling reassuringly, the metallic flavour of blood moving across my tongue as I speak. "I will not punish anyone else for his mistakes." Walking to the bench, I collect a towel, casually wiping the red fluid from my face and hair. I speak as the white towel is slowly dyed red. "Boxing is at the core of my Family. At the core of the *Cosa Nostra*. I realised yesterday that not everyone has the same respect for the sport. You have never been in the ring, no? And so, I insist you embrace it.

"Every Sunday, I will welcome you all to my gym, where a member of your firm will be nominated to fight. I pick the opponent. And Vincenzo,"—training my gaze to his stern but respectful eyes, I make clear—"the Irish will be here too. Our entire operation will be welcome. *Equal.*" I turn back to the bench and begin to pull my shoes on. They will not only be welcome, but participation will be compulsory. I don't need to articulate this, of course.

"The winner will get twenty thousand dollars, and the loser will... also get twenty thousand dollars. We will do business here after. We will bleed here. We will be a *Family* here." I walk towards the freezer chest on the back wall and open the thick lid, white vapour emanating from the gap. "I have a gift for you."

The three men approach carefully, and I watch Lucky Louis peer hesitantly into the steaming cold pit of the freezer. His face relaxes when he sees thick pink legs of pork.

Staring blankly at him, I notice he is fighting to look away from the tightly wrapped meat, still sure he'll see something unseemly. I lift a leg up to offer him, and he sucks a rough breath in when the side of a human head previously hidden beneath the produce comes into view. Dull brown eyes stare absently up at us.

I confirm, "The boy who broke into my warehouse and cost *us* millions of dollars in weaponry. The other boy is below him." I hand Louis the leg, smiling smoothly through the corner of my mouth. "For your family, *Lucky*."

Lucky, indeed.

For now, I might be able to keep their loyalties through fear, but it won't be long before they forget what brought them to my side. Wooed by the green I stuff into their fists; they'll forget about Joe. Enchanted by the life-style my generosity will ensure, they'll become loyal. And they'll be bonded in blood in the ring, intoxicated by the power rushing through them after their first win. But, of course, the lessons they'll never forget after their first beat down—

Constructed camaraderie at its finest.

Nevertheless, I have a war on my hands.

What I need to do now is to get my sisters-in-law, my youngest brother, Xander, and my little deer out of the damn District while I bleed the streets with the biker scum safe-housing Dustin. I need to lie to my family.

To keep them safe.

CHAPTER SEVEN

MAGGIE AND JASMINE NATTER as I pull the scones from the oven. Waves of scented heat suffuse my nose, making me hum my delight. I plop them on top of the counter, panning my gaze over the browning tops in approval.

Nailed it.

Spinning to find Jasmine already peering over my shoulder, the glee of expectation widening her eyes, I smile, not at all surprised by her presence. "Surely you aren't hungry again? These are big scones."

"I've only had a handful of Maltesers."

I tilt my head. "Ah, what about the egg and bacon pie, the chicken and avocado roll, and the jelly cup?"

She arches a mocking brow at me. "That is otherwise known as breakfast, lunch, and a snack. Now, give me a damn buttermilk scone."

I laugh, waving for her to help herself.

Then, the entire house prickles with static. Jasmine twists to face the entrance to the kitchen. Everyone figuratively behaves. The natter quietens down, the enchanted crockery all freezes into place, and my heart flutters to see— Heels make a dominant rapping sound of importance.

My smile slips slightly as Aurora sashays past the kitchen, rounding the counter. Then she is out of sight, but for her perfume, that adds a floral sophistication to the rich scent of the buttery scones.

She has a similar aura to Clay. For a moment... I thought it might be him home from work.

I dart my gaze to the scones, wondering whether I should offer her one. Then I picture her figure so— She is probably a kale and edamame bean girl... Yet another way she is like Clay Butcher. His words float into my ears, coaxing my lips into a smile again. *"I am rather addicted to sweet things lately."*

I untie my apron.

Plucking a scone from the warm silicon mould, I slide it carefully onto a plate with a knife and butter pouch and wander after her.

I find her sitting on the sofa in the living room. Her dark hair cascading like a silky night-time waterfall down her slender figure. Her spine is relaxed to the backrest, her legs folded elegantly, hands set on her thighs with the old book braced softly in her lap, and she looks even more stunning in this effortless evening state.

It's hard to bury the creeping vines of envy; it is hard to ignore her flawless beauty, her potent femininity. It's fucking *impossible* to ignore the huge diamond on her ring finger; the facets create all the colours of the rainbow every fucking time she turns the page.

I attempt to ignore the mocking piece of jewellery as I approach, but just like the fucking crockery in this mansion, it somehow appears animated.

I swallow thickly. "So..." I say to draw her attention. "You don't like cooking, but I bet you like scones."

She smiles politely. "Did you bake those?"

"Yes. Well, with Maggie's supervision," I say, offering her the plate.

She accepts it before glancing at the spot beside her. "Would you like to sit with me?"

"Um." *Yes.* I shrug a little to stop myself from saying that word. "Okey dokey."

"Have you ever read *The Secret Garden*?"

"No." Taking a place beside her, I lean back on the armrest, pulling my knees up to the side. "It's an old one, right? I've read a Colleen Hoover. *Oh*, and Erin Mc Luckie Moya has this Motorcycle Romance series called *The Hell Hounds* and that's really hot and the heroes are all—"

Shut up, Fawn.

"Never mind," I say through a chuckle.

"Well, this isn't a *romance,* but it has elements. Mary has just become an orphan and has been taken in by her uncle and he's—"

I laugh. "Bossy and controlling? Does she call him Sir?"

She chuckles huskily. "It's not that type of story. See, she's in a strange new place. I think you'll like it." Then she starts to read aloud from a chapter somewhere in the middle, and my nerves spark, provoking a twitch in my muscles.

What do I do now?

I shuffle a little.

As Aurora reads, the story unfolds.

Soon enough, I'm transfixed by her and the narrative. It is a unique experience to sit and listen and visualise. It's entirely unique to be read such words in her husky melodic cadence. And it feels nice. So much like what I imagined sitting with a sister might, or even a mother. It feels like family.

I lose track of time as she reads, lost in the garden with Mary and Dickon and Colin as they navigate their differences, understand them, and test each other, form friendships—form something like *family.*

"Everything is made out of magic, leaves and trees, flowers and birds, badgers and foxes and squirrels and people. So, it must be all around us. In this garden—in all the places."

"I like that," I say, pulling the grey mink blanket higher and nestling further into the cream-coloured sofa. "My mother used to say things like that. About magic and Mother Nature."

She gazes up from the worn leather book—and I have decided that all books should be worn and made of leather. Not clothes. That doesn't add up to me, but fashionable worn books make sense.

"Do you miss her?" she asks.

"No," I say as almost a punch to the air, and Aurora smiles in a way that challenges that declaration. "I don't," I press again. "She didn't prepare me for the world and then the world became hard, and people became mean. I never had rules before because, like, who would enforce them? She was never around."

Jasmine appears and kisses the top of my head. "Night, Fawn. I'm going home." She turns to Aurora. "Can I get you anything before I leave, Mrs Butcher?"

"No, Jasmine. That's fine. Drive safely," Aurora says politely, as she turns her large, *almost,* liquor-coloured eyes back to me. "Keep going, Fawn."

I smile at Jasmine as she leaves. "My mum would

appear, then disappear in the space of a few minutes. I was alone so much; that is what I remember most now." I look down at my fingers as I play with the ends of my blonde hair, muttering, "Being alone."

"Well, yes, but you also remember the magic and Mother Nature," she points out, looking back at the book with a peculiar curve to her lips.

"Yeah. I do remember her silly ideologies. The moon has power, ya know? It can cure anything. The earth, too. I embraced the spiritual side of my upbringing for many years, and I—I still believe in some things... to a degree. The moon does have a lot of power. I mean, the tides, that energy, it affects every living thing. We are full of water..." I stop myself. "Anyway, she was just ridiculous most of the time, though. I didn't have time to be ridiculous after she died."

I didn't have time for magic.

Or to miss her.

I don't miss her.

She taps the book cover with her slender index finger, her mauve-coloured nail making a gentle tapping sound against the hide. "Well, Mary is a spoilt little orphan who needed *more* magic and fewer rules, more ridiculous things in her neat un-fantastical life."

I raise an eyebrow at her. "You think I'm like Mary?"

"Well, your stories have similarities. Mary was very attention deprived, but... *No.* I don't think you're like Mary. I think *I* am," she confirms, and I frown, not seeing the comparison between the bratty girl from *The Secret Garden* and the bewitching creature that is Aurora Butcher.

"You're kidding, right? You're—" I laugh dubiously, lost for more words. "Perfect."

Smooth.

"I'm spoilt," she says, allowing my gushing statement about her *perfection* to go unexplored.

Thank fuck.

She continues. "I'm never alone. Wanting for nothing. But I'm entirely *unmagical.*"

"Your life is *magical.*"

"No, sweet Fawn. It's *privileged.* I don't remember the last time I looked at the moon. And I've certainly never believed it to have powers. The only *power* I know is the one wielded by money and demanded with a loaded gun."

"What about your mum?"

"My father had her leave the estate when I was young. They remained legally married, of course, until the day she died. You don't divorce in *Cosa Nostra*; a wife knows too much to be set free entirely. But me and my sisters? Well, he owned us, you see. We would stay here and be raised to be the perfect daughters so he could one day use us like chattel."

I'll never marry Clay Butcher.

The thought comes to me unbidden, like a whisper of unwanted truth. My shoulders sink. When Luca spoke of being the *right* woman for him, somewhere in my hopeful mind, I imagined we might be a traditional couple one day.

I gaze at Aurora, then at her provocative wedding ring, unable to shove down the urge to wince. I can't imagine a better-suited creature for Clay than her. And the truth is, I like her *so* much... but... her statement is just so... *definitive.*

I nibble my bottom lip as she studies my response to her words with soft contemplation. "Clay and I are both locked into this arrangement, Fawn," she finally says. "Don't let it change the way you experience his affections. See it for the arbitrary condition it is. Would you rather wear his ring around your finger every day or his body around yours each night?"

The click of the front door opening and then closing interrupts the intimacy of our conversation.

She glances back to see who appears through the hallway, although we both know it must be Clay as the hour is late and only one strong rap is heading towards us. My heart races in anticipation of seeing him.

Would you rather wear his ring around your finger every day or his body around yours each night? Her words sail through my mind, and I gaze once again at the oddly-animated-inanimate object on her finger.

Shut up, ring.

Had I been able to answer her in our private moment, I would have said, "His body each night."

Of course.

Clay enters the room and with him comes a thick, ominous current. Chills rush straight to the depth of my soul. I hold my breath but can't tear my gaze away from the gruesome image; under his right eye, blood has started to harden in an angry gash. Sprayed across his white dress shirt are frenzied red stains. The kind that came about through brutality, beaten from the source, hitting the material under immense pressure.

His hand grasps a small plastic animal carrier, the cage part covered in a pink cloth. I don't know what to do. Or say. There is something wild about the sight of him.

Contradictory, too.

Clay's eyes shift emotionlessly from me to Aurora and

back again, holding mine for a beat. I don't understand his expression right now.

He lifts the carrier and places it on the table, before unlatching the door and reaching inside to reveal an all-white kitten wriggling in his big, bruised hand.

My eyes widen. I jump to my feet, intent on getting to him, wrapping my arms around his neck and holding him until the callousness in his gaze melts in my love. A thank you. Or support. Anything to break this moment when my man and everything arrives late covered in bloody events but brings me a white kitten to soften the blow.

As I move towards him, he halts me with the subtle lift of his finger. My gaze instantly snagged on the raw skin and blood marring angry-looking knuckles.

He puts the kitten on the floor. It wobbles around, legs wobbly and uncertain, slowly meandering towards me.

I swallow harshly, rooted to the spot.

He nods to the kitten. "Stay. Play." And then he tilts his head to the couch I was sitting on before casually continuing up the staircase towards our room, leaving me in his absence, with a consolation prize.

I lift the fluffy white animal up with one hand, her belly the size of my palm, legs dangling over my fingers. Warmth spreads through me as soon as I feel the soft, fragile thing wriggle and a little meow squeak from her.

I study her. She has heterochromia, just like me. I smile despite the discomfort I have for Clay; she makes me happy. She somehow looks like me. White hair. One green eye and one blue. *I'll protect her.*

I squeeze her to my chest, and look at the empty staircase, wanting to tell him how she makes my skin warm.

How I'll love her, will look after her. How responsible I will be for her.

But he's not available...

I sigh. When it's about me, when my demons are surfacing and toying with our lives, he is like the sun.

Shining on me. I'm the only person in the entire world. But when it's about him, it's an eclipse, and everyone is in the dark, without warmth.

I remember when he tried to leave me after the incident at the pool, when he told me the fate of my brothers, after he took revenge on Lee in some horrific way. He tried to leave me in the dark then too. It was only my own pathetic drama that held him grounded to me. He placed my pain over his need to escape into whatever stoic façade he depends on to survive the evil in his life. Even now—I gaze at the little creature—he ensures I have company, affection...

Aurora stands up, reading me as my eyes flick to linger on the empty staircase where his dark, sad presence still resides. "Follow him up," she says without hesitation.

I drag my longing focus away from the direction he walked and meet her beautiful brown eyes. "He bought me a cat, Aurora. A white cat. My mum would have said she symbolises purity and innocence. She's good luck."

Aurora looks at the kitten, not at all swooned by its presence as I am. "Let's hope she is."

I tuck the kitten under my neck, her pearly fur brushing along my throat and jaw while she wriggles around in my hands. "I can't go after him. He told me to stay."

"He doesn't know what he wants right now. Go up

there and collect his clothes, shoes, everything he wore tonight. Put his clothes straight into the machine—"

I speak through a shake of my head, still picturing the blood all over his shirt, still seeing the violence in each slash of crimson. "I don't think he wants me to bother him."

She goes on as though I never spoke. "Join him in the shower. Remind him you're there. Let him be raw with you."

A sad scoff leaves me. "He won't let himself—"

"*Fawn.*" She steps towards me, getting close enough that I need to arch my neck to stare up at her, a flawless beauty, and my complete *opposite*—olive skin and dark liquor-coloured eyes. A regal expression laced in wisdom far beyond her thirty-something years. She tucks a blonde hair behind my ear, saying, "Just let him know he *can be...* when he's ready."

My heart seems to vibrate in my throat when her soft fingers skate along my cheek. I swallow around the sensation, whispering, "Is that what *you* would do?"

She eyes me closely. "If I were *you,* yes. He's very considerate to take care of *you.*" She glances at the ball of wriggling fluff. "Even when he can't do it himself."

He is. I snuggle into the fumbling thing at my neck. "Do you love Clay?" I ask, the words slipping out unexpectedly and breathy.

She smiles. "With everything I am. But not in the way that will *ever* affect your relationship with him."

The idea of disobeying him stirs inside me, a hot medley of both thrill and fear and disrespect. Not because I'm concerned; he'd never hurt me—*I don't think*—but disappointing him would be the worst feeling imaginable.

"Use your voice, little deer."

I want to be the *right* woman for him. Like Luca said. I place my kitten on the floor. "What about her?"

"I'll have Que organise a playpen for her."

Que, Jasmine's dad and Clay's Houseman, lives here so he is always prepared for what might be requested.

Looking at the kitten one last time, I nod my understanding, because he's using the kitten to distract me, and no matter how much I love her, I love him endlessly more.

He can't pull an adorable fluffy wall over my eyes when he obviously needs me. So I wander up the stairs, leaving Aurora and *The Secret Garden,* and my kitten behind for tomorrow.

In our room, I head straight for the bathroom where there is no noise, no indication of what I might find on the other side of the door.

As I push the door open, my pulse moves from a vibrating mass in my throat to a drum between my ears.

My breath hitches when I'm met with the most breathtaking blue eyes staring at me in the reflection of the mirror. Within the deep sky-coloured abyss, he can't hide the cracks in his pristine manner. Can't hide the crumbling of his control over his own emotions. Is that why he doesn't want me nearby?

I walk slowly towards him, the material of my little nude-coloured dress sliding over my thighs with each step. His gaze drinks me in with disapproval and anger and lust, and the caress of the soft cotton on my skin soon becomes a tangible promise screamed from the darkest depths of the mysterious man in front of me.

Clay's eyes stalk me as I slide up onto the counter, parting my legs to allow for his breadth and desperately trying to ignore the dangerous crack of energy between us. I part my lips to help breathe through his electrified aura.

Contrary to the staunch, hard wall of muscles in front of me, my hands shake as I find the buttons on his shirt and begin popping each one free.

Once open, I slide my hands over the solid rolling canvas of his abdominals and up over the thick hard plane of his chest. I continue over each shoulder, sliding the shirt from his arms and watching it disappear to the floor.

"You're so beautiful," I say to him, and he tries to hide his grimace, but I catch it like a butterfly. It was raw. I don't let it elude me. I saw it. I'm going to put it in my heart where I can protect it forever.

The slice on his cheek looks thick and swollen, the edges curving over a deep valley, the signs of the night's darkness strengthening the mark of pain and over-whelming emotion buried in his gaze.

I love you so much.

Let me in...

Beside me is a neatly folded towelette. I pick it up, soften it with warm water, and dab the nasty wound below his right eye.

And I've never seen anyone suddenly turn to stone before, but somehow even beneath the washcloth, I feel him harden to concrete. The emotions he was barely hiding are now gone completely, swallowed by darkness, replaced with cool, blue detachment.

My eyes fill with tears as I clean the wound. He only watches me. My heart starts to shudder with each burst of emotion, with each moment he doesn't respond. Will he always be like this? *Guarded.*

"Talk to me," I beg, my hand becoming clumsy as I try to clean the gash while the tears break free, clouding my vision. "Please, Sir, talk to me."

Disdain crosses his stern features when he catches my wrist, bringing it down to look at my fingers curled around the blood-soaked towelette. And something, a moment, a memory, flashes within his blue gaze.

He stares at my hand with a strange kind of melancholy that confuses me. I swallow as my nerves twitch, a sure warning to leave him alone while he's acting so chillingly unstable.

He pries my fingers open, removing the cotton from within my curled hand. It is as though he's buried so deep inside his own head right now, I'm afraid he'll struggle to find the surface soon.

"*Clay?*" I sob a little.

His eyes meet mine.

Then he shuts his, holding them like that for a long moment before, *oh God*, his forehead meets mine and he exhales hard. Riding down his breath is defeat—real and honest and painful.

I immediately cup the back of his neck to hold him to me, to accept the sentiment. Accept him. I cry for him—I know he won't—and he lets me do it while holding him close.

"A man gets used to being alone," he says, and I sniffle at the sound of his deep twisted timbre. "Then a little deer comes into his life, and she wants to open him up. She wants to let all that fucking evil out."

"I can handle your evil."

"*No.* You can't." He lifts his head, and I mourn his closeness instantly. "I won't allow such a thing." He leans in and kisses the tears on my cheek, dragging his mouth along the slant of mine, to my other cheek, where he breaks the streams of my sorrow with his lips. He licks a tear clean off my face. "Butchers don't cry," he lets slip, growling as his tongue comes out to lick the tears worshipfully.

And I'm not a Butcher.

Never will be.

That little statement stings, although he can't possibly know that. He adds, "I don't want you to *handle* any evil for me, my sweet girl."

I start to melt, feeling the heat from his body intensify, the burn from his words gathering inside me. "Let me be what you need, Sir. I can be what you need."

"You are," he utters, his tone deep and dripping in anguish, but also a kind of volatile arousal. I shuffle closer. It's welcomed. All of him. His lips on my skin. His hot breath cascading down me, coating me.

And he's going to let me comfort him, so I ready myself for whatever he needs, for what is clear as day in his body—

He tears himself away, taking one step backwards, abruptly ending my thoughts.

I whimper at the loss.

Steeling, he orders, "Now, be my good girl and wait in the bedroom for me."

Aurora's words resonate in me for a moment—"*Just let him know he can be... when he's ready*"—and they help guide me off the counter without allowing his dismissal to hurt my heart further. *When he's ready.* "Yes, Sir." I sober my expression and respect his order, leaving him in his own company.

Entering the bedroom, I immediately slide my gown off and lay it on my pillow. Neatly. I walk to the mirror to confront the girl from the recording, unwilling to let another day go by that I am not the *right* woman for him. To truly do that, I have to accept who I am, believe in myself, and see what he sees... what Aurora sees, too.

How do I help him if he feels as though I can barely help myself? How can I be his emotional rock if he's always mine?

The shower turns on in the bathroom just as I meet my own gaze. Staring at my naked reflection, my figure a slim shape with soft curves, I repeat Clay's words of affirmation to myself. *Brave.*

Resilient.

Beautiful.

His.

Powerful.

My breath vibrates as I sit backwards on the edge of the ottoman, spread my thighs, and for the first time ever, I really look at what was worth more to my foster brothers than me. The part of me that was more prized than the whole.

Is it trust? I had asked Clay this a few days ago. *Is it about trusting my own body?*

My body lied to me.

It lied to *them...*

When I held them to me, when I clung to their thrusts, when I barely fought back...

Tears scorch the back of my eyes as I press the tip of my finger into the crease at the top, sinking in until I hit the sensitive bundle of nerves, and then I slide down the valley. I twitch at the sensation. My skin flushes.

A single tear drops through my lashes. Continuing until I'm above the entrance, I push my finger in, curling my back to aid in seeking the depth I desire. The depth

I'm accustomed to with *him*... Moans sound through a tight throat—*a whimper.*

I whimpered for them.

The sound clogs my airway because that's a lie, too. The sounds of whimpers, mewls, yelps, cries, all lies, so interchangeable, so ambiguous. Am I in pain or pleasure — how do I know?

When they pushed into me, I whimpered and they egged each other on, fuelled by my sounds.

I start to shake under the memory, holding it all in, and then—I don't. I spear my fingers deeper, leaning forward to aid the depth, loving the sensation while sobs racket through my trembling muscles. Tears burst from my eyes, spitting from the pressure in my head, and I sob it all out, because it wasn't my body that lied.

It wasn't my voice.

It wasn't—It wasn't *my fault.*

It wasn't my fault!

Panting, I sit back and slide my fingers from the wet depth of my centre. I breathe deeply. Think about the man who I belong to, and how he belongs—just a little bit— to me.

He thinks this is pretty.

I look at my pussy again. I'm pink inside. *Pretty. He's right.* There are pleats of rouge skin, not unlike a rose; there's a silkiness to the flesh, not unlike the satin feel of the petals.

My mind drifts to the elegant face of Aurora, to the softness of her caress as she brushed my hair behind my ear.

Clay's wife likes women... So maybe if I belong to *Aurora,* too. If I become someone she wants around, likes around, then... I will really be a part of their family. Forever.

I twist my finger.

The muscles inside me cling to the penetration; they are smooth and responsive, and Clay is right about this too; they are *strong.*

When I purposefully clench my fingers, a wave of warmth moves throughout my entire body, peaking at the tips of my ears. I hum softly.

"Completely natural, little deer. Keep going."

Suddenly, the absence of splashing is deafening, and I don't know when that happened, so I jolt my head to the side and catch Clay leaning on the door frame to the dressing room, watching me with the beloved scorching gaze that takes every curl of my fingers up a notch.

"Don't you dare stop," he orders, rubbing the thick bulge of his cock beneath the towel hanging at his hips. He groans as he applies pressure, hissing, "Show me."

"You like to watch?" I breathe the sentence, even though I know the answer. I turn away from him, not that it helps. His energy is potent, and it spurs me on.

"I like to watch *you.*" His lips twitch in a grin; the now cleaned wound under his eye does nothing to lessen such a breathtaking sight. "You're so shy as you first reach between your thighs," he says. "Your eyes widen when you find a sweet spot. You blush but still press down on that special little place, your mouth parting in surprise when your body responds. Then,"—his grin grows—"you smile because you're so proud of yourself... It's the single most endearing thing I have ever seen."

My cheeks warm instantly, but I continue to explore with the soft tips of my fingers, husky moans twisting my words as I speak to him. "You have been keeping yourself from me, Sir. It isn't fair. I miss the taste of you in my mouth."

I hear the arousal in his voice as he says, "So you could find yourself again, sweet girl. What a fantastic result."

"You're so bossy."

"It is my greatest privilege discovering what my sweet, young girl needs. I admit, I didn't anticipate it may be another pretty body like your own to explore."

I gasp, freezing my fingers on the slick swell of my lips. Twisting to face him, I mutter, "What did you say?"

A darkness shifts across his eyes. "You said her name, little deer." *I did?* He takes a step towards me, warning following the meaningful gait. "I don't share *you*."

"I don't—"

"Have you ever been with a woman?"

"No." I stand up, noting the way his eyes drip down my form, drinking in the sight of my body at the cusp of arousal. "You know I haven't."

"Do you like to look at women?"

"I don't know, Sir. *Yes,* I guess."

"Would you like to touch Aurora?"

"I don't—"

"Would you like *her* to touch *you*?" His voice drops. "To kiss your skin, to slide her fingers into your wet wanting pussy?"

I breathe out hard.

God, the man has no filter.

No 'chill' at all.

"I don't know..." I admit. There is no one else for me. I know that. Nothing I want to do that doesn't involve him. It just seems like she is part of him... and being with her — I'm with her as often as I am him.

I clear my throat, unsure of what I'm feeling... *Or mean...* All I know is being away from him all day is too much distance, so when I'm with her— *God*, being with someone else instead of him only twists my heart and lungs into coiled ropes within my ribcage. It's not what I want.

I start to panic.

"Calm down, sweet girl. I told you I would take care of you," he grounds with that cool, smooth confidence that stirs me like nothing else in this world. "That you are *mine*. If it's something you want to experience, then yes, I would allow it. If you ask me very nicely. If you catch me on a good day... And it would be under my supervision. Only *once*. I cannot guarantee the outcome."

With his supervision? So, he'll approve. What is that all about? Does he want to... *join in*?

My hands become fists at my sides. The mental imagery of him with another woman burns through me. It scorches so intensely I'm immediately maddened by it. "I don't share *you!*"

A sly grin slides across his pristine features. "*Greedy*, girl. *Sweet, sweet* girl. No. I won't take Aurora in such a way."

"But—" I falter, shocked. "She's *so* beautiful."

"You gush," he hisses out between clenched teeth, taking another one of those threatening steps towards me. As I peer up at him, I part my lips to draw the thickened air into my needy lungs. "She *is* undeniably stunning, and yet, contrary to the thoughts of simpler people, women and men can have committed relationships that are *entirely*"—he lifts my chin, glaring down at me —"*platonic*. We don't see each other in such a way, sweet girl. Never have."

"And if you see her with me?" I question, nervous he'll suddenly realise the ravishing creature in his house—the intelligent, powerful woman he calls wife is every bit what he desires. "Would you feel differently about me?"

"Never."

"And her?"

"I highly doubt I'll be able to see anything besides another person's hands and lips enjoying my property." He leans down and kisses my mouth hard, his lips stiff and bruising. Breaking away, he leaves me breathless and dizzy from his soul-capturing kiss and his possessive words. "Now, this conversation has me rather on edge."

As he strides across the room, he removes the towel and places it on the end table. I watch his firm arse contract with each step before he turns to sit down on the cushions. Widening his legs with purpose, he looks at me, then at the floor between his feet. "Kneel."

I rush eagerly to him, dropping between his legs, where I'm always the most contented. Settled. Safe. Owned.

Resting my head on his thigh, I gaze up at the most impressive man in existence, even as I see jealousy simmering over an event that hasn't even transpired yet.

Is it wrong to appreciate his love for me in the form of possessiveness? If it is, then I'm guilty over and over again, because being his property is the single most contented state to be.

"Can I suck your cock now, Sir?" I breathe, dropping my gaze to the thick shaft that hangs between his legs. Inches away, but I know better than to touch him without permission when he's coiled so tightly. "*Please*."

His narrowed blue eyes meet my wide, hopeful gaze,

and he says, "You know what your lovely manners do to me. Okay, little deer. *Suck*."

I reach for his large cock, wrapping my hand around it, squeezing as it grows instantly, the strength and breadth of it prying my fingers apart until I'm unable to circle the entire beautiful expanse of him.

Feeding the pink, swollen head into my mouth, I hum around the flavour of him, the silkiness of the crown. I jerk the root as I shift onto my knees to get a better angle.

His fingers comb through my hair with tender adoration as my tongue traces the protuberant vein up and down his length. One of his hands slides down to the curve where my throat starts, massaging the area. "Relax your throat for me."

He cups the back of my neck, guiding me so I'm hovering over his lap. Then he pushes me down, hissing when I groan around his shaft. I continue to pump his root while I close my eyes, relax, and take so much of his erection between my lips that he slides in beyond the back of my throat—*down*.

"Take me deep."

I breathe through my nose. Pressing my hands to his thighs, I brace myself as I bob down and up, his wet shaft sliding in and then slipping through my lips.

Suddenly, the muscles inside each of his thighs tighten and bunch.

"*Christ,*" he groans, and I become ragingly aroused by his deep voice. "That's my good girl. Take it all down... Oh, *yes*. Mind your breathing while I fuck your throat, sweet girl."

Then he starts to pump upwards, still cradling the back of my neck so I can't shy away from the brutal, yet blissful need in each thrust.

I swallow around the penetration, the protruding veins pulsing against my palm as I lure his orgasm out with the strokes of my fist at his root.

His breath comes out fast and fierce. "*Fuck*. You like my cock wedged down your throat. *My sweet girl*. My little queen. Do you want my cum all over your mouth, little deer?"

He suddenly stops thrusting. Griping me tighter at the base of my neck, he jerks me up to straddle him, where he wastes no time in demanding my body to take his cock.

My mind reels at the sudden change.

Trying to find purchase, I whimper and wriggle at the quick invasion. My legs and core surge with pain and sensation at being stretched almost unbearably so.

"Take my cock, little deer. I need to come inside you tonight." He doesn't wait for me to relax, even though I need him to, need more time to loosen, but feral desperation controls his movements.

A whimper claws up my throat as he pulls me down, impaling me deep until my pelvis meets his upward thrusts and the head of his cock batters my uterus.

I cry out.

He straightens to hold me, banding his thick, formidable arms around me. Being too full, too quickly, I tremble within the staunch, powerful cage of his body as he whispers by my temple, "You're okay, sweet girl." Then he bursts inside me with a violent groan, still fucking upwards while uttering words of comfort to me. "It'll be okay. Relax around me. Breathe deeply."

His cum eases the sting of his sudden penetration, dripping from inside me and coating us where we connect. There's a lot. My mind reels. That was utterly out of character for him. He's so very rarely impulsive. At the last moment before his orgasm, he flipped the play as though nothing else mattered but filling me. I've wanted him inside me all week, so now that he is, I revel in it. I roll my head on his chest.

Both of his arms drop, his hands resting on either side of my hips, his long fingers spanning the bones. He holds me there but leans back to inspect me. His cool blue eyes rake down my body to where my pussy stretches around his cock. "Such a snug fit, sweet girl. That was careless of me." He pants as he strokes one of his hands up between my breasts before banding my neck. "Luckily, you were soaking. Tell me, does sucking my cock make you wet? Or was it the thought of Aurora's fingers inside you?"

My chest tightens at the hint of bitterness in his tone. "You're angry with me, Sir. Please don't. I didn't—"

"No." He lifts his hips up as he stirs my pelvis on his lap, his cock flexing inside, forcing a quick soft moan through my lips. "I'm pathetically territorial, little deer. Possessive. So crazy territorial I needed to—" His heated gaze drops to my core, but he doesn't elaborate.

I reach up, touch the wound below his striking blue eye, and try not to wince. "How did you seal it? It needed stitches."

"Glue."

"And this one?" I press my palm to the smooth white scar along his collarbone—tattooed with vines and flowers, the petals appear wilted, at the end of their life. A tattoo equally as beautiful as it is sad. "What happened here? It looks old."

He sighs roughly and covers my hand with his own, together holding the mark that signifies a clearly painful memory.

I don't press him further.

Taking the opportunity while his controlled demeanour seems to be fracturing, I close my eyes, lean in, and pepper my lips along the swollen flesh of his cheek.

My heart balloons when he doesn't stop me but instead sighs roughly, his body relaxing further on the sofa.

Heading down and to the side, my mouth flutters like a feather along his skin until I reach his lips. He deepens our kiss when he releases my hip and threads his fingers through my hair, knotting them in possessively.

Inhaling his breath, I exhale these words: "I love you, Sir. You can be vulnerable with me."

He stills beneath the chaste motion of my mouth, his nose sliding along mine. I open my eyes, meeting his blue gaze inches away. "I am," he states in a way that suggests I should already know this, see this.

I glance at the slice he refused to let me tend to as a sombre feeling shifts through me.

He frowns, seeing the sadness playing across my face. He elaborates, "When I look at you, I'm speechless." His hands tighten in my hair to draw my gaze back to him, to demand my attention. I look into his eyes. "And I'm not often without the right words, sweet girl, but your entire person—" he sighs roughly. "I simply can't believe you were put together with such perfection. I won't apologise for refusing to taint that with my blood and rot."

"You're not rotten!"

"Yes—" He sweeps his gaze over me, "*I am.*"

No. "No," I murmur, heat rushing to the backs of my eyes because how can he talk about himself in such a way when he is the only person on this entire earth who has

given me his time, his attention. He's given me everything, for fucksake! *No.*

I shake my head at him, angry at this life that's so
cruel to him and so neglectful to me... He's *not* fucking
rotten. If he's rotten, then the entire world is the cause,
eating at him, ripping the good away, leaving raw,
wounded flesh.

Emotions bubble within me, but he halts the rising
wave of them when he stands with my legs still wrapped
around his waist. His cock grows inside me, flexing with
renewed thickness and strength.

He cups the back of my head when he lays me down
beneath him on the mattress and begins to roll his hips in
an excruciatingly slow and meaningful rhythm.

I grip his shoulders as he rocks up and into me, dragging his long, heavy body along mine to remain close and
deep.

I'm dizzy from every inch of his steady, tireless
thrusting as the evening rolls on with him inside me.
Close.

Soon, I'm coming with a throaty cry, tightening my
thighs around him, hugging him.

And he comes inside me again.

CHAPTER EIGHT

SHE IS STILL ASLEEP when I take her again with the knowledge that she is ready to accept her pretty body. Forgive her pretty body. It's apparent as I spread her thighs open, her legs flopping lax, trusting, *welcoming*, that she conquered some of her demons last night.

"So snug, little deer," I groan by her ear, sliding into her hot, tight pussy. "Let me in, sweet girl."

She gasps but receives me as I brace my body over hers, pressing in, forcing her to take me to the hilt. I couldn't wait last night, and *dammit*, I lost my mind when I saw her pleasuring herself. Fighting through tears...

Was that for me?

She wants to handle my evil.

I'll never let my evil infect her...

And yet, my lack of self-control with her is a serious concern, dangerous, even. Where I find myself— Christ, seeking a kind of comfort, approval, sanctuary—

"*Clay*."

Groaning, "*Fawn*," I stay deep while she wakes up, my

lips sliding against her sleepy, clumsy mouth and uncertain little breaths.

I start to move slowly. Her arse recoils into the mattress each time I hit the end of her, only to lift and chase the invasion when I draw out.

Such a greedy girl.

And so relaxed tonight...

"*Christ.* You hold me so beautifully. Make no mistake that you are mine." Her tight body is completely covered by mine, taking my measured, deep drives, accepting all of me.

She accepts all of me...

And she smells like me, too, becoming a part of me, still stuffed with my cum from last night, but I need more...

Fuck.

She is so young.

Fuck.

I didn't consider what she might want to do in this new world I've given her, didn't consider how she might want to *experiment*... The image of my stunning wife and my pretty little deer touching each other forces a growl through me as I pick up pace, fuelled by possessiveness.

I thought there wasn't a fucker alive who I would have to share her with...

The arrogant man in me overlooked that my sweet girl might want to experience other sexual practices like most young women do with each other.

The vivid image spurs me on to the point of frenzy, feeling violently territorial, as I know I'll give her the world. Every experience she desires. Every sweet thing. Every pleasure. I despise my love for her because it means

I'll say yes—yes to anything and everything that'll make her smile.

The primal sensation consuming me drives me wild, and she is so fragile beneath me, soft and smooth, and I'm fucking her now with every inch of power in my hips.

My pelvis grinds on hers.

She releases throaty moans.

I withdraw fast.

My hard drives throw her up, her shoulders hitting my forearms with each deep, hard fuck. This is what I can give her that no one else will, and I'll remind her every day of that fact.

There is something else I can give her too. A reason to stack pillows, to bake cakes, and to wake up in the morning.

To be mine. Forever.

My cock throbs, enveloped in her clinging little pussy as she wrings the goddamn sensations up from my balls. I slide my hand to her lower abdomen, pressing down, applying weight until she is overwhelmed by the pressure.

She cries out, "Sir, yes, please," and I eat her words.

Quaking around my cock, her orgasm thrashes within her, forcing her to tense and release sweet, choppy yelps.

My balls immediately tighten, my abdomen bunching to her sweet, whimpering cadence, and I spill into her with a shuddering growl. Demanding I stay deep while I fill her, I feel the sensations of warmth, tightness, and closeness as she ripples around me, sharing my climax.

I rest in her hair, animalistic.

And *feeling* too much.

I need to get her vitamins tomorrow.

CHAPTER NINE

clay

I LEAVE HER TO SLEEP.

Heading downstairs, intent on running off a few rounds in the shooting range, I'm stopped by the sight of Aurora reading in the lounge room. In the corner of the room, a pen houses the small cat. The animal a white ball on a pillow. Setup to be the utmost spoilt creature alive, I am certain.

It's the early hours of the morning now. Staring at my wife, it becomes evident something weighs on her as she escapes into an alternate narrative. Yet, I know better than to press her for details while she attempts to wipe her mind of them.

The lamp over her right shoulder casts a glow across the olive skin on her face and the white pages on her lap. The only illumination to the room. "Were you reading to my little deer when I came in earlier?" I ask, striding to stand before her.

Unfazed, she finishes her paragraph, her eyes sliding across the page one last time before she pulls a ribbon down and closes the book on it. A sly wisp of a smile slips across her lips. "Yes. She likes the classics."

"She likes *you*," I state, fighting to remain nonchalant, stifling the hiss of disapproval that threatens to twist my outward manner. I don't entirely disapprove of Fawn's affections. Watching my sweet girl grow, coming to know what she enjoys and doesn't as she explores her sexuality and accepts her beauty, is my greatest pleasure. I exhale hard, disliking the territorial growl that circles the warning sound.

As always, my wife sees straight through me, saying, "She has a singular taste in companions. Wouldn't you agree?"

"My little deer is awed by strength."

"Yet is so very unaccepting of her own."

I laugh, impressed *and* agitated. "Part of me, as always, is fascinated by your attention to detail." Clapping my hands in front of me, I add, "But I'm not sure I appreciate so much of your *attention* on *her.*"

She rolls her eyes. "She's yours—"

"Yes," I ground immediately. "But she's not entirely contented right now." Sighing roughly, I admit through a tight jaw, "And for the first time in my entire life, Aurora, I have no fucking idea how to fix this damn problem. What do I do with a teenage girl?"

Her dark whiskey-coloured eyes soften knowingly. "You can't expect a young girl to not be the reflection of how she is treated. So... *treat* her."

"I thought I was... What do you suggest?"

"Give her the world, Clay." She stands and sashays to place the book back on the shelf, using the few seconds to hum in contemplation. "Don't keep her locked away from it."

Unacceptable. "I won't choose *anything* over her safety. Not even her happiness," I declare as I track Aurora's movement across the room. "Dustin is only a few miles away, Aurora. It isn't safe."

"You found him!" She whips around to look at me, her dark brows pitched as she processes this recent development.

I nod. "I believe so. In the biker compound. I'm almost certain of it. He'll be coming for her and the baby he believes to still be in her womb. I don't know what he's planning."

She shakes her head slowly. "But it will be a massacre. My father would have had his men and your brothers break into that compound at night and take them all out. He'd call in the force. If he—"

"Jimmy didn't care about casualties. I do. And we won't be putting Xander at risk."

"No. Or her." It wasn't a question. It was a statement of agreement. Aurora doesn't want our family anywhere near this. She doesn't want *Fawn* anywhere near this. It seems my little deer is bewitching everyone.

That makes a smile slide across my lips for a moment before it falls. "This may get out of control, Aurora," I advise. "They may come for you. Or the girls. They may create chaos on the streets. There is no saying what they will do given the chance. I cannot have my family in the city while this is being executed."

"I can tell by your tone you already have a plan. Have you contacted Luca?" Aurora asks.

"I have a meeting with him tomorrow morning. I'll be working from home," I state, my eyes landing on the kitten, a corner smile fighting its way out when those dual-coloured eyes peer up at me. "But we will leave," I say, returning my attention to Aurora. "We must be seen outside the city. I may have a clean image, but Max does not. None of us can be here when the fight breaks out or we will be caught up in it. I won't let another one of my brothers lose years again." My regret clogs my throat. Max lost *years*... "And the women need to be safe so my brothers can act ruthless and meticulous. My thoughts are to spend time in Dubai and then leave the women and Xander under hotel arrest. Max, Bronson, and I fly back to the District... And *we* will take the compound at night with only a few men. We will try to keep it quiet and professional. If we succeed, that will be the end of it forever, and the city will barely blink an eye."

She exhales hard. "Xander will be furious if you leave him out of this. If you trick him into leaving the District."

"My young brother will do as he's instructed. Far be it, I would rather suffer his hate than grieve his death." I gaze at the woman I respect more than most. A person so entwined with my own self, with the construct of who I am today, that I barely know which of my ideals and mannerisms were mine first... and which were hers. So, of course, I know, when I add, "I want you away and safe, too," she will rebut.

"Absolutely not," she scolds, and I grin at her for her predictability. "I won't allow you to execute this by yourself. If any of you don't return, you will need backup. I need to be here to send men into the compound to get you out."

She is right, of course, but I still don't like it. "If they capture us, they may come here searching for you," I challenge, shaking my head. "No. I need you out of the city. I won't put you in danger like that."

"I was in danger the moment I was born." She bristles. "It never bothered my father, so don't let it bother you."

"But it does bother me," I say smoothly.

Squaring her shoulders, she presents unwavering severity in every inch of her posed stance. "You can't expect a woman to not be the reflection of how you treat her," she repeats, and I frown. *Damn woman.* "You have always treated me as an equal. Don't go archaic on me now, Clay."

Panning my eyes over her flawless features, I see the resolve. She is right. Keeping her from this will only fill her with the same disdain she harboured for her father. A man who forced her to accept this life but never gave her a voice. I won't do that. I gave her my word decades ago that I would never pull rank on her.

"As you wish," I agree. "You may stay in the city. Be here to make arrangements should we not return."

"You *will* return, but I'll be ready if you don't." The flare of strength crosses her eyes. "I'll bring every man, woman, and child in until we find you."

"You sound like a boss." I smile at her, liking how well she wears intimidation. How comfortably it simmers just beneath her flawless skin. "And if things get messy," I add. "I need you to control the press. How is your relationship with Lorna? Can we count on her to mediate information to The District News?"

She smiles, unbidden evidence my bratty ex-lover still invokes endearment in my wife. "We still enjoy one another often. I believe we can count on her."

Excellent.

CHAPTER TEN

THE SMELL of coffee rouses me.

I wake to Clay sitting across from me on the sofa in the corner of our room, wrapped in his suited armour, a cigar between his lips, a newspaper going unnoticed in his lap, his eyes on me.

I smile sweetly at him, happily a little daring due to the ache his lovemaking yesterday caused. It reminds me that I'm not just his but a bit of him is mine too. Something I missed these last few weeks.

"You're a creep," I taunt.

"I'm not sure I can argue with that, sweet girl," he states, the intensity of his emotional state last evening seemingly a distant condition, replaced by that smooth, controlled detachment Clay Butcher is known for.

I don't mind; I caught his sentimental butterfly.

I'll keep it safe, Sir.

He inhales the cigar, his eyes unwavering from me, the ember at the tip flaring brightly.

I sit up and slide off the bed, wincing and shifting as I

feel the memory of him between my thighs. Then I remember my kitten and beam. "Can I go play with my kitten, Sir?"

Instantly, he slides the paper to the side and taps his thigh. "After I have played with yours. Lay your sweet body over my lap," he says, talking around the cigar. "I'll help you with the swelling."

A hot flush spreads across my face as I notice the glass of ice sitting beside him, so I quickly do as I'm told, sweet memories of the last time he took me hard and then soothed me after guiding me quickly to him.

Grinning demurely, I say, "Can I at least shower first this time, Sir?"

"No," he states straightaway, "you may not. You can shower after I've had my coffee, read the paper, and enjoyed you."

I crawl over his lap. Settle my head and elbows on the pillow already positioned beside his thigh. Twisting to face him, I ask, "You're going to read the paper while I lay on your lap?"

A cube of ice lands on my spine, and I shudder as it trails down before settling at the well of my arch. "Yes," he says smoothly, using his finger to slide the cube over the hump of my arse and down the crease of my backside so he can use it to circle my lips.

My pussy is puffy and tight, gradually thawing the cube in its heat. He continues his treatment of my aching core, and I bask in the lush sensation of his authoritarian touch.

He treats every slide of his fingers like his duty of care.

It. Is. Everything.

A simmering tingle. A caress that promises ecstasy

but never actually builds enough to deliver the brunt of it. It's perfectly teasing without discomfort.

I'm the spoilt one, Aurora.

So very spoilt.

The smell of his coffee and his cigar circles the room while his hand is reverent in its caring attention. I feel like butter and melting chocolate—all warm and swirly and gooey. "You're not at work," I stupidly say.

"You're very observant."

I chuckle at him. "If you want me to be more remarkable first thing in the morning, then you should probably allow me more than a few hours between—"

His hand connects with my arse in a hard slap. A gasp leaves me before it twists into a long moan, the shock turning that delicious sizzle of pleasure into a buck of sensation.

His big palm rubs the stinging flesh as he says, "I think you have forgotten, *sweet girl*, that you will let me fuck any of your pretty parts I desire. *Whenever* I desire. Now, what were you going to say?

My cheeks heat, probably glowing the same bright red as my backside—a matching stamp of arousal. "Nothing, Sir."

"Good girl." He pushes two cold fingers inside me, easing the swelling, flooding me with pleasure so lovely it curls my toes. "I like watching your toes curl." He scoops both long digits inside me, applying the thick pads to the back wall, stimulating me to flex my arse and groan. "*Yes,*" he confirms huskily. "I'm taking the day off. We can have a long weekend. Have you ever been on an aeroplane?"

Barely focusing on his words, the sensation

consuming my conscious mind, I try to reach for what he said. Plane? *Like in the sky? God,* my brain is useless when he's doing that with his fingers... "No?"

"Don't answer a question with a question."

"No, Sir. I've never—" I start to convulse with waves of arousal when he dips his thumb between the muscles rimming my rosette, while his cool fingers continue their reverent strokes on my puffy lips.

I take fistfuls of the pillow beneath my head and turn my face away from the sight of him with his cigar still smoking from his mouth and his heated eyes glued on my backside. Burying my whimpers within the soft material, I writhe on him.

"Your pretty holes love being full. Did you know that? They suck me in with such demand. Such need. How am I supposed to separate my body from yours when every part of you is so very sweet to me. Hold still for me, little deer." Replacing his thumb now is a cool, hard object that pulls my muscles taut. "Good girl." I flex around it, and he groans. "I can only imagine what it feels like to be held in this tight hole... *Relax.* You remember my present? This is to stretch you, but it's also to help train your muscles so you don't flex too hard when I try to get inside you."

I pant to the hot sensation of being full—so exquisitely stretched. Flexing around it decisively, I moan from deep in my throat. I flex again.

He guides me to a sitting position beside him on the sofa, my hands in my lap and my backside on my heels. The plug moves when I do.

Clay pulls the cigar from his mouth, the tiny remnants of it almost burning his lips. Reaching over my lap, he butts it out in the crystal tray on the table before leaning back casually.

Giving me his full attention now, his eyes roam my face, and he sighs, a smile sliding across his lips. *And* I'm butter. I fucking melt further into a puddle of his making. "This one is smaller than the last one. Not because I'm being generous but because I want you to wear it most of the day. Can you do that for me, sweet girl?"

Excitedly, I agree. "Yes, Sir."

He reaches to the table, retrieving a container of wine-coloured pills and a glass of what looks like orange juice, offering them both to me. "Take these. Every morning."

"Is it candy?" I shuffle my backside in the dip between my heels, closing my eyes for a moment to the sweet agony of the plug moving. I open them and catch his like a direct threat of something primal. I agree to it. "I'm here willing and eager for whatever you want. I don't need candy, Sir."

He clenches his jaw. "Mind your mouth, sweet girl. You may like it now, but I won't always be so gentle with your spanking. Behave so I don't feel the need or desire to show you what pain, pleasure, and discomfort can do when they peak at the same time."

Fucking hell.

Excitement, anticipation, and fear shock my heart into a frantic tattoo, widening my eyes.

Should I start to piss him off now?

Or later?

His easy blue gaze cuts to the container in my hand, then back to my face. "The pills are vitamins, sweet girl. Let me see you take one now."

Okay, later.

I grin at him, a cheeky slant to my lips. "*Yes, Sir.*" I slip a pill through my smile, chasing it with a sip of juice. My tastebuds buzz around bursts of citrus as I swallow.

"Now." He leans back and drapes his thick arms over the back of the sofa, looking powerful even in that casual position. "I'm inside you right now. In your little arse. Remember that because I won't be able to play with you today. You will see me around the house, but I need to—"

"So what? You want me to just pretend—"

"Don't interrupt me," he reprimands. "Yes. I want you to keep yourself busy. Leave me to work. You are a distraction. Be my good girl and look after your kitten. Do some online shopping. Get a suitcase. We will be going on a trip in a few days."

A trip?

"Like, what kind of trip?"

"The kind I will explain when I have all the details." He shuffles to the edge of the sofa, nodding to the spot between his spread thighs. "Stand and let me get a good look at you before I go."

Tiny amounts of warmth creep up my neck as I stand and turn to face away from him, hit with the caress of his gaze on my backside and the little item inside me. Large palms trail the outer swell of my thighs, awakening the tiny blonde hairs on my skin to rise.

"Simply stunning."

One of his hands slides forward and cups my pussy, and my head drops backward on a moan. I press into his palm. His lips touch my backside, dragging along the plump curve, nipping, and sucking the skin.

I rock into his palm as he enjoys the taste of my flesh, all but eating me with small nibbles that shock my nerves and the drag of his tongue that curls my toes.

Then his mouth is gone, and he rises. His suited body

slides up my back, his hands touching me everywhere as they climb with him. They end at my neck, gripping the column, forcing me to crane my throat to accept his lips as he towers above me. He nips me before breaking off from my mouth. "Now you may shower, sweet girl."

CHAPTER ELEVEN

QUE, my first guard and assistant, ever the gentleman in his suit, with his regal manner, enters my office moments after I sit down.

Even though I ran two magazines out in my range before coming here, I'm still tense about what must happen next. The finality of the week ahead, hunting down Dustin, breaking our treaty with the bikers, leaving the women in another country—it coils my muscles to cool, unwavering steel.

A cup of coffee is set down in front of me while I open the building plans my brother Max sent through from the city's database. "Thank you, Que."

"Your father is here, Boss." He pours the steaming liquid, and I nod, abruptly thinking about how Fawn shouldn't have any if I want her... healthy.

"Fawn will need decaf from now on," I state, staring across the polished-wood office table at him. "Don't allow her to drink anything caffeinated."

He nods politely, no intrigue or interest ghosting his

eyes. *Good man.* "I shall get some for Miss Harlow this morning."

"Where is she now?" I ask, although I am one click away from seeing her for myself. I dare say that once I allow myself that sweet view, she becomes somewhat of a perpetual distraction.

"In the lounge area with Bolton and her new cat," he advises and leaves me to my business.

I find myself grinning at the vision of her sitting crossed-legged and playing with the small animal. A soft smile on her face. Shuffling around with the reminder of me stretching her little arsehole. My cock pulses. I relish being her constant thought. Being inside her always. My present in her. My cum still deep and perhaps the building of something else as well...

I stare back at the building plans Max easily accessed as City Architect. And while I don't entirely understand all the information, he does, and I'm confident he will be able to chart a course in and out of the biker's complex. I study the halls and spaces; it's a vast compound with dozens of rooms.

Dustin could be hiding in any part.

If only we had a man on the inside—I sigh, eyeing the documentation—but we don't. Our man on the inside was born and bred District local Dustin Nerrock.

Fucker...

Nevermind.

"Do you have a whiskey for your old man?" Butch enters with my mother, surprising me with her presence. She looks slim, far leaner than the last time I saw her.

Almost sickly.

I stand to greet them, firmly shake my father's hand, and lightly kiss my mother on both cheeks. Hit with a wave of perfume from her neck, I'm instantly reminded how much I enjoy Fawn's natural scent. "Well, now that you're here, it would be ill-mannered for me to not also have one with you."

My father sits, taking up the full breadth of the chair with his thick, muscular physique, while my mother disappears into her one. She crosses her legs, her spine rim-rod straight. She's tense. "So, he's in The Stockyard Compound," Butch muses, usually the quietest man in any room if not one on one, living by the golden rule that words spoken should hold meaning or not be spoken at all. "That isn't good. I never suspected that. I should have." He shakes his head. "I should have but their life-style didn't suit his own, and so... I was misguided."

"Can we get any alliances on the inside? What about the president, Cross? Surely, he doesn't need a war with the Family?"

"He doesn't like Sicilians, son. He is a swastika tattoo away from a Nazi."

I prepare us two whiskeys and sit back down opposite my father. Leaning back in my wingback chair, I rub my jawline and hum. "True." I raise my glass, saying, "cheers." I take a generous mouthful before setting the glass down.

When my mother swallows hard as though she may vomit, I measure her up. She is oddly quiet, holding her stomach in a protective way. "Are you well, Mother?"

She smiles stiffly, even for her. "Very."

I shift my gaze between my father's even stare and her hooded one, sensing a significant issue in their relations. Body language screaming they are amid an argument. Not something I have time for.

I note her tired eyes, dots of blood speckling the

whites. "Are you hungover? Do we need some kind of rehab for you?"

My father folds his arms across his chest. "Your mother has always been a drinker, Clay. You have far more important things to take care of than—"

"Than my mother?"

"I am sitting right here. And I do not have a drinking problem compared to the *men* who have started their whiskeys at 7.am. Thank you very much."

Butch barely reacts as she climbs to her feet and flattens her dress down her thighs before wandering from my office with a slow sway. "Excuse me."

Frowning at her mannerisms, I watch her leave. I don't like that. Pressing my intercom, I speak to it. "Que, get my mother some water and take her outside for fresh air."

Finished with that disruption, I return my attention to my father. "My police informant, Marius, sent over a list of known Patch Members and Prospects that we may find living in the compound. Only ten or so actually reside there on a regular basis, it seems." Readying myself to deliver a regretful truth, I sip my whiskey. He sips his. I chase the burn with the facts. "You will not be needed. In fact, I would prefer if you were not actively a part of these kinds of operations."

Blue eyes stare blankly at me.

I go on, "You may be stronger than most men, but you are not swifter and not stealthier."

Unimpressed, he says, "Never missed a meeting."

A meeting. A hit. Such words are synonymous with large scale execution in the *Cosa Nostra*. My father has been by the Don's side for half his life, offered his greatest years, and his sons to the Family agenda. Now, though, he has earned leave.

I stare at the man who had little to do with raising me, but with whom I share blood and unparalleled respect. "I know you haven't," I acknowledge smoothly. This has nothing to do with his capabilities. "That's the way Jimmy ran things. With you both at meetings. A presence. Intimidation. I don't need you on the frontline anymore," I declare. "Moving forward, my face is the only one they *need* see. And you're *valuable* to me in other ways."

He grips his glass, his eyes cast down, losing focus within the pool of brown liquid. I've undermined him. I know. But this is the way it must be. I won't put him in danger in his sixties. "I'm a liability, is what you mean, son," he firmly states.

"In this case, yes," I admit with due esteem holding my tone. Then I chuckle. "You barely fit in that *damn* chair, and you're going to sneak around a compound at night? Climb through windows? I think not. The plan is this, we fly to Dubai in a few days. That will give me time to organise safe passage and reinforcements while we are there. I leave the women and children there. Bronson, Max, and I fly back. We require only the minimum number of men on this—four others, perhaps. We get in and out of the compound undetected. We finish it. And we fly back to Dubai to get the women. Do I have your support in this?" I ask, wanting the last word on major operations that rely entirely on his sons to be spoken by him.

He assesses me. "And you bring Dustin out with you?"

"Yes. We retrieve him from wherever he is hiding and

bring him back *alive* if we can. To the gym. Where we finish this once and for all."

Setting his whiskey down, he leans back. "You have my support. But let me give you some advice, son. You should not run the *Cosa Nostra* alone. You will drown if you do it all. Who will you rely on?"

"Am I not relying on you as we speak?"

"You are seeking council, *se?* But you need more men. You need *loyal* men,"—He points to the wall, waving his finger, a Sicilian mannerism deeply engrained— "out there."

"I understand. I intend to make these alliances at the matches I've organised. The Irish, the Family, the entire District underground will be there."

He nods his approval, blue eyes fixed on mine. "Allow me to run those events for you, son." He pauses, and the silence thickens with the kind of sentiment my father rarely shows me. Over the last few years, he has changed, admittedly. He is dedicated to his family now, to my brothers, his grandchildren... I consider myself outside of those properties. *But...* his eyes fixed on mine, soften, and my chest tightens.

I don't have time for this...

My muscles coil, wanting to leave the room under this new energy. I clasp my hands. "I need to manage these events," I ground.

"*Clay,*" he starts, his tone a foreign empathetic timbre. A sombre drawl so entirely unfamiliar, I'm thrown as to who is addressing me. "I know I wasn't there for you."

What the hell is this?

He continues, "I know I didn't raise you. I won't tell you how to do this job because you were born to do it.

You are the faultless product of Jimmy. I mean that in the most reverent way, son. But you can't do this alone."

A leader is, by default, alone.

I force my body to still while all I want is to move, flick the discomfort from my fingertips. He cares. I care that he cares. "That's not what I'm trying to do here."

"Yes. You are. You are more comfortable alone." He laughs with derision, directing the contemptuous tone inward, to himself. "We are all particularly good at being impartial. I enforced such a way of life too. I don't deny it. I know. I... struggled, *se*. With my anger. Like Max, it's often better to beat it out. Beat it into a boxing bag. Or put behind walls. Butcher men all have walls, but you,"— his eyes lock on me, and I clench my jaw around the uncomfortable discussion— "you're a fucking island, Clay. You don't even need the walls. A truth that pains me some."

I talk through my teeth. "Anything else?"

He sighs at my deflection, at my behaviour that feeds directly into what he just shared. "Yes." He deflates but continues. "Jimmy delegated brilliantly. You were the link to the city. He was the Don of the Family. Dustin ran the locals. I ran the Family. Your brothers kept the order. I think you need to remove yourself from your official standing in the city. Allow Max to be the man on the inside. Choose someone else to run the locals."

Irritation flares at my temples. I lean forward, press my elbows to the desk and say, "You want me to resign from a position I have worked the last decade to attain?"

"Yes," he states adamantly, and I sink back into my chair, shocked by this new development.

What the fuck is going on here?

"That is exactly what I want you to do," he states. "I

want you to position a mayor of your choosing and be the Don of this Family. It is a full-time job as it is."

Absolutely not.

I shake my head. "I can do both."

"Can you do all three?" He sighs roughly. "Can you do more? I don't want you to be like me, son. *Absent.* Too busy. You'll miss it, son. The time just disappears."

I ask what I already know. "Miss what?"

"*Living.* Watching her become a mother," he states, and my chest tightens unpleasantly. "Watching your sons become men. It just happens." He folds his arms across his broad chest, his white suit shirt stretching around each large bicep. "Do you want children with that girl?"

Damn him.

"How did we get here?"

"You were taking advice from an old man."

Damn him.

It's a truth that comes to me without invite. A phantom need that was coasting through my every action of late. The answer to his question. *Yes.* I want her pregnant. With my sons. Want her round at the hips, growing my heirs. Blood of the *Cosa Nostra* raised by a woman who is royalty and modest but *humble.* Sweet, even.

A sweet girl.

Levelling him, feigning nonchalance, I say, "*Perhaps.*"

Flat blue eyes filled with accusation train on me, their infliction growing like barbed wire beneath my skin. "You will not lie on your deathbed and regret raising your sons, Clay. And deathbeds find us young in this game. You will, however, regret *not* raising them." He slowly nods. "I speak from experience."

Too much.

Damn him!

Rising to my feet, stifling the impulse to lunge over the desk and fist his collar, growl at him for unloading his regret and bullshit on me when I need to focus, I simple smooth my tie down my shirt in lieu of that urge.

"All excellent advice," I say, widening my arms for him, a gesture to indicate the discussion has ended.

He stands, unreadable again but for the pinched brows etched to his forehead, residual of his unreciprocated sentimentality. "Very well. Your mother needs to stay in one of the guest rooms for a while?" he says. "I have pissed her off. She might knife me if she stays in the house with me, se?"

Can't possibly understand why...

I smile easily, and where I would usually decline, I don't. As I'm itching to remove myself from this sentimental energy. "Of course. I will have Que make up a room in the other wing. She will have the entire extension to herself."

CHAPTER TWELVE

"YOU SMELL SO SWEET, LITTLE DEER," he says through a growl that radiates through my bones, "and I'm *starving*."

Those words reach into my dreamless state and draw me from its cloak of darkness. I moan in half-coherence as the blanket slides down my body. Air rushes over my core as Clay presses my thighs apart with his palms.

"Open for me."

The mattress brushes my outer legs when I drop my thighs apart, exposed completely. The air cools the wetness now gathering between my thighs. *His voice.* That is all I need to be completely ready for him. Primed. He wanted to condition me to be ready for him, and I am.

"*Pretty*," he purrs.

I missed him. He was busy all day and gone all night. I missed his voice. His large presence that holds me, envelops me, soothes me. That dreamily coats me in his scent—cigars and gun powder.

Power—Clay Butcher is what power smells like.

My eyes stay closed. My senses are fine-tuned to his

movement and warmth. Reaching down, I find the strands of his dark hair hovering above my waist. He dips down and runs his tongue over my clit in one long slow lap.

"I *missed* you today," I whisper to the ceiling, writhing to the quiet sensation he offers me.

"I know, sweet girl. I had business to organise. And now I want to spoil this pretty pussy." He groans, burying his head into my blonde pubic hair, inhaling me, deep and primal, forcing a flush to creep along every inch of my skin. "But I also want to fuck it sore, fuck it swollen, just like I want to do to your arse one day, and you will allow me. Offer your pretty holes to me. You belong to me."

God.

Firm, authoritarian lips bracket my pussy. I lift off the sheets on a spasm. Arch my back.

He doesn't focus on one spot between my legs like he has done in the past; he is passionately kissing me. He is making out with my pussy, deeply, sucking my lips into his mouth, spearing his tongue in deep, mouthing me.

Not at all trying to edge me in a direction, not at all controlled or measured. Just dirty. Carnal. Strange. Amazing.

I let him taste me, all of me. His tongue venturing down lower until he's fluttering the tip over my arsehole. Then he's back to kissing me and my head swims in the sensation of waking up to this attention.

A loud moan falls from my lips as I arch again. He pulls on my labia, running his tongue inside. A deep hum, a hum ending in a growl of need, vibrates against my wet pulsing flesh.

"Mine. You calm something in me." He flattens his

tongue and uses it to apply pressure to my clit. A zap of sensation spreads from the bundle of nerves up and down. Up and down.

The buzzing following the now meaningful strokes of his strong tongue. "I want to hear you say it."

"I'm yours."

He licks hard. "Your pussy is mine."

"*Yes.*" I shuffle my backside on the mattress, my hips seeking, needing, desperate, but he pins me down.

He slides his tongue upwards, dragging it between my hipbones, leaving my pussy beckoning in his neglect. "This body"—he peppers kisses along my lower belly— "is mine. To use. To fill. Say it."

"My body is yours, Sir. To do anything you want with."

He dips down again, licking once. "To use."

"*Yes.*"

Twice. "Fill."

"*Yes!*"

"Don't move then, sweet girl. I want your little pink clit vibrating on my tongue."

His thumbs slide to either side of my lips, he presses down, parting, and his warm breath beats down on my now exposed swollen clit. Within a second, he is using the pointed tip of his tongue to stimulate the buzzing bundle of nerves in hard, purposeful flicks.

"*Oh God. Oh God.*" I gasp. "*Please. Please, Sir.*"

"Let me have it all, sweet girl," he demands, dipping his kiss lower, moving his thumb to press down on my clit so he can lap the wetness from me as I start to shake, convulse.

A thunder-strong sensation shocks through my core, to my soul. My thighs tighten.

My stomach muscles bunch.

I release a long, uncontrolled moan as I give in to the waves and come apart for him. *"Sir,"* I breathe his name like it is air, life, reason, *everything...*

Clay hums and sucks me until my muscles slow their intense contractions, my pussy stops pulsing, and all my wetness is licked from my folds in a way that suggests he wants to savour the taste of me, to not waste any.

Rising over me as I roll my head from left to right on the pillow, he presses the thick, warm crown of his cock against my opening. "Now to fuck it sore and fuck it swollen. Now to fill you."

CHAPTER THIRTEEN

"YOUR LUGGAGE IS HERE." Jasmine peeks around the corner of the French doors to my position on the new outdoor lounge suite by the poolside. "I'll take them to your room. Want me to pack for you, Fawn?"

I gaze over my shoulder at her, dropping my line of sight to her hand, hoping she has the new luggage for me to see. She doesn't, and I don't want to leave my kitten or order her to grab them, so I say, "No. I can do it."

"*Righto,*" she says in her English accent, forcing a little chuckle from me. I never had any acquaintances who weren't Australian born and raised.

She disappears, and I look back at my kitten. It's been three days since Clay brought her home. And, well, tonight, I've been instructed to meet Clay at the airstrip, meaning I won't see her until we get back from wherever he's taking me.

I need quality kitten time.

She rolls around, her white fluff shedding all over the dark-grey cushions, her needle-like claws plucking the occasional seam out of place.

Kittens are so full of life—the epitome of playful chaos. At odds with so much of what Clay Butcher—the Devil's prototype—embodies. She meows and meows.

Squeaky sounds.

She likes her own voice.

Smiling, I see similarities too. There are two things that my kitten and Clay have in common: vocalisation and honesty.

I like cats because they are always honest. If they don't like you, you'll know it, if they want space, they demand it, and if they want attention, they'll take it.

The confident little creature stares up at me, tilting her head, her ears flicking around. Cats also consider everything in their path as though it belongs to them—just like the kitten is doing with me right now.

Like Clay always does.

The mild breeze touches my legs, my white shirt-dress ruffling around my waist. And I'm warm on the inside as well.

Sweeping my long white-blonde hair over my shoulder and twirling the ends around my finger, I smile at a memory. The vision of when I first saw this elevated area, overlooking the crystal blue waters of the pool and canals, I thought to myself that if I ever lived in a place like this, I would sit here every morning and enjoy the view. Take time to appreciate it.

And I would get a cat.

I shuffle.

Stretching me, the plug he placed inside me this morning forces *aware*, my mind perpetually drifting to Clay Butcher. He ensures control—consuming me—even in his absence. And between my thighs, the ache of his passion remains too.

"You must be Fawn," a woman says from over my shoulder, and I glance behind me to see Clay's mum in a pink matching sweater suit and jacket, gold jewellery dangling from her thin wrists. The woman who created the most impressive man I have ever met.

Kudos.

She is in the jamb of the French doors, her blue eyes assessing, her pursed smile not entirely unfriendly but not pleased either. *Unreadable...* like it's a fucking Butcher trait.

"Hello," I say softly, hearing my voice smaller than usual as the matriarch of Clay's family moves around to stand in front of me. I try not to think about what Luca said. About his infidelity. About loving another woman—

"Yes. That's me." I internally roll my eyes at myself. *Clever girl, Fawn.* "It's nice to officially meet you, Mrs Butcher."

I go to stand, but she raises her hand.

"Please, don't get up on my account. You look far too comfortable."

Okey dokey... I lean back. And yet something about the way she said 'too' feels as though it stifled further articulation... Like, "you look far *too* comfortable in my son's house." Maybe I'm reaching...

She considers me for a moment, somehow stripping me bare. Under her gaze, the thought and sensation of the crystal plug force blood to my cheeks.

Fuck. Don't shuffle, Fawn.

I'm becoming increasingly uncomfortable...

Thank you very much.

"So"—I clear my throat— "you're visiting—"

"You're very striking, Fawn," she cuts in. "With those eyes." She looks down at the kitten; her lips pinch and then twitch. Then she returns her gaze to me. "And you're the daughter of Dustin. Not just anyone... are you?"

"Yes. I'm his daughter."

"And yes, I'm staying in the far wing. You shan't see me. And don't worry, I cannot hear anything over this side of the building, so you and my son have absolute privacy to engage in whatever it is that makes him happy. You *do* make him happy, don't you?"

I have no words, my mouth flapping in shock. She knows about me—about *us*. She did see him fondling me in the kitchen the only other time we met...

God, what must she think of me? Maybe, Clay's marriage is a known ruse within his family. Yet with that knowledge, she has managed to say nothing offensive, yet somehow delivered discomfort to my very marrow.

"I hope so."

Gah.

Smooth.

She smiles, but it's flat. "That's very good, Fawn."

My breathing picks up pace. It is as though she just awarded me a gold star for giving her son orgasms... This is getting awkward.

Glancing at the kitten, I use her distracting little meows to contemplate what to say. I want to ask Clay's mum to sit with me, so I can understand her better. Maybe learn about Clay as a child. Maybe laugh at a story or two, pull out the baby book, all the silly, sweet things I've seen mums do on the television. *Only* on the television.

Because mums in real life don't always do those things. The media gives people unrealistic expectations...

I'd like a mum, too, though; I'd like a relationship with her. Maybe I can pull her stone-like façade down.

Maybe she'll let me call her mum one day. Maybe she's just guarded because the life she's lived has been cruel, *maybe...*

Mine too!

I can relate to that.

Hopefulness fills my chest. "Would you like to—"

I halt my tongue on her retreating back. She's already walking away from me, passing through the French doors, and closing them on her shadow. Done with me.

"Cool," I mutter to the breeze. "Next time then."

CHAPTER FOURTEEN

THE WIND SHIFTS through my hair, the long blonde strands interrupting the view of the flat horizon only divided by a long black tarmac.

Ahead, dusk gathers, rushing lines of silver down the pearly metallic paint on the luxurious private jet.

I'm awed.

I'm also fucking nervous.

My stomach churns to the sound of the jet ahead, but I block it out. Slipping into an automotive state, I stride towards the private jet.

Henchman Jeeves rolls my new pastel pink Louis Vuitton luggage behind him. I know that's a *thing*. Louis Vuitton. When I saw them in the flesh on my bed, I raced over and couldn't stop swiping my thumb across the small grooves creating a perfect *LV* in the cream handles.

Ahead of me, two young women in power suits wait by the stairs as I cross the runway. I take bigger steps towards the open craft, knowing within the rich interior is Clay Butcher.

Between my legs, I've been throbbing and wet all day.

This is my third day wearing the plug. He puts it in me each morning and removes it when he gets home. It keeps my mind beneath a blanket of perpetual arousal.

Today, *I* removed it—only a few hours ago. Fumbling around, I didn't like taking it out myself, but I came on his sheets as I did.

I focus on the craft.

After the awkward encounter with Clay's mum, I used his laptop. He'd set up a guest account for me. I know he has some kind of *child-lock* on it, although I haven't faced any restrictions yet. I don't think I mind... he believes he's protecting me. Whether I need it or not, the premise is new, foreign, and makes my heart soar because someone cares enough to do so. I know that to many people this kind of behaviour raises flags—bright red flags—but to a girl who spent her entire life without her seat belt buckled, without a phone call to see what time she'd be home, without a meal for three days, without a second thought... it's like finally being *seen*.

The Beginners Guide to Flying, and although he told me that it was *"far from necessary or relevant in this case, little deer,"* given we are taking a private jet, I memorised the main points anyway.

Some still matter.

One: arrive early.

That one doesn't matter.

Two: wear easily removable shoes.

What shoes aren't easily removable?

Three: Wear comfortable clothes.

I gaze down at the white lace *'poplin dress'* Aurora bought and hung in my dressing room, the seam lightly feathering my upper thighs. It's short, cute, and Aurora was right; I do love it.

Four: have identification handy. I realised when that one came up that I don't have any identification of any kind. None that would secure me a passport anyway. I struggled for a moment with that, along with the irony of having little *identity*—never to be a Butcher nor accepted as a Nerrock and only momentarily a Harlow—but drowned that thought. I'm going to be many things now —the most important, the *right* woman for him.

The jet engines roar as I grow nearer, my pulse kicking up a notch with every step. This big column will be in the sky soon, hundreds of kilograms of weight, hurtling through the clouds with squishy, fleshy human beings on board, only protected by the metal walls, only held up by velocity—

It doesn't seem safe...

Swallowing thickly, I climb the stairs dutifully. Staring at my nude-coloured sandals—easily removable shoes—making sure I don't miscalculate, I take two steps then I hear his voice over the droning of the jet, "Take my hand, sweet girl."

My hair sweeps across my face as I peer up and into blue eyes that rival the silver lining of low hanging clouds above a descending sun. The eyes of the most formidable man in the city. The most beautiful. Deadly. I remember when I compared him to a villainous Batman, and the District to Gotham.

The Devil's Prototype.

He's not falling out of the sky.

I grin at him and take his outstretched hand, feeling my nerves settle immediately. His hand swallows mine with a protective dominance that warms everything inside me. Guiding me up until I am on the deck with him, he then steps backwards for me to precede him.

We enter the warm lightly humming cabin. Clay's presence behind me is hot and electric, as I pan my gaze over the luxurious, lavish interior. It looks just like I imagined it. White leather recliners set by the small windows. One facing the other. An aisle through the middle.

Taking a seat opposite the one already leaning back, guessing that's his spot, I place my hands on my lap and watch him sit opposite me. While the chair is spacious around my body, it is snug around his much larger form.

He stares at me, and I glance away under that penetrative gaze. "I have cameras in my room. I saw you take my gift out of your pretty arse."

I gasp, twisting in my seat to see if anyone can hear. The women are nowhere to be seen. Neither is Henchman Jeeves.

"They are all in the cockpit," he deadpans.

I glance back at him, my face on fire. Squirming, I almost moan at the memory paired with the imagery of his cool blue gaze watching me. "I came."

His lips form a tick of smooth, confident approval as he praises, "I saw. Such a good girl, humping my pillow while you removed it. Moaning my name. You never forget who to thank for your orgasms, whose name belongs between your gasping lips when you come."

Oh. My. God. I cover my face, groaning my humiliation through my fingers. "You have no filter with me, Sir."

"How would that benefit me?"

I talk to my palms. "*I'm embarrassed.*"

"Don't be. You must have known I could see. You'll never be without my eyes on you. Find comfort in that, little deer. You put on such a pretty show for me. With your pussy grinding on the pillow and your fingers playing with your rim. Tell me, do you want more of that? *Much* more?"

I swallow. The thought of him mounting my back, his heavy body pressing into mine, his cock thrusting through those muscles until he is so deep the sensation dances on pain—I nod into my palms. "Yes, please, Sir."

"Good." He shifts his expression to one fitting casual conversation, his tone losing a hint of guttural arousal as he says, "Now, my father spoke to me this afternoon, sweet girl." I drop my hands to stare at him, the heat from my cheeks cooling instantly. "It appears you two had quite an interesting conversation a few days ago."

Hopefully not about *'fatherhood'* or being the *'right'* woman or his marriage or—I shuffle in the now *strangely* spacious seat.

He goes on, "Do you believe we hold you accountable for Dustin's betrayals? That has simply never been the case. Why didn't you discuss this with me?"

Oh. That's the part they discussed. I relax a little. "I don't want to disappoint you."

A man says something in another language over the speaker. Clay stands and moves to belt me in, testing the tightness across my chest before sitting back down and belting himself in. "I want all of you," he states simply. "I want you to come to me with every issue. Every pain. Every uncertainty. No one else. Ask me now. We have all night."

All night? On this craft?

The plane begins to move. "But I didn't even realise I felt that way until Luca and I were talking," I admit. "It just came out. I feel like the—*your*—enemy... by blood at least."

"You are mine. You're not his."

"But I was the enemy at the beginning. Right? You had this big secret while I thought you were helping me, but you were using me... Even Xander was a part of it."

"*Even* Xander?" He articulates the *even* with hints of contempt. "Is his involvement in this betrayal somehow more impactful than my own?"

I can't hide the hitch of a smile at my lips. "This jealousy thing is really becoming of you, Sir."

"*Territorial,* sweet girl."

The plane speeds up, rolling over small bumps, and my hands go to the balls of the armrests. I squeeze, pressing my spine into the seat and peering out the window. The night has swallowed the twilight, making the runway glow spectacularly.

I thought I'd be more nervous than I am. First time flying. First time in the sky. I have done everything alone in my life. I would have done this, too. But there is no fear now that I am with him. He will never let any harm come to me. Never put me in danger. Never let anyone hurt me. There is power to this man greater than his body. Greater than the plane. The sky. And even any storm.

It wasn't always so, though. Weeks ago, I was simply the daughter of his enemy.

I look back at him. "What were you going to do with me at the beginning? That first day when we met?"

His brows tighten. "Once I found your father, I was going to pay you off and send you on your way."

"How did you know I wasn't working for him?"

"I obtained your records," he says, unwavering and unaffected by that admission. "In amongst the documentation was recordings of your interrogations with the police. I watched them. Watched *you*. Many times. More times than necessary, I admit. I liked watching you. I knew about your mother's suicide. Your brothers. I knew about that fucker's death." He studies my response to his words, adding, "Don't be upset by this, little deer. I don't take chances with my family, and you were living under my roof. After watching you, I was convinced you were innocent in all this."

I nod slowly, sorting the information behind blinking eyes. I knew he would do some kind of due diligence after I arrived at his house. And I remember he took a swab of cells from my cheek the day I arrived, so I suspected he'd have information on me, but footage from—

The plane suddenly tilts.

My body flattens to the seat, and I hold my breath along with my thoughts.

My lungs expand as we take flight. Then we are soaring upward through the sky, steady and smooth, to get closer to the stars. To the moon. My mum's magical moon.

Staring out the window into the black void only lit by the red light on the wing, I smile. "*Woah.*"

"When we arrive in Dubai, the sun will be just rising," he advises, and I turn to him in shock. *Dubai?* "And you can watch the world light up from above it..." He pauses. "Like my queen. Will that please you?"

"Dubai? *Woah.*" I try to recall everything I know about the place but come up short. It's in the Middle East. I think? That's the extent of my knowledge. "Yes."

"Good. Accept that part of your life is over. Accept who you are and who you belong to." The plane levels out, and he unbuckles his seat belt, saying, "Do you have any more questions for me? Don't be shy."

Who am I going to be to you? Will we have children? Will I be part of your family, with your brothers?

Am I the right woman?

I glance down at his thighs, wondering whether he'll let me sit at his feet and rest my head on his knee. *Am I allowed?* I don't know private jet protocol.

"Would you like a beverage?" One of the suited ladies appears at our side, her eyes politely on Clay's face. I tilt my head, wondering how she stays so respectful and calm when he is so striking, such a force of masculine prowess. Then I notice her chest rises and falls fast, and the roll of her throat follows. She *is* susceptible to his magnetic pull.

"Whiskey," he states, offering her a smooth smile.

"Oh." Beaming at the thought, I quickly say, "Same for me, please."

"No," he states, his eyes dropping the length of my torso and up again. "No alcohol. Juice?"

My shoulders deflate. "But I had whiskey the other day with your dad. I like it."

The muscles along his jaw pulse. "No. Alcohol."

I frown, thinking about Aurora nursing a glass tumbler, and sipping her whiskey without his refusal. A little grumble leaves me. "Fine."

"Grape juice?"

I raise a brow at him. "Funny."

As the lady leaves his side, he leans back a little further, eyeing me with intent and amusement. "You like whiskey?"

"Yes. I really do. It's fucking amazing. Like drinking liquid fire, somehow. I won't have much. Just one glass. Ya know? Experience the whole plane thing properly," I press, appealing to the side of him that wants me to experience things and use my voice. I grin. "*Please*, Sir."

A smooth, charismatic smile works in the corner of

his lips, and my stomach bursts with butterflies just like the first time I saw him. "Another time, sweet girl. I promise. For now, juice and focus." He nods at the spot between his feet.

My sigh of contentment cascades like a wave. I do as I am 'nodded' to do, unbuckling my belt and jumping to my feet.

I sit between his legs on the floor.

I settle in, and he combs his fingers through my hair. "You have been very brave tonight, little deer. I'm proud of my sweet girl for her first time flying. I admit I was trying to distract you. But using your voice is important to me. So, do you have any further questions for me about your father?"

It did work, Sir.

Resting my head on his lap and staring at the red light on the plane's wing as it flashes, I think about this life of rivals and enemies and, as Luca put it, *'bad blood.'* I don't mind what the answer is... I just want to ask it. "Who is the villain in this story? Is it my dad?"

"I'm the villain," he states, and my chest tightens. My first assessment of him being *the Devil's prototype* comes tumbling back into my mind. "Your father is the villain," he adds. "We are all evil in someone else's narrative."

I don't mind that he's the evil in someone else's narrative. I like his power. Control. His morally grey exis-tence. I've lived with *'good'* people—my foster mother, for one. I've asked *just* people for help—the police. People who wear a façade of pristine correctness to hide the pollution inside them.

I gaze up at him. "You're not evil in mine." I look into endless blue eyes that send shivers of warning and excitement through me. "You're *everything* to me, *everything* I ever wanted, Sir."

His lips take on a warning curve. "*So sweet*," he purrs. "And what do you think evil really looks like, little deer?"

I breathe out hard. "I don't know."

"Everything you ever wanted."

CHAPTER FIFTEEN

I READ all about Dubai on the way. It was a barren wasteland once, and now it's a living organism, pulsing and flashing with colour and luxury.

As the sun rises, the streets seem to glitter in dashing lines of gold and red and orange—the veins of roadways. A moving sea of energy.

Above the streets—buildings like columns of wealth, their glass windows rolling in colour in the newly gathering dawn. Bright-blue man-made beaches, rivers, and estuaries, cut through the lavish cityscape. White sand on the banks. Fountains propel neon water into the air, reaching for the clouds.

In a desert.

Dubai.

The wealthy man's holiday destination, the corrupt man's escape, and to an orphan girl, it's Wonderland.

With my face basically squished to the cold window, I watch the plane land. We exit the conditioned environment of the jet, stepping into a stifling heat that seems to wrap around every inch of skin, immediately forcing sweat to the surface.

Henchman Jeeves and another henchman follow us across the tarmac, where I remain silent as we are ushered in a state of urgency to an awaiting black vehicle.

We set off, and the driver takes us through the overlapping channels of roadways. Clay's hand rests on my thigh the entire time, his thumb moving over my skin, sliding in the gathering beads of perspiration.

When the driver crosses a bridge, there is no mistaking our destination as on the small island before us stands one thing—an over-the-top hotel shaped like a sail.

We pull in and are escorted into the lobby. It all happens so fast; I only manage to register a moment of rich humidity, and then we pass through the entrance and into that perfectly fabricated temperature.

I turn to see Henchman Jeeves and Henchman Noname close behind. *Are we avoiding someone? Everyone?* The thought comes to me in an unwelcome wave. I'm forever going to be his dirty little secret. Will it always be this way? I imagine plastered across the news tomorrow morning: "Mayor Butcher and his young lover check into a hotel in Dubai."

My self-doubt stills as my sandals clip over the polished flooring, and I peer up at the golden columns in the lobby. "*Woah,*" I mutter to myself.

Fucking hell.

This hotel certainly doesn't skirt the limits of decadent excess. No. It spills the fuck over such limits.

I try to keep up with the pace of the *'yes'* men and swooning women now filtering in and out of conversation with Clay. His smooth voice sails around, delivering greetings and demands.

I stop for a moment to gaze at a painting, but Clay grips my hand reassuringly, guiding me away. Smiling at his touch, I look down at his long fingers entwined with mine. "Are you hiding me?" I ask, but he only squeezes my hand in response, his attention on the elegant man who has appeared at his side.

"They have already arrived," the man says, falling into stride with us as we head towards the elevators. "We have secured both floors. We will have men on the lower level and the upper one. Your suite is ready with all the changes required for your stay. And Mr Butcher..." The man stops, forcing us to still. "Mr. Futtaim is eager to see you before you settle into your room. He's in the lounge."

Clay's gaze shifts to an area beyond the lobby and he nods in a respectful way. "Very well."

We slow our steps slightly as we enter a room draped in red and gold striped curtains. Scattered across the recessed lounge area, people sprawl out on plush sofas with golden carvings. The smell of incense circles the space, and it's so intense and delicious I imagine myself in a cartoon where smell can be seen in ribbons of colour slithering through the air.

Across the room, a bar glows behind a man sitting on one of the stools, his eyes fixed on us. Immediately, the butterflies in my stomach stir.

This man is powerful. Rich too. Such a statement is in the drips of gold on his long-sophisticated robe and the penetrative demand of his wide assessing eyes.

He smiles at Clay. It's friendly, but that doesn't gentrify the vibe of superiority he radiates.

"Greetings, Clay."

Clay's hand slips from mine. Without that anchor of what to do, I'm left not knowing how to behave... *Should I offer them privacy? Or stand quietly? Shake his hand?*

The striking, brown-skinned man stands and clasps both palms around Clay's firm shake. "So wonderful to have you here in Dubai. And to accommodate you again."

"Likewise. Next time it will be for leisure."

Is it not for leisure this time?

Or is that just something businesspeople say...

I fidget beside them. Wealthy people still make me uncomfortable. They see the poverty in my own mannerisms just as clearly as I see wealth in theirs.

Holding my breath as they talk, I sense my temperature rise from standing in the shadow of these two men who exude such potent and dangerous heat.

Absently, I chew on my bottom lip, and the man Clay is conversing with looks at me, catching my eyes on him.

I look down beneath his gaze. I'm not sure what it is about him—perhaps it's the unapologetic way his eyes cut through everything they land on... the current destination, my blushing cheeks.

I exhale hard, realising *both* men have fallen quiet and now have their gazes glued to me.

"Hello," I say stupidly.

Clay grips my elbow, and I realise that I'm twirling my hair around my finger. I drop my hands to my side. "Malik asked if this is your first time to Dubai, sweet girl."

I smile forcibly at Malik. "Yes. It's like Wonderland."

Malik smiles wider, his eyes dark tunnels set ablaze by amber flames. "And you fell down the rabbit hole." His accent makes all his words seem curt and adamant, but I like it. It reminds me of power. Just like Clay's voice does.

"Ain't that the truth." I laugh nervously in response to his brilliant smile and uncomfortable attention.

"Well, I'm terribly sorry I'll be taking your friend away from you for a few hours tonight."

"My friend..." I glance at Clay, my throat tightening. "Yes, we are very friendly," I bite out through tight teeth.

Malik's grin grows.

Clay only displays that stunning practised contentment he shows the world. A man of utter control. Smooth and unaffected by others. "We haven't seen each other in many years, sweet girl, and you'll be exhausted soon. You barely slept on the plane."

Right.

I'll be exhausted soon by the sheer damn will of Clay Fucking Butcher. And I'm still *his pretty little burden.*

After a few pleasantries and a drink shared between the men, Clay guides me into the lift and up several floors.

A man stands at the entrance to a room, holding the double doors open, awaiting us.

Clay is quiet and unreadable now as we pass through the threshold to our room—No. Not a fucking room.

I gaze around the elaborate floor. Opposite to the entrance, a kind of lounge area with a large, recessed spa and love-seat style sofas overlook the vast Dubai cityscape.

I wander into the centre of the floor as Henchman Jeeves and Henchman No-name bring in our cases. Spinning a little, I take it all in.

The flooring to my left is gold and beige marble, while to my right, is a rich magenta carpet leading to a raised four-post bed draped with satin and silk, covered in pillows.

Camouflaged in front of the purple and gold encrusted wallpaper, a guard is stationed at every door.

Three doors.

The scent of smoke coming from a fancy kind of pipe on an elaborate stand in the lounge area awaiting Clay, I imagine, teases towards me like that brightly coloured cartoon smoke.

Dashing over to the window, I press my palms to the glass, peering down the edge of the building—the drop straight. The fuck. *Down.* My mind throws my body off the brink to experience the fall... It's surreal. Experiencing this devastating height and drop without the risk of falling weighs down my chest. "*Woah.* Dizzy," I say, stepping backwards.

The door shuts behind me, and I chase the sound, landing on Clay watching me intensely.

He doesn't smile, and I wish I knew why. "Do you like your room?"

I beam at him, hoping my happiness will find his hiding away inside his serious façade.

"I've seen better," I tease, walking towards him, reaching up to touch the light bristles along his jawline. "Why are you so grumpy right now, Sir? *Whatcha* hiding from me?"

He ignores my questions. "I have entertainment planned for you, sweet girl. But you can do anything that pleases you as long as it isn't dangerous."

"Bummer," I mock, trying to lighten this dark, breathtaking man, "because I very much like doing you."

Classic, clever, one of my best, and yet it goes completely unappreciated as he zeros in on a desk in the corner of the room. My hand slips from his cheek as he strides over and takes a seat in front of it. "I'll shower then... if that's okay, Sir?" I call over to him, unable to stifle the bratty tone circling each word. *Is he pushing me away again?*

This is such bullshit.

He calls me the "teenage girl" but has the grunts and disinterest of a teenage boy sometimes.

Around the room, we are not alone. Four foreign henchmen, HJ and HN converse quietly.

My new Louis Vuitton case lies on the bed, and the lady who put it there is busying herself unpacking and hanging up my clothes. What do privileged people do for themselves?

Shower, I think.

I grab my toiletry bag from within the silk-lined mould of the luggage.

As I near the bathroom, I catch Henchman Jeeves' attention and shrug questioningly. He nods in an "it'll be okay" kind of way.

Whatever.

AFTER MY SHOWER, I lie on top of the sheets, facing the wrong way so I can watch Clay at his desk. He's magnificent even as he ignores me—neglects me.

That's pathetic, Fawn.

He dotes on you.

The little girl with abandonment issues in me experiences the burn of his lacklustre attention. I need his eyes on me like I need air. It isn't fair on him, though.

His mind is somewhere else—not on me—furrowed brows screaming his concern etched to his masculine face.

I sigh, willing the pathetic self-doubt away. I can't be arduous work for him, or he'll realise I'm not worth the trouble.

The rational side of me reminds me of our conversation on the plane. How he reassures me at every turn that I am his. That I'm safe.

But why did he bring me here if only to work?

It's a selfish question, coming from the girl with nothing to do—not even unpack her own suitcase. I want to ask about his work, but there is a battle going on in my mind, wanting to please him, not *burden* this important man because I'm needy-as-fuck and he'll realise that and wish he'd never told me to speak my mind in the first place because maybe I'm better as something quiet to look at— *God. Shut up, Fawn.*

But then he did tell me to use my voice...

Or does that only apply to issues regarding me?

Or can I ask him about his business?

"What is worrying you, little deer?"

I smile; his voice is like a smooth blanket sliding along my thighs and legs, reminding me that he sees all, and knows everything. He's perfection.

How did I get this lucky?

As I sit up on the bed, my long blonde hair cascades over my robe, the ends skimming the mattress. I swallow around the lump in my throat and answer him honestly, "You're so quiet, Sir. It's making me feel invisible."

"I'm working," he states nonchalant, his eyes unwavering from the document on his laptop screen.

I pout petulantly—hating that I'm inclined to do so—and reposition myself, shuffling to draw his attention.

Only then he says, "What would make my sweet girl more comfortable?" He swivels in his large black chair, pinning me with his blue gaze, and I smile at his attention. At his X-men ability to see through me, just like he can somehow see from the corner of his eyes. Must come in handy in his line of work. "Would you like to sit at my feet, lay your head on my lap, and suck on my cock until you feel better?"

My heart balloons. "Yes, please, Sir."

He nods at his henchmen, who dutifully turn to face the purple and gold wallpaper. *The Clay Butcher nod.* "Grab yourself a pillow and come here," he orders me, tapping his thigh once before returning his attention to the computer atop his desk.

I scurry from the mattress and rush to him. Dropping the pillow at his feet, I sit on it and get comfortable. He continues to work, and I slowly slide his zipper down to release his large length. Weighted and swelling in my hand, a bead of pre-cum surfaces as I rub him to steel. He's smooth like satin, yet hard and unyielding. I lick the salty bead, rewarded instantly with a hiss from him. "Good girl. Now suck. And remember who you are to me."

IT'S HOURS LATER. I'm sure. I don't know how much time passes, but when I come to, I'm so perfectly tucked into bed that I'm basically Cryovac packed. And I must have fallen asleep on his lap with his cock in my mouth.

Through the window, the city is lit in the night-time sky. I frown. I somehow slept through the entire day.

Peering around, I try to recall the moments before I fell asleep. I rub my tired eyes before dragging my hands down my face.

My half-masted gaze lands on a small white box on the bedside table and a handwritten note.

I tuck my legs behind me, kneeling on them and reach for the box, which is white, silk, and *God*, I think it's a present. I don't get presents. Ever. I don't get pointless presents like expensive jewellery.

How do you know it's expensive, Fawn?

How do you know it's jewellery?

Shut up and open it.

Heat behind my eyes threatens to boil tears until I release them. Nope. Not happening. I read the letter instead:

"Remember who you are. My queen. And you never leave my sight."

I dart my gaze around the ceiling line, searching for a camera. I notice two small globes like little upside-down spaceships. My mum would have had all sorts of theories about them... *"Cameras are deceitful, Fawn. You never really know who is watching you. Or how many screens there are."*

I'm reminded momentarily of Benji's room in the basement, the camera, and the recordings, the night of the incident and— I shake my head, dislodging the unbidden recall.

I know who is watching me today, Mum. And I've never been safer.

I smile brightly at one of the little upside-down spaceships and lift the box to show Clay, who I can almost sense watching me from within the dark, ominous void.

Taking a deep breath, I open the box in my lap. My

eyes widen on the piece. Within a silk cast is a rose gold necklace with a beautiful pendant encrusted with little pink, white, and peach gems. My hands start to shake. It's a monarch butterfly.

Beautiful and poisonous.

The queen of the butterflies.

I unthread it from the base and turn it over in my hand, feeling the weight, the cool metal, loving it so entirely my heart balloons to uncomfortable proportions.

Then I see that on the rear side, engraved along one swooping wing, the words, "*My queen.*"

A tear bursts from the corner of my eye, and I wipe at it immediately.

Another tear rolls down my cheek and over the swell of my lips, as I reach between my hair and my shoulders and fasten the clasp at the nape of my neck.

I'm never taking it off, Sir.

No more than a few seconds later, the phone beside the sofa rings. I race to it. Grabbing the ringing handset with a start, I answer, "Hello to you, Sir. I love it so fucking much."

"Then why are you crying?" he asks in a smooth, rich timbre that slices through the deep laughter in the background. Voices I recognise and loud music so crisp I could be in the same room as they sail through the speaker between his words. "I don't like to see it."

"They are overwhelmed tears," I admit, pressing my palm to the butterfly now resting over my heart. "Is it expensive? Not that it matt—"

"What do you think, sweet girl?"

I talk through a grin as butterflies, *way bigger* than the one settled into the dimple at my neck, bash around.

I squeak excitedly, "Are they diamonds?"

"Yes."

Woah.

Never in my wildest fantasies did I *ever* imagine owning a *real* fucking diamond. *Fuck.* What if I lose it?

What if the chain breaks while I sleep?

This is a huge responsibility. I need to look after it! Should it be in a lockable box or— "I need to get it insure—"

"It is insured, little deer."

My heart swells. "Of course it is." I release a long, dreamy sigh. "I couldn't love it more if I tried."

He deepens his voice. "My feelings precisely."

And he's not talking about the necklace. My expanding heart fills all the space in my chest, leaving me breathless. "I miss you, Sir. You left without saying goodbye."

"*I* said goodbye. You were exhausted after barely sleeping on the flight. You need to sleep when you are tired, sweet girl. That is important to me. Sleep. Nutrients—"

I chuckle. "You're not sleeping. And I doubt any nutrients are being ingested, *Sir*. That is important to me," I mock, talking through a small smirk.

"Even a business meeting sounds like a carnival when my brother Bronson is around. I assure you, I'm as uncomfortable with our distance as you are."

I smile at that. "So, Bronson is with you?"

"Yes, sweet girl. My family is here."

My stomach sinks a little. Am I his dirty little secret? And while he is out with his family, I'm hidden away in here.

Is Aurora there?

On his arm?

Gah.

I touch the pendant, willing my mind to remain in the contented, loved state from moments ago.

Seriously, Fawn?

What more do you want from this breathtaking man?

Everything!

"*So...*" I chew my bottom lip, blurting out, "Is your wife there with you too?"

Smooth.

"*Little deer,* stop those thoughts."

Wiping at my wet cheeks again, I remove all the happy tears, hearing a rough sigh leave him.

"You have company," he states at the exact time a soft, hesitant knock draws my attention to the double doors. "I will see you soon. Put some clothes on before you let the soldiers in, but they must stay inside the floor when you are awake, Fawn. They have strict orders."

Then he's gone.

Soldiers... I've never heard him refer to them as that before. And I always call them henchmen because '*soldiers*' sounds like they're going to war. My stomach knots up for reasons I don't care to analyse, so I slip from the mattress and throw on a robe and rush to the door.

The silky material whispers around my legs as I walk. The luxurious feel of expensive fabrics is still new and exciting to me.

I swing the door open.

Surprised, my eyes land on Clay's sisters-in-law Cassidy and Shoshanna, and I grab the tails of the robe, tightening them around my waist when I see they are fully dressed.

As is appropriate at 6:00 pm, Fawn.

I smile. *They aren't out with him...*

Cassidy is dressed casually in a yellow t-shirt and yoga pants, while Shoshanna is in a red halter with jeans, the denim fashionably ripped open around the thighs. She understands the worn-but-new-trend, and with her curves, the strategically faded denim clings to her body, stretching and drawing my eyes to the plump parts of her I wish I had more of—

"*Hey*," I say in a long, drawn-out way, forcing my gaze from her thighs as I leap over the line for the appropriate time spent ogling someone you aren't dating.

"You seem surprised," Shoshanna interjects, combing her fingers through her silky dark hair.

Cassidy beams. "You had no idea that we were in Dubai too. Did you?" Before I can answer, she snort-laughs. "Classic Clay. Need-to-know basis for just about everything. Max is the same. Getting information that isn't immediately important is like pulling teeth from a bear. I just got, "Pack for Dubai, little one," without much explanation. He does always pack for Kels though, because we forgot her favourite shoes once, and I didn't fret. She's not even four, ya know? She'll get over it quickly. But every. Single. Tear. Is devastating to Max. He can't handle them. He spoils her... *Sorry*." She giggles again, outwardly far more awkward than me. "I ramble."

"No. It's fine." I say, gripping my forehead, cradling it. "I'm sorry. I had no fucking idea you guys were here. I'm glad you are though."

"We came on a different plane," Cassidy says. "Your first time flying so—" She shrugs a little. "I guess he wanted you to have privacy or something."

Clay's statement on the phone tumbles into my mind as if for the first time: "Even a business meeting sounds like a carnival when my brother Bronson is around." Of course. If his brothers are here, then so are their partners. That aspect of the conversation didn't really materialise, drowned out when he had said, *"I assure you, I'm as uncomfortable with our distance as you are."*

I smile, rolling my eyes at myself. "Actually, I should have known you were here. Clay told me on the phone just now. He said Bronson was there with him."

"We have come to have dinner with you," Cassidy says, engulfing me in her small but strong arms. "Kids are safe and tucked-in bed. The ladies will eat and play."

I stiffen.

Combating my body's predisposition to push her away, my skin reminds me I'm not a fan of touch these days. She is practically a stranger. Her entire torso is touching mine. Besides Clay, I'm not sure I've had another person touch me this closely, for this long—*will this cuddle ever end?*

She finally releases me and skips into the room, and I cloak my uncertainty by smiling harder than feels normal.

"Room service fricking rocks. Frick," she coos through a laugh. "This suite is amazeballs. I love these little carvings. And this view! Shoshanna, look, you can see the fountains. They'll be down there somewhere. Being menaces, I bet."

Shoshanna follows her in, both soon making themselves comfortable on the sofa. I see the *soldiers* waiting expectantly, and I attempt the Clay Butcher nod for them to enter. They do. And I'm kind of chuffed about it.

Immediately finding a place along the wall, they once again become one with the furniture.

I close the door behind them.

"You have a lot," Cassidy says, following my attention

to the men around the room. "I have a few as well. My main guard is Carter, but he's watching over Kelly and Stone at the moment. Shosh has guards too. She has more than she knows about," Cassidy quips as though she has the intel.

"I have *Henri*. Predominately. He watches over my sister as well," Shoshanna grounds, before gazing at me, her tone shifting in a formal way, in a clinical way, bringing to the front of my mind the memory of her performing my ultrasound—a lump builds in my throat —and my *Pap Smear*. She's a doctor. *Dr Adel?* I think she introduced herself at the time. "How are you feeling today?"

"Ah. *Fine...* Why?"

"It's been a very stressful few weeks, and stress can do strange things to us," she confirms. "And your first time flying, too. That's a lot. If you ever need anything, I'm always here for you. Okay?"

I chuckle a little. "Did Clay put you up to this?"

"He just asked that I check in—" Then she grins candidly, figurately dropping her doctor's hat for me. "And has asked that we make sure you eat something."

"*Shosh*," Cassidy reprimands, turning to me with a cheerful appeasing kind of smile. "He cares. That's all. These boys just have a... *funny* way of showing it."

"A funny way?" Shoshanna questions. "A primitive way." She laughs as she lifts the hotel phone and begins talking to a person on the other end. The words 'steak' and 'cake' seeps into my ears. *I could definitely eat.*

As always, with my limited girl-to-girl social skills, I come back blank with what to say. Agree with them.

Fit in.

Are his ways primitive?

Maybe... but I'm not like these girls. I didn't have the luxury of learning independence, of proving I was ready and then fighting a guardian tooth-and-nail for the freedom to do what I wanted, ready to be pushed from the nest—I was abandoned in the damn nest. *'Alone and surviving'* is my standard. That condition was all I'd known.

Taking care of myself feels a lot like being a child in a caravan with nothing but a promise that the moon can heal, and the world is beautiful, and I'll be a butterfly one day. Nothing but hippy bullshit, two-minute noodles, and peanut butter sandwiches. It's not refreshing to make my own decisions or rely on myself—it's brutal.

Clay sees that.

But I don't argue or try to explain. I simply say, "Are Max and Bronson the same then? About eating and stuff?"

"Ah," Shoshanna drawls, hanging up the phone. And the two women share a meaningful glance in contemplation while I join them on the opposite sofa.

"Different," Cassidy finally says.

"How so?" I ask, watching her pull her legs up and cross them on the sofa.

"Well, Max won't directly say anything," Cassidy offers brightly, "unless I press for it. I just know when there is something wrong."

Shoshanna laughs, a deep husky sound that is confident and full of unapologetic truth. "I've known these boys for most of my life, and what Cassidy means is, he's a grumpy arse, and she has to find out why he looks like he wants to snap something or someone in half."

"No," Cassidy insists through a smile that defies that word. Clearly, Shoshanna is right. "He is just not a big

talker. If he thought that I wasn't eating enough, he'd probably take me out for lunch and then watch every mouthful I take until he's happy with the amount. And I'd see right through it." Then she bursts into giggles because she must find that as endearing and as strange as I do. It makes my heart warm for her.

"And Cassidy will never say a bad word about her Max," Shoshanna quips but seems pleased that it's true.

"And Bronson?" Cassidy eggs Shoshanna on, righting herself from her small fit of laughter.

"Well..." She leans back, settling in. "Bronson would probably tie me up and force feed me or make a joke about providing adequate nutrients by shoving—" She stammers, and Cassidy's eyes widen above an excited beam. "By *other* means..."

I smile at them.

Girlie banter.

I can do this...

We spend the night talking, and Shoshanna trims my hair because she can't seem to stop. She's an over-achiever. Well, both she and Cassidy are, really.

I recall comparing them to cultivated roses, and me to a grass flower. I'm not sure if I feel like a rose just yet, but I also... I don't feel like a grass flower anymore. I reach up and touch the butterfly pendant hanging over my heart.

"You're my pretty little queen."

A monarch.

"I cut Bronson's hair too," Shoshanna says, pulling the strands taut down my back so she can trim the ends, redirecting my attention away from butterflies and roses. "I'll just take a few inches off the bottom." The blunt end of the scissor glides along my lower back as she talks. "It makes sense that I'd be good at this, being a surgeon.

Usually, I'm cutting through tissue though." She pauses, and I hear her smile as she says, "And there is more blood." *More?*

"I've got litres of blood. It's all good."

I look at Cassidy as she fills her mouth with a burger bigger than my palm and definitely bigger than her trim stomach that must be a black hole. "You like food. Where do you put it?" I ask.

"In. Ma. *Belly*," Cassidy croons around the food while gazing at the beef burger with adoration.

I laugh. Titling my head to the side, I say to Shoshanna, "So, doctor, surgeon, hairdresser. What can't you do?"

"I had to learn," she admits softly. "My sister Akila had an accident that left her with— Well, it's complicated, but basically put, brain damage and paraplegia. She wouldn't let anyone else touch her for years, so I learned how to do it."

My smile falls. I blink ahead, not being able to see her expression, only able to hear her tone tighten. Wishing I hadn't assumed... I don't know. Wishing I hadn't made her sad. "I'm so sorry, Shoshanna."

The mood shifts, hurting my heart in my ignorance.

She starts to brush and then snip, brush and then snip. "It sucks. Sucks even more that I couldn't let her go when she wanted to. I'll never do that again. It's no life to live. I knew better as well. It's just not a life."

"*Shosh*," Cassidy whispers, having swallowed her mouthful and placed the burger down on the plate.

"It's fine, Cassidy." She clears her throat. "What can't I do?" She repeats my question from before, her tone upbeat once again. "I can't cook for the life of me. Bronson cooks everything in our house. He's like an old

Sicilian *nonna* in the kitchen. That is, if you can ignore the *kiss-the-cook* apron and the fact he's usually naked."

I laugh, imagining his butt peeking out from his apron.

She adds, "He'd be a nudist if he could."

Thinking about the warm fragrant mist from the oven and a wave of scent blanketing me, I grin widely. Cooking resonates in the maternal side of me, in my soul. It's special. Underrated. Putting different textures and different chemicals together, culminating in decadence.

It's chemistry.

It's magic.

A week ago, Maggie taught me how to create the perfect crust on a pork belly. I watched Clay bite into it, his dark brows rising in satisfaction in a moment he couldn't hide. It was the best feeling. I waited with bated breath to hear the crunch of his teeth as they sunk through the skin, and then I pictured the salty juices spilling around the morsel. "I love to cook," I quip dreamily.

"I love to eat!" Cassidy sings, and we all chuckle a little, letting the conversation lighten.

CHAPTER SIXTEEN

IT'S my new favourite song. Cassidy and Shoshanna went back to their room half an hour ago to sleep but I slept all day, so I'm still wired. *And he isn't home...*

I lift my arms up, making little circling motions in the air above my head with my fingers. The silk of my dress rises to my underwear seam, the fabric caressing my skin, that sensual caress of silk on flesh arousing me.

Closing my eyes, I hum to the melody just as the sound of a door opening snatches me from my dreamy state. I open my eyes and meet the owner of a heated blue gaze. My heart fills with love for this man. My everything. A guardian. A boyfriend. A lover. A teacher.

He frowns at me, and I smile a little harder. Happy. I'm so happy when he's close. When he sees me.

"Who touched your hair?" he asks smoothly, but he might as well have asked who broke my arm because his body takes on a predator's cold, alarming stillness.

Continuing to sway my hips under his penetrative stare, I ask sweetly, "Don't you like it? It's just a few inches shorter."

He lowers his head, staring at me through his top lashes. "Do *you* like it?"

Swooning at his protective nature, I nod, still dancing seductively. "Yes. I do."

"Very well. But next time, little deer, you ask me before you change *anything* about yourself. Give me the opportunity to prepare for that change. Do you understand?"

"Yes, Sir," I agree as he takes a measured step towards me, his potent energy filling the room.

His attention seems to have tangible depth— *God*, it can slide along my skin, squeeze my flesh. I roll my head as the reverie of his touch forces a soft hum through my lips. And as he traces his lower lip with his tongue, my nipples tighten.

Absolute control.

Even from this distance.

I've never danced for him before. I skim my hands down the side of my face and over the front of my dress, rolling my hips as my palms slide over the now aching pointed beads.

He deadpans.

Then he's not looking at me.

I drop my arms immediately as I follow his gaze to one of the foreign henchmen standing across the floor, dutifully at his post, but transfixed on me.

I look at Henchman Jeeves who is staring ahead, not at me or Clay. He isn't oblivious though; the tic in his jaw is proof enough that he knows what is coming.

Time moves slowly now as I flick my eyes from him to watch Clay stride towards the man. Across the floor.

I look at the guard; his eyes haven't left me. *Stupid.* To Henchman Jeeves, who is now closing the gap between us. To Clay Butcher as he passes a cabinet. Back and forth. The man's attention is still fixed, ignorant to the slow, quiet movements that have death and danger circling him.

Stupid—

Clay reaches for a thick based bottle of alcohol. Then everything speeds up, and he's on the man instantly, smashing the bottle on the wall beside his face, brown liquid glistening with shiny shards. The man breaks from his trance, startled.

The sharp blades meet the underside of the henchman's right eye. He is now pinned to the wall by Clay Butcher's formidable form, and I hold my breath.

"See something you want to taste?" Clay hisses, leaning in, but suddenly Henchman Jeeves steps in front of my view, hiding his boss. Yet, I still hear the man howl even though I can't see what's happening. "I should hollow your eyes from your skull."

My eyes shoot to HJ's tight features. My friend. My guard. The man shielding me from witnessing something I may not be able to handle, but I *can* handle it.

"Move," I order, trying to step past him. He refuses. I don't need nor desire his protection in this case. I understand this. I'm not that soft. "*Sir,*" I call soothingly, hoping my voice will somehow break Clay Butcher from his state of feral possessiveness.

HJ twists to see his boss, so I take the opportunity to sidestep from the blockage of his body. Clay's back bunches as I speak. The glass is an inch inside the man's flesh. "Tell him to leave so you can come here and touch me," I plead in a breathy cadence, experiencing a thrill and love and a kind of intoxicating power stir within me.

I watch Clay lower the bottle to his side. We are both

learning how to be together. What it means... All these *feelings*. I miss him. When he's away it sickens me.

And then when he comes home, returns to me, there is this euphoric moment. The moment I need. A passionate display that he cares. I'm insecure... I know.

How can I not be?

"Apparently, she is allowing you to keep your eyes," he states, his tone somehow smooth and commanding, but also flaring with a snarl of restraint. "Leave. All of you."

They don't waste any time.

All three henchmen leave.

I glance at Henchman Jeeves, the last man to exit, closing the door behind him and he nods at me.

But my breath hitches when I look back at Clay. He's staring at me and then at the door HJ disappeared through, his shoulders squared and stiff. His jaw pulses and I realise the interaction just now—*HJ nodding at me*—bothers him.

With Clay's eyes fixed to my body, he places the smashed bottle on its side, blood dripping from the shiny surface. Not a lot. Just enough to explain the man's choked howl of anguish.

Leisurely loosening his tie, his tall, dark, muscular figure walks confidently over to me. He takes a firm hold of my chin, his fingers dipping into my cheek, arching my face up. A harsh hold to foreground a serious message.

Leaning down so that his lips talk against my puckered mouth, he says, "Do you need some kind of reassurance from Bolton, little deer?"

My heart thrashes in my neck, but his mouth is so close to mine, his energy sparking in volatility, I'm quivering with need for him. Finding his feral state of jealousy seductive.

Breathing deeply, I pull away from his grasp, provoking his fingers to give and allow me reprieve.

Softly, slowly, like edging towards a growling dog, I reach up and touch his face. "Have you ever been in love before, Sir?"

His jaw clenches beneath my palm, while his eyes are intent on mine. "No, sweet girl. I don't believe I ever have. Until now."

My heart grows, and I beam, unable to bridle my smile at his honesty. He loves me. I know. He knows too. "Scary, isn't it?"

He grins, and it's devilish and cunning, and my knees buckle from the devastating beauty of it. "For the world, sweet girl. It is incredibly *scary* for the world."

He scoops me into his arms, and I gasp at being so easily manhandled by this terrifying man. A commanding force who is suffering the volatility of love for the first time. He walks with me, cradled to his chest, over to the mattress.

He crawls on, bracing the nape of my neck and head in his large hand before settling down with me under him. One of those trivial things that I love so much. The hand behind my head. Protecting my neck.

And then he kisses me.

His lips slide over mine, and my chest fills with air, my moans and his, and my ever-growing heart. Leaving my lips with a small nip, he drags his down the length of my body at an excruciatingly slow pace. Skating over the silk of my gown, he is soft, and I arch my back off the mattress, wanting more pressure from him. Clutching at him. Wanting to be bruised with his intensity.

He stops at my waist, quickly kneels, grips me either side of my hip, and flips me so I am face down on the mattress.

My dress slides up with the motion, the air now touching the lower globes of my arse cheeks. He slaps the side of my arse hard enough to send a sting through me, but it's only a passing action as he is now pulling my underwear down past my knees.

He stuffs a pillow below my hips. Listening to him remove his belt and drag his pants down, I push up on my elbows to see better. His large hand meets the centre of my back, spanning out and pushing me back into the cushioning beneath me.

I groan at being pinned as his other hand slides to dip inside me, priming me. He growls when his finger slides around my arousal. "So wet. *For me?* I hope."

I frown. "It's always you, Sir!"

With that, he feeds his cock below my arse, between the delta at my thighs, and slams in fast and deep with one long, possessive thrust. "Pretty little liar."

I cry out, taking him so quick.

There is a message in his depth.

A warning in his formidable presence.

"Your body"—he starts to fuck me, his hips dragging a gasp and then a groan from my parted lips—"is so"—my pussy clings to every thick inch as he moves relentlessly, pointedly, purposefully—"fucking *dangerous.*

"So pretty, men risk their eyes for the view." He sweeps my blonde hair to the side, jack-hammering a message into me from behind. "Love from a man like me isn't just scary, sweet girl. *My* brand of love is *lethal.* I will *hurt* them."

I fist the sheets as he works out his possessive

demons using my writhing body for therapy. I know what he's saying, but I ask anyway, the question expelling in bursts that match the pounding of his hips. "Hurt." I gasp. "Who?"

His lips meet my ear, his voice dark, while the rest of his body only tenses and powers through with more unyielding focus. "The men that you *let* look at you."

A pulse begins low in my abdomen, and I pant while taking this fierce man's thrusts. "I didn't."

"The men that you blush for."

"I don't."

"Smile for."

"I don't!"

"You blushed the prettiest colour for Malik," he growls, laying his large body on my back, his thighs locking mine in tight. It's an intimidating hold, but the pulse in my core only becomes more erratic. More stirring. The energy moving lower. Seduced by the growl in his tone, the weight of him, the heat of his feverish skin. "And I don't care that he's one of the richest men in Dubai, little deer." His lips touch my spine. "If you flush under his smile again, I'll gift him to you in small pieces."

He goes on roughly. "You did this on purpose... Pushed me to the edge of my resolve. Testing your boundaries. Admit it to me, little deer. Don't lie."

I roll my head from side to side against the pillow. "No."

"Lie." He slaps the side of my arse, forcing a cry through gasping lips. Pain and pleasure surge and wrestle for dominance. He drops his voice further, saying, "You did it in the dressing room when you panted Aurora's name. And kept touching yourself for me to see. You wanted me to take you. You didn't like that I kept my cock from you while you healed."

"No. I didn't even realise I said her name."

"Lies." His palm connects again, a sting ripping through me. "My sweet girl who wants to *experience* and *experiment*." He slows down, teasing the muscles inside me with the perfect rhythm. "And smile at other men and drive me out of my goddamn mind. Do you want to lie again?"

I only shake my head, but it's enough to earn me a slap harder than before, and while he takes my body in a way that roars it's for *him*, the sting on my arse cheek reminds me that he holds me accountable. That he sees me.

That sensation is for *me*.

The thought of his affections, of his attention, throws me into pleasure's grasp. I begin to tense, my orgasm cresting because of the perfect pace and—

He rams into me and holds, halting the sensation—my climax—from building further, from peaking.

No!

Bastard.

He did that on purpose!

I whimper at the loss.

He begins again, his rhythm brutal and abrupt.

"*Admit it*, sweet girl," he growls, shoving me up the mattress with each pound of his hips. "Admit. That you. Want me. Like this. *Territorial*. Obsessive."

"Fine! I do!" I relent.

He stills. A long guttural moan escapes my lips, warmth from my breath hitting the pillow, heating me further. Defeated. I'm fucking defeated. I want him like this.

I want you jealous, Sir! Dammit.

I want him jealous like I am! He's married. He's married, so he's not mine. His words from the past hisses at me. *"I'll never be yours."*

Fuck.

He knows everything. He always knows, and I'm the stupid girl who can't keep up with this impressive man.

Bastard.

"Good girl." He softens. He threads his fingers tenderly through mine, leaning on his elbows to give me a big breath of air. Humming his approval, he rolls his hips upwards, hitting the twitching bundle of nerves inside me.

He understands my body.

With his approval, I start to come even as I shake from the truth that he wrenched from me. The acknowledgement to who owns my pleasure, expels me as a deep throaty groan muffled in the plush fabric below my face —*Sir.*

He works his cock in and out, dragging the full, throbbing length along every muscle, and I clench around him, holding him to me in a way Aurora never has. And never will. And for a moment, that is enough... I breathe out that lie. A lie. It's another fucking lie.

I want all of him.

"This is *my* sweet, young body," he says smoothly. "I've felt your heartbeat. Tasted your pussy. Touched your blood and licked your tears." His breaths become heavier, and I'm now burnt out, spent, from his words, from the pumping of his cock inside me. From the honesty he fucked from me. *Yes,* I was enjoying the attention—even from Aurora. I want to be close to her to be closer to him. I want to be a part of every aspect of his life.

I. Am. Obsessed.

I am the one obsessed, territorial, and crazy because he is my fucking *everything*. "I just want you," I cry out, utterly overwhelmed.

His warm breath blankets me. "You have me, little deer. And you're going to be swollen with my children soon."

What?

Soon?

A deep groan rumbles through his chest as his words seemingly spur him on. His hips become rhythmic, chasing. "Another way you'll have me. Play your games. But remember what happens when you do. I'll fuck you until you feel me rattle your goddamn bones."

My moans break from me. "Oh. Oh."

The packed muscles lining his powerful physique tighten against my own soft body, his thighs bracing my legs harder, and with a possessive growl, he comes inside me, shaking us both.

Groaning, he holds himself buried deep, the pulsing of his release making me swim in the pleasure he's experiencing as if it were my own. "*Fuck.*"

He slowly winds himself down by rolling slowly, wringing out every powerful burst of cum. I feel it inside me. Wet. Thick. Powerful.

I wriggle on the pillow stuffed below my hips, so entirely enjoyed and possessed by the man holding me down. I pant deeply, my own orgasm a trickling sensation now.

Still breathing hard, my brain reaches for the sentence he uttered about children. "Did you say *soon*, Sir?"

"Don't move, little deer," he says, easing himself from

me with gentle precision, so as to not drag his cum from inside me. "Be a good girl. Stay nice and still for me."

He kisses down my spine, and I close my eyes, feeling each gentle touch of his lips on my back like the promise of a future. Like the gift of our forever. And emotions build, tears rising. *He wants to have a baby with me.*

His declarations to keep me, care for me, spoil me, have never been so concrete, so real... He wants to have a baby with me. Not like before. Not just accept the responsibility of the one already growing inside me when no one else would but to actually make one.

With. Me.

God.

I start to sob softly, tears wetting the fabric beneath me. "Are we going to have a baby together?"

"Yes, little deer. " He kisses my spine again. "Don't cry. It pains me. You asked once if I could love someone who found their accomplishments in being a good mother. You spoke of this in your grief. And I promised to spoil you. You want to be a mother. I want to watch you swell with my babies, watch you nurse them and bring them comfort. Be *sweet* with them. Give them all the things—" He stops talking but I hear his mind whispering, '*All the things we didn't have.*'

All the things we didn't have.

A sense of home.

Luca admitted to his inadequacies as a father, but what about Clay's mother? She seems to adore him. Was she really that terrible a parent? A neglectful woman, maybe?

I sniffle a little as relief reaches out and wraps me in a weighted blanket. I didn't realise just how much I wanted this. Yearned for this. How I found a sense of purpose when I was pregnant. Like the baby gave me a new life...

It's why I want to cook and stack pillows and make spaces comfortable and fun.

It's because other little girls laid in bed, held awake by their father's snoring and the sugar-high from their mother's freshly baked cake, and they imagined their future of fame, of degrees and doctorates, of money and wealth. Of being successful and independent.

While I imagined being them.

I'm an orphan.

My fairy-tale is family.

And Clay Butcher knows it.

CHAPTER SEVENTEEN

"DON'T MOVE, SWEET GIRL." Rough fingers slide along my forehead, my loose hair tickling my skin as they sweep it from my face. The smell of cologne and warm clean male flesh rolls over me. "You should sleep for a few more hours."

I slowly bat my lashes, opening my eyes to the dim room, and find him sitting beside me on the mattress. Feeling my body in that perfectly tucked-in state that means he's taken the time to cover me, and position me, I smile sleepily.

"I have to go."

What?

I squint at the breathtaking man looking down at me, my eyes panning his slightly damp hair, his clean-shaven jawline, and his pristine black suit.

I jolt up, rolling the heels of my palms along my eyes, working them into focus. "What do you mean? Why are you dressed?" Darting my gaze to the window, I see the sky is still a black abyss dotted with multicoloured lights from the city. "What time is it?"

"I said don't move," he deadpans, and I fall back on the mattress as he hovers over me, a serious look in his eyes. "Don't be frightened, but I have to leave."

The quiet circles us, the hum from the air conditioner the only interruption to our breath.

"What do you mean?" I ask, my heart suddenly beating unevenly, my hands shaking uncomfortably. A silly response to the possibility of being alone when it's such a natural state for me to be in. It's not about me, though. This racing heart... It's— "I thought we were going to spend time..." I trail off.

His dark, strong brows draw in, creasing his forehead, displaying glimpses of his age. He looks tired.

Did you sleep at all, Sir?

I reach up, and he turns his head, accepting my touch on his jawline. His softness sends vibrations of breath through my throat. Something is wrong.

"Don't panic, little deer. Listen to me and then drift back to sleep. My brothers and I went out last night to be seen," he states, his voice carrying faux indifference. He's not indifferent this morning, and he's failing to mask it. *God.* I don't like this feeling at all. "To be photographed in Dubai."

Words cling to my tongue.

"Sweet girl, I don't want secrets between us."

I swallow thickly.

"I believe your father is in a motorcycle club's compound," he states firmly, and I squeeze my eyes shut. Holding them still to focus on my breathing as his timbre rips the air from me. This is happening. *Now.* I'm not ready. "He grew up in the District," he points out. "My father, the name Butcher and Storm, did not. My father grew up in Sicily. Jimmy too. Which is why we aligned with Dustin in the first place. He has alliances all over the country. It's true that some of the locals fought back during the Family's takeover. The bikers were the first to disapprove, but they followed one of their own. They followed Dustin. I have good reason to assume they have been protecting him for some time, and that he is planning something. This can't wait." He pauses, his voice strangled as he says, "Protecting *you* can't wait."

He leans down and kisses my eyelids. One, and I take a big breath in. He moves to the other eye, so I can exhale on contact. Then his lips touch mine quickly, provoking my eyes to open when he draws back, my skin mourning his warmth.

A deep clear-blue stare, full of wisdom and severity, pins me in place. "We are going to take the compound as soon as we arrive back in the District tonight. Finish this for the last time. Then we'll fly back here immediately after and be seen in Dubai within twenty-four hours."

I try to wrap my head around his words, intent on understanding his dealings in a business way. In an emotionless way. Like him. "You're using the media."

"Propaganda, little deer. The issue with being at the *top,* sweet girl, is that you're always a *topic.* I had to give them a headline so they would be looking here and not in their own backyard."

I blink over his shoulder, shuffling the information around, ignoring the ever-growing rate of my pulse. I fight the panic that rises. Swallow it down. "So you hid me on the way in, but then went out to be seen last night?"

"Yes."

Nodding mechanically, fighting the bubbling of tears, I whisper, "And Cassidy and Shoshanna?"

"They will be here. With you. And Xander, also."

Xander too. So, it's too dangerous for his little brother?

God, breathe, Fawn.

He'll be okay.

Don't go, Sir.

"Why Dubai?" I ask, my chest beginning to strain the more I understand the situation. The gravity of it. My chest heavy with pressure, my lungs collapsing with the need to control my rising panic.

"Because, sweet girl, despite how I feel about that pretty glow you gave Malik, he adores money nearly as much as I adore you. Of which, I believe he has no greater love affair. I will be giving him a lot of it. So, he is going to protect you. *All* of you while we are out of the country."

And *we* need protecting because this is not safe, but while we are heavily protected, who is protecting him?

The shuddering of my heart surges through my veins and overwhelms me. My panic for the win.

Send someone else.

The guards, soldiers, henchmen.

Whatever!

Anyone else!

Abruptly, I push up, forcing him to lean back to allow me the space. His eyes turn to thin slits, glaring at me as I command, "Don't go!"

"Calm down—"

He made me rely on him.

Obsessed with him.

Love him.

Now he's going to die!

"To hell, I'll calm down, Sir." I shake my head, scurrying along the mattress until I am standing. Putting a bit of distance between us, I square my shoulders, bare and exposed for his perusal, as always, open and available. "Could you die tonight? Could you leave me—"

Projecting feigned composure, he twists to face me, his features smoothly set into that practised expression. "If you continue to raise your voice, sweet girl—"

I laugh hysterically at nothing—it's not even the slightest bit funny—cutting him off. His jaw pulses as I say, "How about, *fuck you, Sir!* Fuck you and your orders, and your fucking cooing and soothing. Fuck you!"

He clasps his hands in his lap, and I hear his knuckles crack under the pressure of his brewing temper. *Good.* He can't bury his sentimentality from me, and he can't drown mine in a charming smile and fussing tone.

"Eccentric girl," he mutters to himself.

"*Eccentric?* I'm so fucking *simple.* Don't lie to me! That's all. Don't bullshit me. This is *dangerous.* You're so willing to risk your life. You come home with a cut like a fucking axe wound in your face, that I can't tend to, and blood all over your clothes that I can't clean for you. You keep yourself an island while making me so utterly vulnerable and available to you. It—"

He rises to his full height, creating a formidable wall of muscles cloaked in a pristine black suit. "*Goddamn it,* Fawn," he bites out. "I'm doing this for you—"

"You think you're so fucking clever, Sir! And I'm so dumb. Like I won't see this for what it is? I'll just let you take the most important thing away from me. Well, I won't. I'll fight you *for you.* I'll fight to keep you."

Fight to keep him, Fawn!

I think quick.

Desperate to keep him here.

Slanting my hips in a seductive way, borderline insane and eccentric and desperate, I whisper, "Don't you want to stay here and play with me?" My feigned breathy voice shakes with emotion, but my posture earns me a hiss from his lips.

"Stop that."

"Don't you want to touch this *pretty pussy,* Sir?" I touch between my thighs, pressing into my palm. "It's yours."

"*Careful,*" he rumbles, his chest thundering beneath smooth dark material, his breath building in anger and arousal.

Unable to pretend further, I snap, "What?" Throwing my arms in the air, I repeat, "What will you do?" *God,* I hope he unleashes himself on me. Hope he grabs me. Manhandles me. Punishes me. Shakes away the blood-curdling fear coursing through my bones, my muscles. "What will you do to me if I'm not *careful?*" I shout. "Have me suck your cock until I calm down? Spank me? Reprimand me? Make me accountable for my words and bad manners?"

I start to tremble with fear of losing his attention, of losing him, tears spitting from my eyes. "Care about me? Give a *shit* about me? *Love me?*" I scream at him, my body a vibrating figure, a vessel for more grief. "*Love me.*"

I drop to my knees.

Cover my face.

And sob helplessly into my palms, wailing. "That'll all be a bit hard to do when you're *fucking dead.*"

Instantly, he is beside me, his body curling around mine, straightening me from my huddled position. He cups my face and forces me to look into his fierce blue eyes. "I won't die, little deer."

"Promise me," I beg, tears filling my mouth. "You're

my *number one*, Sir. My number one good thing. Promise me I'll get the other two *with you*."

"I won't *allow* myself to die," he states through gritted teeth, cradling my wet cheeks. His gaze, darkened by large demonic pupils, howls he'll claw his way back from hell to be with me. And I revel in that notion.

He kisses my lips, then peppers his affection down on my face. Touching each tear. "I won't allow myself to die before I give you all the things I promised you, sweet girl."

His lips slide down my face, crashing with mine. With a jolt of desperation, I accept his kiss. Crawling onto his lap, kneeling either side of his thighs, I connect our bodies. Our mouths consume my whimpers and his possessive groans, refusing to pull away to draw in air.

His hands knead up my spine, gripping with protective intensity, pushing me hard so I arch into him. It feels a lot like sadness and vulnerability.

It feels a lot like goodbye.

CHAPTER EIGHTEEN

MADONNA MIA.

This damn girl.

With her eccentric, teenage tantrum, screaming about making her accountable for her lack of manners, for her disrespectful attitude, all the while she reminds *me* to be damn accountable for my promises... I made the *damn* promises! The assurances!

Were anything to happen to me, my brothers would give her their protection, my sisters-in-law give her company, my wife—*fuck*—would love, touch, and keep her supple body warm at night... *I am sure...*

My teeth lock together.

I treated this order of business with Dustin, with her father, like any other—with minimal sentiment. Impartial. Measured. Controlled.

But Fawn is *mine.*

And no one will care for her with the diligence I will.

Yes, little deer.

You've proven your point.

Christ. It's on me.

It's not until now, while she sobs in my lap at the premise *I* may die, that the concept of my own mortality becomes unbearable in the light of her sweet existence.

She is *my* responsibility.

Pushing off the floor with one hand, I stand with her supported by the other. She kisses my face with wet, tear-soaked lips, trailing across my cheek to find my mouth as I walk her to the bed.

Bracing myself on one arm, I carry her to the head and lay her down gently. Our lips stay connected, and I consume her moans for more love. More treatment of gentleness. More affection. My sweet, affection-hungry girl. I've never kissed a woman as much as I kiss her—

My cock stiffens in my pants as she slides her pelvis along the bruising length.

So needy, my little deer.

She believes she can keep me here with her body. With her tears. With her love.

Christ... She can.

Irritation growls from me.

She is.

Brat.

I wanted to leave while she slept. Peacefully. Hopefully, growing my baby inside her young womb. After having heard and been satisfied with my explanation, accepting it like a good girl, she should have let me leave.

Her arms tighten around me. "Don't go."

The concern now shifting through me is distracting. Not that this is the most dangerous thing we have conducted. Well, perhaps it is, but— *Fuck.*

For the first time in my entire thirty-five years of life, I have a reason to live.

Not simply a reason to die.

The Cosa Nostra.

My brothers—they were always good—worthy—reasons to die.

Needing to be inside her while she steals my breath in her mouth, while death warrens through my brain, I unbuckle my belt, hissing at the urgency. I should have woken her up earlier. Fucked her thoroughly.

There is no time.

Her hands fall above her head, where I pin them to the mattress, my weight pressing on her wrists as I release my cock.

Breaking our kiss, I look down and circle the glistening outer folds of her pretty pussy with the crown of my erection.

She is slightly parted and slick as always. Such a beautiful gift for me. Pink. Glistening. A thin, soft coat of lovely blonde hair. My hips rock back and forth as I view her pussy stretching wide, sheathing me until I'm completely swallowed by her. The sensation demands a whimper to break from her lips. Her eyes roll back.

"No one else will ever be inside you like this," I state, luring her eyes to gaze down at the way I fill her snug opening. I push her thighs to the mattress; her legs slip open easily. "Such a pretty, agile body. See how you swallow my cock, sweet girl? Accept me inside your pretty body? You hug me in such a lovely way. It's breathtaking."

She pants under my gaze. "Don't go."

"I won't die, sweet girl." I lean down and take her mouth before she can ask again. As I thrust roughly in her, I slant my lips in a demanding kiss, filling her mouth with my tongue and her yelps to overthrow the begging that will be my undoing.

I start to fuck her tight little hole.

Leaning back, I leave her lips swollen and red in my wake. I take her all in as she rolls her head from side to side, overwhelmed by sensations uncontrolled by her. Arousal looks pretty on her. A crimson gloss mars her chest and cheeks. A plumpness to her panting mouth.

She takes me so beautifully, curving her back, squeezing her eyes shut and gasping each time I punch her depths. "That's my good girl."

Warmth rushes along my thighs, pleasure sitting heavily in my abdomen as I rub my throbbing erection through her channel. All her powerful, smooth muscles enveloping me twitch, clinging and kneading.

I groan, thrusting in relentlessly, uncertain how she manages to accept me with such grace, such pose when she's wanton, open, and giving.

My sweet, ravenous little deer.

Against all odds, she is still incredibly innocent even as she lets me fill her with my darkness and perversions.

"Mine. Who do you belong to, sweet girl?" I dive in deep with the onset of that question, holding myself at the depth of her. Her hips recoil under the pressure battering her cervix. "Say it."

"Yours," she cries out, and I draw outwards along her gripping walls before rolling in at the angle I know will have her quivering within moments.

I need her orgasms.

"Who do you love?" I demand, cursing the question that came unintentionally from me.

"I love *you*, Sir."

Concentrating, I start a rhythm that immediately sends her into a frenzy of seeking her own pleasure. Her body wriggling around, hips becoming needy, careless, uncertain, as she chases me and then becomes over-whelmed, retreating.

Needing to stop her passionate, clumsy motions, I withdraw from her, sending cries of disappointment through her lips. My cock is coated in her juices, sliding down her thighs as I take hold of her hips. I flip her onto her stomach to stop her frantic gyrating.

"Good girl. Grip the sheets." Laying my body down against hers, I feed my fingers between hers. The slender digits tighten around the soft material below.

I enter her wet pussy again and pump in and out at the perfect pace for my little deer to meet her pleasure. Her thighs locked between mine, her body unable to protest under my weight. She is mine to use.

I kiss the soft white skin of her neck.

"Mine," I declare, my tongue sliding out to taste the salty perspiration gathering. To lick her. To coat her. "I will return for what is mine."

She trembles beneath me.

And I wring her orgasms from her, shudder by shud-der, as her gasps become my name. *"Sir. Sir."*

Her choppy pants and writhing motion befall my own catalyst. Her perfect pussy chokes at my cock as her orgasm tears through her body, sending warmth pulsing through me. Heat like wildfire rushes up my thighs and brews inside my balls. My own release crests.

Tightening and growing, I fist her fingers and the sheet within her palms to fuck my cum into her. Grunt with each pulse. My vision floods with a haze of ecstasy. Then suddenly, my own death slams through that black-ened moment of desire, pushing through the image of a baby boy with her dual-coloured eyes, of her alone in our bed with him, of her a single parent like her own was—

Fuck!

Of all my broken promises. I roar my orgasm out into her, biting back the petulant fear. I'm fucking poisoned with it. Fear of failing her.

One final thrust, and I still on top of her, my panting gushing from me in warm waves, hitting her spine.

I slide my hand between her abdomen and the mattress, cupping between her hipbones, and say, "I will come back for what is mine, little deer. You can do this. Be my strong girl. Let me finish this for my brothers. For you. For our son. And be my brave girl while I'm gone. Be the blood of the *Cosa Nostra*. My queen. Their queen. I know who you are. Do you?"

Her strained breath vibrates on sobs, before she declares, "Yours," ripping my stone heart in two.

"Yes, sweet girl. And *so* much more."

I LEAVE her in her slumber—now late—and go straight to the airstrip. Finding the jet ready, idling, yet empty of passengers, I board alone. My brothers seemingly have their own goodbyes delaying them.

Taking a seat, I recline and pull a cigar from my jacket pocket, in need of the mild flavours that have always relaxed me. Lighting it, I draw the smoke in just as I catch sight of Max and Bronson heading across the tarmac towards the jet above the low light of the runway.

The sky is still consumed in night-time blackness. Early morning lines of silver are barely visible along the horizon. Looking out the window as the ember flares in the dark reflective glass, I imagine my sweet girl in the penthouse. A small, foetal-positioned body on a king-sized bed.

It's only twenty-four hours.

I'll be back for what's mine.

I'm inclined to pull up the footage on my phone and check on her; such a habit is always twitching my hands. I resist the urge, drawing the port-scented vapour into my lungs and loosen my tie. Settling in.

When Bronson climbs into the cabin, vivid tattoos exposed at his forearms and neck, I nod to acknowledge him, earning me a wide smile that is anything but wholesome.

There is a swiftness to his predatorial gait as he moves around, his eyes glowing green. I don't know what goes on behind those unhinged irises, but there has always been a demonic side to Bronson. One that is often so powerful it can't be restrained. Not alone. His woman and his son, Stone, keep him sane. So now more than ever, while a physical divide separates him from them, I'm sure the darkness is surfacing in the imminence of their bleak absence.

I sigh hard, disappointment rolling down my port-laced breath. I failed him most of all. With my absence. With my cold shoulder. Where I thought the separation was for the best. For them. For *Cosa Nostra*. For me. I'm not entirely sure that was the right way. The only way... For while I was being trained to lead, at some point during my brothers' childhoods, Bronson lost his mind and Max lost his hope.

Max follows Bronson into the cabin. Together they approach me, sitting on the opposite seats, both in expectant silence. Waiting.

I lean back, eyeing them, then smother the ember of

my cigar in the ashtray. "Are you confident in explaining the landscape of the compound to the soldiers?" I ask Max, getting straight to business, and receive a curt nod in response.

Which is enough. My brother isn't a conversationalist, but he's the best damn architect in the city and his comprehension of building plans is second to none. Where I see flat, linear lines, he sees entire three-dimensional spaces. I need him on this. I trust him. "Did you use the building records to sketch a direct path in and out of the compound?"

He nods again.

"Good. Remember, if we can avoid it, no gunshots. Get us in undetected while most of the fuckers are asleep. We find Dustin and slice throats in beds until we do. I don't need gun residue or evidence scattered in the dark. We want it to look like a rival gang. Make it sloppy. Messy. Gruesome."

Bronson smiles.

It's his kind of raid.

Max looks down at a tattoo running the length of his finger, cursive writing that reads, *Ardente One*, then to his tattooed wedding band, his dark brows tightening as he says, "Dustin is mine."

"Yes, brother," I agree, and his stormy grey eyes rise, locking on my face. For a moment, I'm reminded of a time when I was eighteen, when Max wanted to stand by me, comfort me, in the way a broken boy comforts another broken boy, but I threw his concerns in his face. He never looked at me the same way again.

I ram the unbidden memory and the sentiment attached down. It will only drag me down, haze my course. "You will get your revenge tonight for what happened to Cassidy," I assure him. "But for now, get some sleep."

Dustin's death is for all of us, but to Max, it's a promise he never kept.

And I can't imagine a darker place to live than in the pits of a broken word... *Christ.* There would be no crueller existence. I did that. *I'm sorry, brother.* I sat by when Jimmy allowed Dustin to remain a partner in *Cosa Nostra.* I couldn't understand love—I couldn't fathom that level of affection.

What it does to a man...

What it means to a man...

To men like us who were barren of its power.

I retrieve my phone and open the footage to the penthouse, catching a sweet girl in hysterics. My heart twists as she hurls pillows around the room, crying in fits that shake her small shoulders. Emotions and feelings far too big for my little deer to handle control her movements.

She needs me, and I need her.

And I've made promises too.

I intend to keep them, sweet girl.

CHAPTER NINETEEN

A FLUTTERING *inside me steals my breath. It's not butterflies. Unless they have managed to break from my stomach and into my uterus... I press my hand between my hipbones. My face stills, my eyes losing focus while my mind becomes attune to the whooshing—no, rolling sensation.*

Then I realise what it is.

Squeezing my eyes shut, I home in on the feeling, forgetting about Clay for just a moment so I don't miss this. I thought it was too early, but I'm small so maybe... I think, the baby is moving inside me. I can feel something strange.

"What's happening, Fawn?" he orders, his voice finds me in my daze, pulling me from my focus.

I open my eyes to his full of a kind of stern interest—on anyone else's face, it may be considered concern. I smile at him, training my eyes on his devilishly handsome face, ignoring the fact that he's little more than a stranger, intimating, all that, and just eager to see if he feels it too. "I feel something."

Without thinking, I throw the silky lapels of my gown open. Pulling his much bigger hand away from where it has a death grip on the counter, I press it firmly to my lower stomach. His hand almost flinches from me, stiff and defiant, but then he stills with my hand on top of his. Exhaling heavily, his long fingers span out to cradle my abdomen with a protective dominance that causes a rabble of butterflies to take flight inside me.

I stare into his eyes as the strange sensation happens again, but it's too early to be movement... isn't it? His eyes narrow to the sensation. Then meet mine. I smile wider, breathing with excitement and rapture, knowing he feels it as well.

He smiles too.

That. Is. Everything.

THE SOUND of knocking stabs through my unconscious state, throwing me back into the hotel room, into the empty bed with only my small frame curled into a sideways ball.

I slowly sit up, regaining my senses as the knocking continues. The phone rings. It is an obnoxious chiming that is surely to alert me of the other obnoxious sound coming from outside the room. All the noise slams within my skull, forcing a groan from me.

I grip my forehead. Cradle my brain as it shrivels under the dehydration my tears left. My eyes burn as I blink them open. Tracks from the streams of salty tears pinch my cheeks as I work my mouth open and shut.

The noise continues.

Then the dream leaks in...

HE SMILES TOO.

That. Is. Everything.

IMMEDIATELY, I cup between my abdomen to protect the hollow centre. A punch of anguish beats through me as I place myself in this moment with an empty womb.

An empty bed.

I gaze over at the far wall, seeing a stack of pillows. The image of me from this morning rips a sob from me. After he fucked me, he waited and then left the moment the waking world eluded me. But my sleep didn't last long. Seconds. A minute, maybe, before I dragged myself back with dread being my guide. Dread that the click I heard in my half-conscious space was the door. That it was him leaving, that he was—I sat up in despair.

He was gone.

No. The memory alone hurts.

I flung the pillows around the room—needing to ruin the fabricated world he'd created for me—broke a vase potentially worth more than my foster mother's house and then dutifully cleaned up the glass fragments knowing I'll probably step on them if I don't.

Then I stacked the pillows.

It felt ridiculous, *needed*. The entire scene ripped apart because it wasn't real without him. The hotel floor. The perfect view. The concept of a holiday together. All bullshit.

"Be my strong girl."

I shake the memory. The knocking at the front door continues as I slump to my feet, wrap myself in a robe, and wander over to swing the double doors open.

I'm met by an emotional-looking Cassidy and a stiff,

unreadable Shoshanna who is swaying, rocking her son, Stone, in a colourful cloth baby-holder wrapped around her torso. They stare at me from the hotel corridor, and none of us have a smile to exchange today.

Cassidy's arms are around me before I can take a breath; this time I mimic her embrace. She's close to Clay; his sister-in-law, so I hold her tightly with that knowledge.

Peering over her shoulder, I meet Shoshanna's amber eyes that flare with red flames. Yet, beneath the deep amber pools of fire, her anger seems an overcompensation for gut-wrenching fear.

I recognise it immediately.

That was me last night.

Something touches my leg, so I peer down. Clinging to my thigh like a baby koala is Cassidy's daughter Kelly, copying her mummy, cuddling me too.

It isn't comfortable to be touched so much, but it doesn't stir me any more than the realisation we are alone without the men we love. That connects us.

And they are in danger.

Don't cry.

Don't cry.

A sob wants to break through my lips, but I clench my teeth to hold it at bay, an ache splaying through my gums instead.

"Hey," I force out, patting the golden bundle of hair on Kelly's crown. Appearing oblivious to the tension-thickened aura, she peers up, an endearing naivety set in her grey-coloured eyes. Just another day for the little girl—

How can that be?

Cassidy must lock her emotions up tight, keeping her reactions quiet and contained.

Unlike you, Fawn.

The image of the pillows being hurtled around the hotel floor, of the vase shattering, casts a sad reality in my mind.

Eccentric.

I sigh.

Fuck.

Maybe I won't make a good mother at all. Is that what my mother would have done in my *easily removable* shoes? I remember the emotional breakdowns... *So many of them.*

Check out that apple by the tree, Fawn?

Looks a bit like you.

Irritated at my own inner monologue, I snap my eyes up from Kelly's hair to the hallway. Lining the corridor walls are *soldiers*—that's what they are to me today—including HJ and two other men who are dressed slightly different to the rest. They converse quietly.

I shudder, butterflies like goddamn bats beating their wings inside my stomach. I haven't felt them this intense for weeks. This scene is plucked straight from a crime series. A hostage situation, maybe.

Don't cry.

My hands set to tremors, so I pull Cassidy and Kelly into the room. Shoshanna follows with heavy footsteps.

I shut the door.

Immediately, Kelly rushes over to the pillow stack, claiming the debris of my emotional collapse as a stage for her to play on. She dives into it. Despite the sombre energy, the barking tears, my lips twitch with a smile for her.

"Did you know?" Cassidy asks, risking a glance at her daughter before continuing. "Did you know they were going to leave us here?" Her voice is soft and defeated.

There was nothing provocative about her question. It was spoken with genuine, caring interest.

I walk over to the window, gazing down at Dubai, a sense of dissonance finding me as I reflect on the last few days. Think about the wound below his eyes. The way he seemed dead-set on using my body often the past few days. And... the last-minute holiday.

"Be the blood of the Cosa Nostra."

Glancing back at Clay's sisters-in-law, I watch them move around the suite, positioning themselves on the sofa where they wait—

Are they waiting for me to do something, say something?

What brought them to this room?

To me?

At first thought, it was a babysitting mission. The whole 'ensure I eat.' Behave, even... but now I'm not so convinced that's the whole picture. "Clay told me last night," I admit to them, wishing I had more information to offer as uncertainty thickens the air between them, as they look at me with intent.

Shoshanna sighs angrily, focusing now on cooing her son to sleep, a visual declaration to deter questions. So I turn to Cassidy, asking, "Did you two know that they were going to leave early this morning?"

"Only last night," Cassidy confirms. "Max told me he was going to get revenge—" She pauses, hesitation holding her tongue while pity softens her gaze on mine. "Are you okay with what is happening?"

I'm not sure what she means. About my dad's involvement? I think. *Like, am I entirely on their side?* The urge to stand by Clay's decisions seems to solidify inside my spine. Needing them to see my irrefutable loyalty, I simply say, "Yes."

She swallows hard, uncertain. "Has Clay explained everything to you? About—"

"About my dad? Yes."

"And what he did to me? The attack. How he tried to have my brother killed?"

"I know all of it."

She looks down at her fingernails as she peels a film of pink from the surface, saying, "Max apologised to me, ya know? For it taking so long. Like I care. Like it's been on my mind all these years. That was him projecting his own guilt and regret on me. Not mine... *God*, he was in so much pain last night." Her voice wobbles, and she bounces her eyes to her daughter, who is now building a three-wall cubby with my 'emotional-support' pillows. Cassidy looks back at me. "I don't want them to kill your dad, Fawn. Of course I don't—"

"I don't know him," I state straightaway, defensive, and wishing I wasn't, but I need them to know who I stand beside. I'm not a victim here. Not collateral damage. I don't want them to lump me in that camp. I'm the same as them.

"When Max needs to do something..." Cassidy trails off, muttering to herself through a small nod. "I need to let him do it." She peers her sad hazel eyes up at me. "He carries so much inside, so much weight. He just... he has all these contradictory pieces, ya know? He's so sweet. So... *gentle.* My big gentle menace. And then he's so... *cold and hard.* I don't pretend to understand, but I support him and whatever he feels he *needs* to do. Stopping a man like Max Butcher from doing what he feels is right would be like wrapping his heart in chains. I could never do it. It's part of him... And I love and accept all his parts." She suddenly gazes at Shoshanna, who has relaxed her shoulders, as if the anger is no longer twisting her muscles tight. "We don't need to understand them, Shosh."

Shoshanna seems pained as she says, "Bronson is too fragile to do this alone. He needs me. He knew I'd fight him on this. He knew I'd want to go. To help. I can help. I'm a doctor for God's sake. What if they need me? What if *he* needs me—" She looks down at Stone. Then inhales angrily and exhales hard, enforcing calm. She lowers her voice. "The crazy son of a bitch didn't even tell me."

My heart hurts. "He just left?"

Her expression softens, letting her guard slip. "I should have known. Last night when he got back, he had this look in his eyes. They were *so* green. And when they're green... Well, *crazy* happens. I thought it was a *moment*. He has them sometimes.

"After everything he's seen, done, been through with that cunt Victoria, it's like there are days that the darkness consumes him. Circles him. And he needs me to hold him for hours sometimes. Like a child. My six-foot-five tattooed, bearded man-child. *God*, I love him so much. I —" She covers her mouth to smother a sob, then forces it away. "I was wrong. It was a lot more than a moment. Then I found a single rose and a note on the dresser this morning."

"What did the note say?" Cassidy asks.

She smiles tightly and gazes down at her sleeping babe, her amber irises swimming in tears now. "It said 'think about my boy.'"

Cassidy exhales hard. "That's a good note."

A tear drops from Shoshanna's eye, her hand wiping at the unwelcome little bead as it trails down her cheek.

Clay's words float back to me with her sorrow: *"Let me finish this for my brothers. For you. For our son."*

Bronson and Shoshanna's son, Stone, is the reason he left, and the reason she can't. Just like Clay's and mine. I get it. Immediately, my hand cups my lower abdomen, praying there is life beneath my palm. The heir to an empire. A prince. A little boy I will give sweetness and magic to—

Wait. What did she say?

"—been through with that cunt Victoria."

Their mum...

"What has he been through with his mum?" I breathe the question out, and both girls suddenly still. "You just said *Victoria*. That's their mum, right? I've wondered for a while what her deal is."

Shoshanna answers, "She's a bitch."

My brows pinch, and I think about the way she interacted with me. I didn't understand it. Or her. "Neglectful or something else? She seemed super nice to Clay the one time I met her. And she was... I dunno, pleasant-ish to me."

"Pleasant-ish?" Shoshanna drawls. "She wasn't pleasant. Trust me. And she isn't nice to Clay. She's a *sycophant* with Clay because he's the Don of the *damn Cosa Nostra*. Her perfect, fearless heir to this dynasty."

I don't know what sycophant means, but placed in context, I imagine it means she's a brown-noser. I don't argue with her. "She does seem cold."

"Believe us," Cassidy insists. "She's not a good person."

"Dammit, Xander!" A man barks, the words freezing

us, our gazes now darting to the closed double doors as our answers lie beyond them.

Shoshanna leaps to her feet like a mother who heard her own son's name screamed. She rushes over to the door and swings it open to reveal the soldiers darting through the corridors, throwing orders to one other.

Something is going down.

Is Clay injured?

Did the plane go down?

"What happened, Carter?" Shoshanna asks, gripping the arm of the biggest man I think I have ever seen. He twists to acknowledge her, unveiling his face from the shadows— I suck a breath in. His skin is curled and cavernous, his expression taut with the kind of anger only dread can provoke.

"Damn that boy! I should have known," he says to Shoshanna. "He's gone. He bloody slipped us."

I move towards them. "What do you mean?"

Carter steps inside at my utterance, stopping before me as a soldier would his commanding officer, with a respectful and orderly manner. It throws me a little.

"My queen."

"Miss Harlow," he looks reluctant as he says, "he slipped us. We don't have eyes on him."

He knows my name...

I'm not Clay's dirty little secret.

"Xander," Shoshanna breathes, the word choppy with concern. "What is he hoping to achieve? To go back?"

Cassidy gasps. "You have to find him, Carter."

"We'll search the city, Mrs Butcher," he says over my shoulder to Cassidy, in a far more familiar way. *Her* 'Henchman Jeeves', I think.

"Carter, I need a juice boxy," Kelly says to him from

her pillow fort, either oblivious or immune to the commotion.

"I'll get you one in a minute," Cassidy says, her tone is effortlessly soothing and motherly.

I don't know how she does that. My mum kept everything bubbling shallow—anger, delirium, despair. I experienced them all.

Carter trains his gaze to me, and where I usually experience the shift of the patronising stare from men like him, he's different with me. He considers me as though I'm somehow taller than his seven-foot goon self.

"This is on me," he offers. "I should have known. I've watched over that boy for his entire life. This is exactly like him. I should have—"

"No." Craning my neck to see him better, I realise on a closer look that he isn't as monstrous as I first thought. The skin on his face is smooth like melted wax, glistening and silvery like the moon. He is quite beautiful, really, in a tragic way. "It's not your fault," I confirm. "Has Clay been contacted?"

He shakes his chin stiffly. "We only just realised he wasn't in his suite seconds ago. I don't know how long for. We had men outside the entire time."

I nod. "Call Clay immediately."

"Yes, Miss Harlow."

Their queen.

CHAPTER TWENTY

IT'S NO MORE than two hours into our flight when my phone rings, luring me from my state of restless sleep. From the nightmarish reverie of Bronson tied to that damn chair, of Max demanding the *Cosa Nostra* give him Dustin's head, of my little deer screaming for me to punish her.

Protect her.

Stay with her.

When I'm beside her, below that *damn* dreamcatcher, my vicious memories seem to pardon me. Her ideals are a ridiculous comfort, and her soft body settles my pulsing heart.

Blanking my mind.

Sleep a quiet state.

Without her, I'm pulled from this half-dream condition and sit up. Retrieving my phone, I frown at a notification in my inbox from an unknown number. The beginning of said message visible: I have the little—

Ignoring the ring, the incoming call from Carter, as it beckons me to answer it, glued to the message—

Immediately stilled. Ice slides through me. My world blurs around the edges when I open it.

It reads:

I have the little Butcher.

All I can hear is my heart between my ears, not the humming of the plane or the engine. Only a deep, thundering drum of hatred in my mind. Carter continues to call, but I decline, and instead dial the unknown number.

"*Clay Butcher*," Dustin's deep voice rumbles through the phone, his delight hitting my ears like a blade, cutting through ice. "It's been many years."

"Talk." I lock my teeth around the word, staring dead ahead, unable to form further conversation while also appearing in a state of calm. Indifferent. Impartial. That's the power stance, and I'm balancing on the cusp of my control.

Don't feel.

I hiss the rage through my teeth, and Bronson and Max both become alert to my change in demeanour. They watch me closely, and I stare ahead with rage a red blanket over my focus.

He goes on, "The security you have in Dubai is impeccable. I applaud you. I'm, of course, disappointed you didn't seek a safehouse in Indonesia. I would have been happy to see you there. But you knew better. Vinny gave that away. That was a pity. I was fond of him."

"Talk."

"You see, I picked your little brother up trying to get back to the District on a commercial flight. He's slippery, isn't he? A little too clever. Even for you. Even for Malik." He laughs loudly. "Even for dozens of your soldiers." His chortles continue, stoking the fire inside me. "The only way *we* caught on to him was because we saw a young man wearing Malik's hotel staff uniform, with the remains of a boxing match across his *face*. Swollen eye. Split lip. On closer inspection... blue *Butcher* eyes. It was the little legend, for sure." He pauses on another condescending huff of amusement, and my knuckles run cold, losing blood, as I fist the phone. "He always was the invisible Butcher, wasn't he? The forgettable one."

I bite back words, using my silence to speak volumes as nothing productive can come from the turmoil heating my Butcher head to an inferno.

"Okay then, Clay. Let me make this clear. It's a simple one. Bring me my daughter, and I'll trade you your little brother. Seventy-two hours. That'll give you time. Meet me out past the docks. There is an old campground. The fire circles it but for one entrance in and... one out. Be there. Come alone but with your brothers and bring my daughter with my unborn grandson. In return, I'll give you an unharmed little Butcher. But if you don't, if you play me—"

He pauses, and my eyes mist over with red dots of rage.

"I'll pluck your little brother's clever brain out through his nostrils while he blinks up at me."

The phone call dies, and my hollow stare crosses the plane, meeting the dark gazes of my brothers. Their sense of danger fine-tuned to the discomfort in my usually unaffected manner, to the shaking of my rage-filled body.

I've failed them.

CHAPTER TWENTY-ONE

NO ONE SPEAKS on the flight back to the District, to the city with so many secrets. The plane is a droning vessel of grief-stricken silence. I want to curl into a ball and sob. Want to moan at the possibility of our loss.

I want Clay.

My mind is drowning in blame.

Xander...

He's gone. Taken. I dart my gaze to Cassidy, who is staring heartbrokenly out of the plane's port-like window while an exhausted little Kelly lies in her lap. Cassidy combs her daughter's golden hair with her fingers.

Then I look at Shoshanna. She is rocking the bassinet in front of her with her red sneakers—easily removable footwear—while punching buttons on her phone, concentration furrowing her brows.

What must they think of me?

Sorry.

Sorry. It's a word I don't say often anymore because Clay despises the way it slips from me unbidden. But today, I *am* to blame.

I'm so sorry.

God, I'm so sorry, Clay.

He was so busy protecting me...

He'll regret that one day.

Regret me.

When we land, there is a car waiting for each of us, and I separate from Cassidy and Shoshanna without a goodbye. Striding away from them with hardly an upwards glance, I'm unable to bear their feigned expressions that hide screams of accusation. My presence is like a nail in Xander's coffin.

Does my dad want me?

It was meant to be me.

Xander...

He was the one who taught me good things come in three— Where the hell are his? I try to breathe, to fight the boiling heat in my eyes, as I slide into the backseat with HJ. The door closes on us.

Twisting my hair around my finger, I swallow around the rising bile in my throat. I'm sick with grief that knots and twists inside me. That renders guilt and self-blame to my very marrow, to my core. To the parts of me that wanted to believe in Xander's advice.

There is no sequence of good things, Xander.

Only bad. This is number one.

Xander: Number one.

Gazing out of the window at this city, I watch the blissfully ignorant citizens filter the walkways of Connolly under the early morning sun. The separation between me and them, a thin pane of tinted glass, a soundproof and bulletproof partition—and knowledge.

At the house, I climb out of the car. Under the constant cover of guards, I rush inside, needing Clay so I can ask, '*What now? Are they still taking the compound? Are they waiting? What did my dad say he wanted?*'

I'm halted by Clay's voice, the sound of him so in control easing me slightly, needing that infallible assurance he is going to take care of this. He's going to get Xander back. He'll fix everything.

Within the room, I hear another voice, too. His brothers'—I can't tell which one.

I wander slowly to the closed door of Clay's office, leaning my shoulder against the wood and bating my breath. But soon, Carter and HJ appear beside me, and I glance guiltily at my feet, having been caught eavesdropping.

Carter only indicates for me to slide to the side so he can enter while HJ stands across the room, eyeing me.

"He knows you are home, Miss Harlow. No need to hide," Carter advises as he walks into the office. Even so, I tuck behind the wall until the door closes again. Then I ignore HJ's uncertain stare and press my ear to the wood.

"Good. Carter is here." Clay's voice nestles into my soul. "Is *everyone* back safely? And where they should be?"

"Yes, Boss."

"Let's get this sorted out," Clay orders. "I'll drive into the campsite alone, and Carter will bring Max, Bronson, and our men in through the flames behind Dustin's flank. Undoubtedly, he'll have the Stockyard members there, but they'll be on vehicles. You'll be on foot."

Through the flames?

A voice that I think belongs to Bronson says, "Gonna get myself a new bike on the way out. But it's all lit up in red. How do you know where our yellow brick road is?"

"The marked red is *heat*. Smoke, mostly," Carter confirms. "But I can get you in at this burnout site here.

There is an old service road connected to it that runs around the campground. The trees were cleared for the pipes. It should have created a narrow fire break through the inferno. Not visible from above."

"Should have?" Bronson asks in a quiet, unnerving way. "Can't have my beautiful brothers burning their faces now. We need to be sure."

"Nothing is for certain with fires, Boss." Carter's voice carries regret. "But I've seen worse than this fire. I was a smokejumper for two decades before your father hired me. I'm confident I can get you in and out."

Bronson says, "We won't bump into any fire-fighters out there, then? We don't want innocent eyes around us."

"The fire is contained," Clay states, and his voice still catches my breath every time I hear it. "They have no need to be out there. No resources to put it out. It's too large. State services are letting it run its course, and it'll go out by itself come the wet season. I have all the roads blocked off. Services are at the head near homes, nowhere near the campsite."

"He's a clever son of a Butcher, isn't he?" Bronson states, humour laced in his voice that doesn't seem genuine—they are all on edge.

"And Dustin won't see you coming," Clay states, back to business, assertive and systematic. "You will enter from behind the campsite. Wait for my signal. Take the bikers out. If anything happens, if we don't come back, Aurora will organise a hunting party."

"We bring the girl!" someone states, his voice already tight and uneven with sentiment.

Me? I'm going—

"No, Max," Clay dismisses. "We don't."

"We can protect her," Max grounds out. "But the girl needs to—"

"*Fawn*," Clay corrects smoothly. "And I said *no*—"

Max cuts in. "If Dustin asks to see her, and you don't have her, he'll put a bullet straight into Xander's head."

He's right.

We can't risk it.

I can't—

I can't risk it.

"This isn't about Fawn." Clay's foregrounding voice leaves no room for emotion. "He doesn't care about her enough to risk his own life—"

"This is about Xander!" Max snaps, and tears slide down my cheeks, followed quickly by more. They are painful now, after having shed so many over the last twenty-four hours. They leak in thick hot rivulets down my face.

Max is right.

Please listen to him, Clay.

"This is an execution. This is about *us*," Clay states with that cool indifference that hides his true intensity. I need him to think about Xander now. Think about his brothers.

"*No*," Max repeats softly, hoarse, making me shiver.

"You're angry. Tired. Take a moment—"

"No—"

"Damn you, Max," Clay hisses, his temper simmering in that sound. "I will not hand over Fawn. This conversa—"

"We're your brothers!" Max's voice breaks, and the talons of guilt circle my throat, tightening around the column as I listen to the Butcher brothers turn on one another.

For me.

Because of me.

Max bites out, "He's your little brother—"

"Would you trade Cassidy? Think about what you are asking of me," Clay says, a lethal dare stalking his words.

His tone buckles my knees, forcing me to slide down the door until I hit the floor and wrap my arms protectively around my legs. *You can't choose me, Sir.*

Not over them...

"And what about Xander? What about Bronson?" Max's voice rises with each forced word. "The one you made do all the dirty work? What about when we were just children?" Max growls, straining to continue, as though he is fighting with honesty. "Dammit! We needed our big brother! What about then?" He laughs contemptuously, bringing anger to the forefront to veil the honest declaration that a man like Max Butcher needed his big brother. "I don't know why I'm surprised by this," he goes on. "I thought maybe you'd changed. Without Jimmy holding your strings. But I see I was wrong. You're still the same self-important prick you were when we were children."

"*Max.*" Bronson says his name so quietly it could be a ghost moving through the room.

Clay reasons, "I will get him out—"

"He'll kill Xander," Max states coldly, all his emotion smothered into bitter-ridden detachment. "He'll kill him because he can, and I'll kill you because I can't stand to share your fucking air."

Seconds later, the door slams into my spine, sliding me across the floor. Wincing, I climb to my feet as Max's formidable body appears in the jamb. He steels when he notices me, nothing but venom in his assessing grey eyes.

Then he strides away, his body taking him quickly from the thing he despises. *Me.*

I exhale hard, shaken to my core by his hatred.

It looks familiar—the disdain. A look so becoming I'm prickly and self-conscious like the old Fawn again. A Harlow. Not a Nerrock. And definitely not a Butcher... My fingers meet the cool surface of the Monarch butterfly pendant hanging around my neck.

I brush my fingertips over it.

My dad can't hurt me. No one can hurt me except Clay. Nothing will hurt more than to see my everything's eyes flash with that familiar contempt-filled look.

Needing to see his eyes—

See *reassurance.*

See *love.*

With my breath uneven and forced, I walk on hesitant legs to the opening and stand there unnoticed. No —ignored.

Bronson has his shoulder against the wall, so motion-less he could be a sculpture as he stares at Clay while lost within his own green gaze. He's a little frightening like this...

And Luca is sat, silent, his eyes glazed over as though he is staring at something far in the distance.

I shift my sight across from him to the other side of the desk where I once watched footage of my own assault. Carter is conversing with his boss, earning himself all of Clay's attention. Clay rubs his jaw in contemplation, but he's glacial in every inch of his powerful suited body. His eyes are glued to the monitor ahead. He's getting the job in order.

Dutifully, without emotions.

So very Clay Butcher.

And he doesn't look up.

Not once. But he knows I'm here. He always does—

My stomach twists.

He's ignoring me on purpose. *Maybe...* he knows he is making the wrong decision but simply can't bring himself to change it... maybe? He's so heavily wrapped in the promises that binds him to me.

To protect me.

To keep me.

To choose me.

"I'll always choose to protect you, little deer."

That he can't see what needs to happen. I gaze at him, adrift for a moment in his beauty, the tense lines of his sharp jaw, the gravity of his blue eyes. He's spectacular. I was half right: belonging to him is the sweetest of existences but being loved by this man... I sigh. It's like starting anew with wings.

My eyes well up.

I can't accept his choice. *God,* I wanted Benji to choose me, my mum too, anyone, but I can't accept his choice, not when it's at his own expense and not at Xander's.

It's a cruel fucking joke, but I'd rather lose him, lose myself, lose this whole wonderful life than have him *lose* Xander and blame himself. He already carries enough guilt. I can't allow it. I'd rather be a sweet memory in his mind. A sweet girl who he was very fond of once...

Who he loved...

I smile at that.

I won't allow him to endure Xander's death. Won't let it start another sequence of bad things. Not this time.

Moving away from the door, I find myself walking in the direction Max disappeared, Henchman Jeeves as my shadow.

CHAPTER TWENTY-TWO

I GRIP the corner of the doorframe, peering around the wall to see the back of Max's large tense shoulders. The room—an office of sorts—is furnished but staged in a way that suggests it doesn't get used. I've never been in there before.

Max is sitting, leaning forward on his knees, staring at a glass of whiskey on the table in front of him. I wonder if he's crying. *Does Max Butcher cry?* I wouldn't know.

There is sadness in this room, that's for sure. It's chilling. It sweeps around me like a current across a harsh plane. The kind that precedes snow and then a frozen wintery grave. It's lonely. Like, he keeps it to himself. I remember something Cassidy said about him: *"Stopping a man like Max Butcher from doing what he feels is right would be like wrapping his heart in chains."*

I sigh, thinking about how well Cassidy understands Max. Maybe more than he understands himself. I imagine Clay's emotional state right now. The entire city is his responsibility, his brother and me... how does he not crumble beneath his duties. *"Trust me, little deer."*

Maybe he *is* crumbling...

Maybe I would have seen the splintering of his resolve if he had looked at me moments ago...

He doesn't see it yet, but if something happens to Xander, he'll never forgive himself. I need to protect him from this mistake... I need to be at the campsite. I need to go with Max. And I need to get HJ off my damn heels.

Taking a big breath in, I close the door. Heading to the lounge area, I see the play pen. Inside, my kitten tumbles with a ball of wool, flipping around with it, the static of the wool caught in her needle-like claws. I pick her and the wool up, hold her to my face and fight back tears.

I whisper, "I'm sorry I can't play with you today." Then I put her back in the pen, and with my shadow—HJ—making a poor effort to give me a wide berth, I search the halls.

As I pass a few guards, I nod at them, trying to act as natural as possible but failing miserably as I never nod at them. Mostly, I barely notice them...

Smooth.

Today, they are everywhere.

Thankfully, I see Jasmine flitting around the halls. "Hey," I say, grabbing her elbow and tugging her in for a —completely unlike me—cuddle. "Can you do me a favour?" I whisper in her ear, holding her tightly so she can't push me away.

She lifts her arms, but they are uncertain as they return my embrace with loose pressure. "That depends entirely on what you are about to say."

"I need you to get me your hoodie and then pretend we are talking about private things because I'm upset, because there is a lot going on, and I'll tell you everything later but... I need to sneak out the staff exit."

"No."

"Please?"

"No, Fawn."

"It's important!" I whisper-cry, burying my face in her hair a little to muffle the words. "I just want to talk to Max. He's upset, and I don't think he'll talk to me if he thinks H—*Bolton* is listening..." I hate myself for this, but I need her to do this, so I manipulate the side of her who pretends she knows things she doesn't, who pretends she's worldly when she's not. "You know what men are like." I chuckle, a sound so utterly forced that it hurts. "All macho around each other."

"Can we have some space, please? You're like such a space invader," she calls over my shoulder, hopefully to my pain-in-the-arse tracker.

He retorts, "You best not be up to anything."

"Well, my girl is sad and shit. She doesn't need an audience for *everything*. You lot treat her like she isn't a grown-arse woman." She talks back into my hair loudly, saying, "It's okay, Fawn." Then she drops her voice. "Why is Max upset?"

"I promise to tell you everything after. Please, we have to go now. He might leave before I have a chance to talk to him properly."

"Okay. Okay." She wraps her arm around my shoulders, poking her tongue out at HJ, before steering me into the changing room.

He doesn't follow us in.

Jasmine goes to her locker. Quickly pulling her black hoodie out, she hands it to me. While I pull it on, she eyes me with scepticism. "Your hair is very noticeable."

I pull the hoodie up and tuck my blonde strands into the back and out of sight. "I know."

"Are you going to get in trouble?"

I lie. "I just want to talk to Max."

"Can I play with your cat?"

"Sure."

She half grins. "Can I name her?"

"No." I think about her white fur and multicoloured eyes, her uncertain little manner. "She isn't ready for a name just yet."

Jasmine tilts her head questioningly. Not at all understanding why the kitten that looks a little like me isn't ready to have a name. And I don't waste time leaving through the back door and navigating the staff quarters to get to the unused office, hoping Max is still fuming and eager to act.

Checking the passages, I enter the room quickly and close us inside. I exhale hard. Hurriedly, I turn to Max, who has twisted in his seat, his stoic grey eyes landing on me.

I take a big breath in and say, "I'll go with you."

Dark brows furrow, but he only returns his gaze to his whiskey, ignoring me completely.

I frown, rounding the seat and table to stop in front of him. "Did you hear me? I'll go to the campsite. We can meet them there. But we have to go *now.*"

"No." Is all I get from him.

My pulse races. "We have to go *now* while Clay is talking to Carter and Henchman Jeeves thinks I'm talking to Jasmine about how horrible this entire situation is."

Nothing.

He focuses on his untouched glass of whiskey. His jaw

is set hard, his anger evident in the pulsing muscles beneath.

"Fucking hell, Max! We don't have time for this. You were right. You are right. We have to go because they will be searching for me soon and because I can't let Clay choose me,"—I hear my voice losing strength with each word—"because no one has ever *seen* me before, Max. No one has ever looked at me the way Clay looks at me, and if something happens to Xander—" I catch my breath as he glares up from the glass to meet my gaze. "No one ever will again. He'll be gone. He'll never forgive himself. You'll lose both your brothers." My heart shrinks. "He is choosing wrong, Max. He should choose Xander."

He stands, his body forcing me a step backwards purely by his presence, his heat hitting me even from this distance. "I'll keep you safe," he assures, dead serious.

"Keep Xander safe. " Swallowing around my nerves, I nod. "*I'll* be fine." I always am. I survive.

"Stay to my left," he states, and we stride back through the staff quarters, hugging the walls, and heading towards a different exit. I hang close to his left with my head cast low.

Trying to keep up.

Pushing the staff exit open, he guides us forward. I pull the hoodie down my face. We walk across a gravel road, and the small loose stones shuffle below my sandals. My eyes sting thinking about my pretty new sandals.

I dart my gaze quickly up to see we are in the staff carparking lot, keeping my nervous gaze away from my sandals and all they symbolise.

Then I hear the static of male voices and the scuffing of rushed, heavy-footed people.

We start to jog.

I follow Max.

The sound of shoes beating the floor chases after us.

Closing in.

My heart spikes. Panic sets in, and I almost slam into the bonnet of a red car when Max grabs my elbow, steering me in another direction—

A gunshot blasts my ears, ripping a yelp from me, forcing me to duck and cower low.

Did they just fire at us?

"Fuck," Max bites out, sweeping me in front of him, blocking the direction of the bullets with his form. He stoops with me still in the sheltered cave of his body, hiding us by the side of the car. Another bullet sounds.

They are firing at us!

Gasping as a third round is fired, hitting something metal, the ting of sound like a jet flying past my ear, I try to calm myself down. Think straight. I squat lower, peering around the side of the vehicle's black metallic paint.

Tears consume my eyes when I see Clay rip a weapon from the man firing at us. He's frantic as he slams the handle into the guard's face, barking, "That's my brother!"

Then our eyes lock.

His gloss over.

Mine gape at the vulnerability.

He calls out to me. "Fawn!" His voice reaches right inside me. "Fawn!" He shakes his head meaningfully, and my breath vibrates in my throat when I hear the strain in his timbre. "Come to me, little deer. Walk to me now."

I can't. I sob once but suck it in. My whole body starts to quake violently under the restraint of those angry, wanting tears... I touch the pendant on my chest, pressing my palm to the meaningful gift.

Remember who I am...

Clay's face twists in anguish, an expression that strips the calm, controlled mask away and reveals utter defencelessness to me. My heart thrashes. I want to go to him, to my everything, want to rush into his arms, the arms that held me while I bled, that rock me while I sleep, that protect, that defend, that love. His arms.

But I don't.

And it kills me.

I defy him for the first time, splitting straight down the centre, tears filtering out the seams of my existence.

I'll see you soon, Sir.

I'm resilient and brave.

The blood of the Cosa Nostra.

I can do this!

Clay curses, spinning in anger, gripping his neck before turning back to aim the gun at the car, his deadly stare focused on something low, homed-in like a predator to prey.

My wolf.

His deer.

My soul wants to leap from my body to be held by his, comforted, coddled. I can feel his resolve melting away even from this distance, seeing the evil that lives so comfortable beneath his skin move to the surface. It doesn't change anything. I can't run to him when I know he'll never let me go. I can't go to him—

Don't cry, Fawn.

I have to do this. I will force myself to stay strong. Defy him. Break our bond. Change everything... *God,* but a memory is better than the constant reminder he did.

He actually *chose me.*

I watch in horror as he points the gun in our direction. The pathetic, bruised remains of my heart like a bass between my ears. Waiting.

"He doesn't miss," Max states as he jumps to his feet. Opening the car door, he lifts me up and ushers me across the driver's position to the passenger side.

What is Clay aiming at?

Without caring that we are in the line of Clay's weapon, Max starts the engine. *He wouldn't shoot at his brother...*

Would he?

One shot!

A tire hisses.

My body shakes.

Max tears out of the parking lot, and now in the lonely, agonising safety of his car, I sob hysterically. My chest is cavernous, my heart a shrivelled, thrashing lump of flesh.

I cup my face and bawl, the tears creating a pool against my palms. My mind's eye desperate to see him one last time. In case something happens. In case.

The pull of Clay's gaze grapples me, so I twist in my seat and stare at him still bracing the gun, still pointing it at the vehicle, still wanting me to "come to him."

I can't see his expression.

But I can feel the second he breaks.

CHAPTER TWENTY-THREE

DON'T FEEL.

Pain shoots through my fingers as they lose blood while I choke the handle of my Glock, my bones swelling beneath taut skin, the gun cracking under the pressure, and I lose sight of her...

I. Lose. Sight. Of. Her.

Aurora shouts from behind my back, "Follow that car! Keep an eye on them." The sound of her heels approaching me is the last thing before everything goes deadly quiet, as though the air itself has crystallised around me.

I lose focus.

Losing her—

She's gone.

The gun shakes harder. That I can feel. The sight still pointed at the end of the driveway as cars flood out. That I can see. But no noise. There must be commotion. Shouting. Tires.

I hear nothing.

"This is the last thing."

"This is the last thing. I will drag God himself to hell before I let you hurt again."

"I will protect you."

"I will choose you."

"You have to trust me."

Don't feel!

Rage like pure evil boils through my veins, red hot lava, burning up everything rational as it surges into my muscles, feeding them with volatile need. Need to hurt. Need to fight. All the "don't feel," orders and lessons in remaining unreadable, in control, in being the wolf, the heir, the District Mayor, the family man, the controlled man—

I don't fucking care.

I. Fucking. Snap.

Growling as tears flood my eyes, their presence creeping dark pools of hatred across my vision, backing me into a corner of near volatility and vulnerability and —Fuck!

Someone touches my shoulder and when I whirl around, they punch my wrist, knocking the gun from my grasp. I cut my fist through the air, throwing a faceless person backwards.

There are soldiers all around me now, blurred shadows in my peripherals that want the calm Clay Butcher. The reliable one. He's not here—I don't fucking care.

They let her leave.

They had one damn job!

I roar, "You fuckers let her out of your sight!" I charge a body, jabbing quickly. Movement behind me jolts my attention. Ducking, I spin low and punch a solid wall of muscles three times until it falls away.

Someone else grabs my arms to stop me, and I still. Straighten. Taller than the guard now wincing, I use my weight and drop my fist hard into his face. Another soldier at my flank attempts to lock my arms behind me, to control me.

Who gave that order?

I growl and fight back.

Hearing my anger.

In my head.

But nothing fills my ears.

The fuckers get a grip on me. Three soldiers bracing my arms behind my back while others shift around in front of me. I can barely see them, the who, not important.

Bucking and gyrating as another body fights to restrain me, I tense, flex my muscles, and throw the fuckers forward. They fall into a pile ahead of me. I'm a fucking animal right now. Bared teeth.

Deaf.

Blind. Rage.

Suddenly, pitch-black coats my irises, and I fall forward on my knees, a hard knock to the back of my head stealing the strength and sight from me.

I shake the hazy dark from my vision, slowly regaining a grainy view of the parking lot.

Growling at the gravel, I try to push up with my hands, but I'm kicked in the side, the boot of someone throwing me over.

I'll kill them.

I roll onto my back as fuckers circle me, and one face comes into view. I should have known.

Only one man can control his fist, the meticulous

placement, the precision of pressure, the exact amount of both needed to render a man immobile.

Luca Butcher.

"Calm, son." My father drops to his haunches, blood spilling from his nose. Compliments of me, I presume. "That'll do." He grips my shoulder as I regain my senses, hearing the calamity of my men hit me square in the fore-head. Hearing Aurora shouting orders. The cars leaving.

The parking lot emptying.

My father is still gripping my shoulder... And I'm certain he has never held me for such a time. And he is staring at me again with that uncomfortable intent. With regret. And *empathy.*

I frown at him. What does that look mean to me? It reminds me of an eighteen-year-old boy after his first kill, after murdering a young girl. Of being rejected such empathy. It retells a moment of need, of wanting such understanding.

"Don't feel."

"You're a leader."

"A leader is always alone."

Perhaps he never said that. It was teachings from the *Cosa Nostra.* It was my mother... And it was my old Don. It was *Jimmy Storm.* And I made his words synonymous with my father's, but they never were... were they?

Jimmy encouraged the segregation.

And I, I hid in it.

Christ.

I squeeze my eyes shut to the sensation of his fist gripping my shoulder. I've lost my mind. My absolute control, my logic, rationalities, utterly waring with my emotions. "Max," I hiss through my teeth.

"He will keep her safe, son."

Seeing only red in my mind, I open my eyes to find Bronson has moved in beside my father, a look of both volatility and pride firing within his glowing green gaze.

"Well, well," he almost sings. "There you are, my beautiful brother. And what a sight for sore eyes you are."

"We have to find them," I say darkly.

"We don't have time to chase them around the city, brother. So get up. Wipe your pretty suit off. And let's go get our brothers... and *our* girl at the campsite."

CHAPTER TWENTY-FOUR

I FIST THE WHEEL. We go ahead with the plan. Bronson is with Carter somewhere in the thick, dense bush. Aurora waits at home with Luca and the men, ready to initiate a recovery operation should we not come back tonight.

And I drive alone.

Thick grey smoke rolls along the bonnet, icing the dark metallic sheets in white and brown soot as I drive through the debris of the bushfire.

To her.

And I'm feeling.

So fucking much.

It's dangerous.

Distracting.

Blackened trees border the road. The national park fire is a 360-degree glow of orange. The heat is immense, contracting the metal of my Chrysler. The fibres shrinking within this woodland furnace.

I head further into its depths, towards more scorching intensity. Ahead, I can only make out mere metres. Cracks rattle my bones as branches snap in half in the vast distance.

This is red, hot, earthly hell.

I roll down a dirt track, steering towards the meeting site. My mind drifts to the text message I received thirty minutes ago as I geared up. It read:

> "We will be there. I will keep her safe. You have my word, brother."

She's out in this heat, too.

Without me.

But "a leader is always alone", and I have never felt lonelier in my own presence than I do in her absence... *Christ.* I'll die before I let anyone take her from me. I'll crumble the world around her body.

The corridor of charred trees is narrower now, black limbs reaching over the track, the higher ones disappearing into the smoky air.

Passing through a scorched gate, I enter the campground. My fist tightens on the wheel as the glow of lights drill through the grey abyss. Ominous dots. One beside the other. The row of bright headlights alerts me to the barricade of bikes ahead. The dense fog hazes my vision of much more.

Flanking them will be Bronson, Carter, and three soldiers, on foot, navigating their way through this terrain.

Dammit.

They won't be able to see a fucking thing. Won't see my signal. And I can't get an aim on anyone. My heart thrashes hard under this premise. I won't lose them. I can't.

Unable to measure the distance between my car and

the awaiting lights, I pull over. Fisting the wheel on a final thought of her, of the sweetness she gave me, the hints of what life and love could be, I inhale hard and exit the vehicle, feigning a smooth unaffected manner.

Still suffering it all.

All the way in my veins.

Rounding the bonnet, I open my arms wide, welcoming, calling out, "Now you have me. Let's talk about why we are really here." Honing my ears, I try to decipher movement, chatter, orders, anything, but the silence hangs with the thick smoke around me. Their engines are killed.

Interesting...

They are not in any hurry to get away. Not wary.

"Are you tired of hearing the name Butcher?" I go on. "Tired of seeing the name Butcher all over the news. Tired of having men refuse your business because of us. Of hiding from your own city."

"Where is my daughter?" I jolt to the north as his voice punches through the smoke from my left-hand side. The dark silhouette of a man appears through the smoulder, followed by the hazy outline of several in his shadow.

Dustin.

And I know this is an execution.

The tightness of my bulletproof vest below my suit reminds me they'll need to aim true. I press my hand to my collarbone. Hold the scar that mars it and recall what he had me do when I was eighteen. What I did for him. For Jimmy. "You don't want your daughter. You want me."

He scoffs. "I have promised her to one of these men behind me, you see, and he'll be rather unimpressed if she's not here."

"Don't lie." I face them straight on. "You don't want your daughter. You want me. You can have me. Let my brother go. I'm bored of this. Of the theatrics. I'm the one you want.

"My dad fucked your wife, and she grew his heir in her stomach. You raised the boy as your own..." I say, stepping to the side, trying to see through the smoke. I try to force an emotive response from him. A passionate man is a vulnerable man; I know this most of all today as it's boiling inside me. "Did it hurt when you found out he wasn't yours?" I continue. "Then I fucked your daughter. Butchers are infesting your life, your city, right? I'm the head of this Family. It's me you want. Why aren't you just shooting me? I'm the one you need to make this all stop."

I know the answer, of course; he wants us all. All of Luca's sons dead. Our bodies forever ash in the national park.

"Clay Butcher, the Don of the District," he mocks, and the sound burns fierce hatred through my Butcher head. I realise he's the impartial man. I'm the one on the cusp of volatility today. "Still a self-centred son of a bastard. You give yourself too much credit again. You can *fuck* my daughter as much as you want, Clay. Please, she's on the house."

I hiss through my teeth.

"You see," he says, "there was a time when I would have handed you the cigar afterwards. We almost had an understanding between our families. I knew that I needed to marry my girls off to one of your brothers, or my part in this empire would be overthrown as soon as you took over.

"You married Jimmy's daughter. And well, your brother, Bronson, is damn out of his mind. It had to be

Max. But then the Slater girl got involved. And she got in the way of that. And she brought the Slater boy into the light to remind me of what your father did. To show him off. And now—"

He walks towards me until I can see the shadowed edges of his face, the sharp lines cutting across his cheeks and jaw. I haven't seen this face in years. I once said that Fawn bared no resemblance to him, but— I lock my jaw. Now all I see is that his eyes mirror the same shape as Fawn's... I want to remove them. He doesn't deserve her likeness.

"I'm no fool," he says, his tone circled in hatred. "It doesn't matter that my daughter takes your cock each night. You won't be making me a boss under your leadership."

"While I'm still alive," I implore, wanting to reach the fifteen or so metres between us and pull his tongue out through a slice I make in his throat. "It'll end with me."

"No, it won't," he deadpans, and I hear feet shuffling. The rolling of rocks below uneven steps.

My smooth outward armour slips right off when I see Xander hauled towards me by a leather-clad biker. I recognise the thug as the Sergeant at Arms, Crow. Or *Colin Marone* for when he's a civilian filling in his papers at the City Building.

I know them all.

"Clay." Xander searches the area around me, blood rushing from his face as he takes in the scene. Me, alone. No sign of an ambush. "Clay..."

Dustin grins and raises his gun, and when he presses the nose to Xander's temple, a desperate sound rumbles from my throat. A second. That is all it will take. A second and my baby brother will have his brain misting the thick, pungent smoke. "My daughter?" Dustin insists, and as I stare at my brother, blue-eyed and bruised, a stab of affection, of protectiveness so intense slides into my chest. I realise I chose Fawn over him. I can't not... choose my little deer.

We lock eyes. *"He always was the invisible Butcher, wasn't he? The forgettable one."* No. He's the right one. The perfect one. The good one. I'll die in this park for him, with the hope he'll live and one day understands why I chose her. Hope he accepts with sad melancholy that it does not lessen my absolute loyalty to him and my family.

"*Here.*" My body stiffens. Max's voice seeps into my blood, setting it to boil, my muscles pulsing to claim what he took from me—*her.*

With my fingers curled to the point of searing pain, I turn slowly in the direction his voice comes from.

Squinting through the thick grey haze, I watch Max appear like a ghost, shielding my little deer with his body. They came on foot. They. Came. On. Foot!

"Hello," Fawn says softly, speaking to her father for the first time in her life. My muscles convulse with need —a need to wrap my arms around her. Protect her from the smoke. The heat. *Him.* Everything.

She must be so overwhelmed. Confused. I need to get to her, but then she steps forward, provoking words to claw through my clenched teeth, through my waring resolve. "Step back, Fawn!"

She gasps at the sound of my voice, squinting through the dense atmosphere, stilling her gaze on me as smoke parts between us. Her mouth moves as she breathes my name. "Clay." The haze brings the word to me. Not *Sir.* Not today.

Dustin laughs, and I know I've lost the war of wills. Shown him everything I should have meticulously guarded. I revealed my affections, my moves. *Lost.* I fucking lost.

Unable to wait, unable to signal Bronson and the others, I edge towards him through the smoke as Fawn has captured his attention.

Still with his gun to Xander's temple, he says, "Let me get a good look at you." Eyeing her, he takes in her appearance—skin pinkened and slick from the heat. He regards her like a prize colt he might purchase and race, wear to the ground, and then put a bullet in once it has served its purpose.

"Well, aren't you lovely," he finally says, and I hear my growl rumble between my ears. "I understand why Clay Butcher finally thawed. Don't you want to give your daddy a kiss hello? It's polite, after all."

He waits, but she tilts her head, looking at him as though she is trying to recognise herself in him. When she doesn't respond, he says, "No? Well, we can work on that."

I still my creeping forward when he looks back at me. He frowns, his stare shooting to the trees behind me. "Order Bronson and the others to move where I can see them. He wouldn't have missed this. I know he's in there. I can *feel* him. I can always feel a Butcher."

Fawn takes another hesitant step toward her father. My little deer, seemingly unafraid. Intrigued, instead.

"I wanted to meet you," she almost whispers, and my heart aches from hearing her sweet, honest cadence. He never deserved her. "I came all the way here to find you. But I found Clay instead. Do you actually want to trade Xander for me? Do you want to know me at all?"

Xander suddenly drops his head back into Crow's face, provoking a grunt from him. Quickly, he twists to grip his shirt, whirls around using the thick dazed biker as a shield, and ducks behind it just as Dustin's gun goes off.

A bullet meant for Xander appears like a red portal in the centre of the Sergeant of Arm's cheek.

Chaos breaks loose.

Rounds suddenly echo through the hot, coasting fog. The thick smoke lights up with small flares from the firing weapons ahead.

Dustin growls, turning his gun towards us, firing through the haze. Shooting at everything. Anything. *Anyone.*

Only ten or so metres away, Max shields Fawn. Suddenly, his arm jolts backwards as he takes a bullet for her. It must have hit his bone, or it would have broken through his flesh and landed in her face.

He grunts and cups his shoulder as blood spills through the webbing between his fingers.

Fuck!

"Max!" I roar, rushing to them. Reaching for my little deer, I grip her close, drop with her to ashy debris, and cover her body while unseen bullets soar around us.

"Max? Talk to me," I call out, unable to see him while I guard her beneath me.

Fawn whimpers within my hold. The sound of ammunition hitting the dirt around us forces high-pitched yelps of terror from her. She covers her ears.

I lift my head to assess Max's condition, but he's crawling along the dirt towards Xander, moving with strength, unaffected by the wound. That's my brother.

Xander meets him on the ground, and for a second, they embrace, and I smile with relief.

Then I hear Bronson's laughter ring from somewhere inside the circling black mist, a manic sound that follows a gurgling howl, then a roar of hysterics.

"Seven lil' bikers all in a row, seven bikers in a row, " he sings, and I catch a blur of his silhouette and another's dashing around behind the headlights across from me. "Take one down, what do you have"—A man groans —"*Six* lil' bikers all in a row."

Max is on his feet now, charging straight towards an oncoming bike. He throws himself at the rider, slamming the body to the dusty ground. Soot and debris rise around them. The two wrestling figures are swallowed by smoke. The smacks of skin to skin follow them.

Assessing the immediate area, the unknown location of Dustin unnerving me, I pull Fawn with me as I crawl over the ashy dirt on my elbows towards the Chrysler.

I hide her behind the tyre, cup her cheeks soaked in tears and soot, and kiss her lips. Feeling too much. *Damn her.* I love her too much. Then I rip open my suit shirt, tug the bulletproof vest from my body, and fasten it around her.

She clutches at my shirt. "I'm sorry. I'm *so, so* sorry."

I punch kisses over her face. Anger towards her surfaces. Now she is safe. Now she is in my arms. My hands twitch. "Don't ever do that again, little deer. Don't ever defy me—betray me again!"

My choice of word throws her—betray—her breath catching on it. "I'm so sorry. I couldn't let you choose me."

"Dammit! I will *always* choose you!"

Her small fists shake, still curled around the fabric at

my chest. "Maybe I can talk to him." She wheezes, and the word *betrayal* takes on new meanings as her concerns shines in tears. No. She's just desperate. Confused. She knows this has to happen. "Yes. Yes. Maybe he will stop this. I can convince him I'm worth knowing and that we are in love and—"

Fuck. You're worth knowing, sweet girl. He's not!

But I don't have time to coddle her as the war continues around us. Shaking my head, I say, "He shot at you, sweet girl. He shot at you."

Her lips wobble, and I curse, ever fuelled by the need to make him pay. *Goddamn it.* I don't have time for more sentiment, so I drag myself from the sweet, little hands desperate to keep me close.

"*No*," she cries as I head back into the open. And it dawns on me that it may not be my safety or her own that causes her to suffer through that cry. Perhaps it is for her father. That the reality of him, his existence, and the slight similarity in the shape of his eyes may have altered the idea of him for her—he's real now.

Fucker. Drawing my Glock, I find purchase behind a blackened trunk before moving to another.

I hear Bronson sing again. "Take one down, what do you have"—another groan echoes—"five lil' bikers all in a row."

Upon me, a biker appears through the grey clouds and throws a fist into my face. I hiss on contact, dropping my gun. I curse.

He gets in close, so I pull him in further by his cut and slam my forehead into his nose.

The biker thug stumbles backwards, and I use the reprieve to claim my knife from my belt and slice him from ear to ear, the sound of gurgling vibrates through the slit.

Then I hear Fawn screech and ice slides through my veins. I dash to her place beside the tyre. My heart thunders in my throat. She's gone. "Fawn!"

I hear her gasp, and my brain fractures. I charge straight towards her frantic sounds as the thought of losing her tears my stone heart in two. I'll die for her.

I'll take every bullet, all the pain, the beatings, and it'll be my greatest pleasure to suffer them for her. To die devoting my life to her. So if there is a fucking heaven and by some crazy instance, I am allowed to visit from the pits of hell, I'll hold her unborn baby for her because I am devoted to her even in death.

I rush to the sound, dodging trees, jumping over the wreckage of a bike on fire. Passing Bronson on his knees, straddling a biker, sliding his blade upwards into the fucker's mandible.

Abruptly, I see them.

A burning branch lays over Max's leg, pinning him to the dirt. Flames flick around his body. Across from him, Dustin approaches with a knife raised and—

"Fawn!"

She jumps on his back, grappling her father, one arm around his neck while the other slaps hysterically at his face. *My bratty queen.* Dustin bucks around, but the knife—

Fuck! I get there just as he attempts to stab her, carelessly slashing, trying to leave her with holes in her shoulders and neck.

I see red. Growling, I catch his arm, giving her relief to release her grip. Dropping to her feet, she rushes to Max. Xander has found him, and together they manage to heave the scorched trunk from his thigh. Max rises to his full height.

In one quick succession, I snap Dustin's arm at the elbow, the limp ulna and radius bone hanging pendulously.

He howls in pain.

Max is upon him instantly, kicking Dustin's kneecap in, crumbling his leg, making him a wailing pile of backward-facing bones.

"*No* lil' bikers left in the row." Bronson emerges through the smoke, streams of bloody carnage sliding down his face and forearms, a knife in each fist held out wide. "Hello, beautiful brothers."

He stops by Xander, and the national park is suddenly swept in eerie stillness, only interrupted by Dustin's cries and groans. As though the entire forest has quietened down for our revenge.

My brothers let their demons out tonight, let them free to roam the national park until they must be reined in again. For my brother's women and children. For their sense of peace. For each other.

Carter and our men are close now too, watching from a distance as large unharmed mist-covered figures.

I reach for my little deer, pull her in, and cup her cheeks, staring into her uncertain dual-coloured gaze.

"Are you hurt?" I don't wait for an answer, examining the ash-iced skin at her neck and shoulders. Small cuts mar her flesh from the tip of his knife, rocks, twigs; it doesn't matter what. I clench my teeth. Dirt, dust, and soot cover her face and clothes, and I need to get her home. I need to care for her.

"You put yourself in danger," I say tightly, finding her blue and green gaze. "I should bend you over my knee, little deer. Expose your arse and pussy and spank you until the thought of leaving me—" I choke on that admission. *Dammit.* Correcting myself, I say, "Of *defying* me, will make you tremble."

She touches the bristles on my unkempt jawline. Her lips tight, and her eyes soft as she reads me. My sentiments play out on the surface despite my attempts to conceal them.

"I will always choose you, Sir," she says breathlessly, and my chest fucking throbs with affection for her. Her eyes widening, they slide past my shoulder. "*Clay...*"

Turning to follow her gaze, I see Max stalking Dustin as he tries to scoot backwards on broken limbs. Max's large muscular frame creeps over the fucker's crippled body.

"Stop. I'll leave," he begs. "I'll leave the city. *Cross?"* He calls out to the President of the Stockyard MC—otherwise known as Brock Riley—and is greeted with silence. "Cross?"

"Gone," Bronson states smoothly, wiping a stream of red from his lip with the back of his hand.

"You're alone, Dustin," Xander confirms. "Can't you *feel* the Butchers all around you?"

"Fawn! Don't let them kill your daddy—"

"Don't say her name!" I hiss, nodding at Max, who kicks Dustin's jaw shut. The sound of snapping teeth echoes. The knock sends him into an almost unconscious state.

Pity.

Dustin's head lulls along the dirt, his eyes rolling around like marbles within his skull. We may have taken him back with us once, drawn out the revenge. Not today. The bushfire will end this. The bodies charcoal soon.

I hear my sweet girl's breath hitch faster. This is not for Fawn to see. I pull her face into my chest, protecting her from the murderous scene. She can be my queen without witnessing her own flesh and blood die. That action doesn't rip away her strength. Nor undermined her bravery. It allows her humanity.

"He's yours," I say to Max. "Finish him.

Bronson and Xander look on from my side, and Max glares down at Dustin as the rarest of smiles creep across his face. Time becomes longer, stretching, as he hovers over him. The glow of the fire sets the backdrop. The grey smoke circles Max like the phantom of each betrayal readying itself to reap the consequences.

For the kidnapping of Konnor.

The attack on Cassidy.

For being undeserving of his daughter.

"Silence him, Max," I order, not wanting to lead Fawn from my clutches to the safety of the car but not wanting her to hear his howls of pain either.

Max squats slowly, hovering over Dustin. A shadow cast over the crippled body of his enemy.

He reaches down and tears a piece of Dustin's shirt, removing a strip of soiled fabric. Dustin comes to with a hazy groan as Max shoves the ash-covered material into his mouth, muffling the guttural sounds that rumble out.

Dustin begins to choke, the smoke and soot filling his pulsing throat, provoking it to contract and fight for air.

"I don't like his eyes," I say in Sicilian, holding the trembling body of my sweet girl, only further driven by her sorrow. Further angered by his effect on her.

Max's smile widens.

Dustin gapes as the shiny blade approaches the first glistening orb, his black pupil darting to follow the skew just as it connects. Sliding in with ease, the blade spears the brown eyeball straight through the centre.

A few twists later and Max has the first orb impaled and plucked from Dustin's skull.

He flicks the wet ball to the dirt, where it lies on its side, sizzling in the charred dirt, wide and watching as Dustin vomits around the cloth. Muffled rasping sounds curdle within his clogged mouth and throat. His body shakes with horror.

Max leans in for the second one, slowly lowering the blade closer and closer until the tip dips into the fluid coating Dustin's last eye—the last one that looks like Fawn's.

He plunges in slowly.

A fraction at a time.

Then he slams the knife down until only the handle can be seen bobbing and swaying with the eye it has impaled.

My brother is not a man of words, but he still hisses by Dustin's ear, "No eyes. You must really *feel* the Butchers all around you now... And a Butcher is the last thing you will ever feel."

CHAPTER TWENTY-FIVE

THE WEBBING of trees makes a near-black tunnel that envelops the car as Clay drives us from the campsite, from the dead bodies, ash, and debris. From the executions.

Everything happened so fast.

As though I had only just whispered, "*Hello*," to my dad moments ago, then someone hit fast-forward, a blur of events flashing behind my eyes in an instant; the vision of Max taking a bullet for me, of Clay dragging me beneath him. Of bullets flying. Of people dying. Of flames and smoke and ash, and then it stops. And I am dropped into this seat.

In this gliding car.

Where everything is still: the glass blocks the smoke, the tyres roll gently on the windy road, and the man beside me is as cold as stone, but my heart—

My heart is still on fast-forward. Still mirroring the events that have somehow ended just as they began.

I look down at my body. Belt on.

When did that happen?

When did I get in the car? In this suspended space between the first hello and the last death, I sit, experiencing my body as though it's been detached.

I feel—*the adrenaline.*

Feel my heart jumping into my mouth, feel everything inside me moving at a million miles an hour while nothing but the car moves... My body is still back there.

Hands shake.

Legs tight with fatigue.

Skin hot and sweaty.

A growl that should seem otherworldly but in this tunnel of fire only fits the ominous scene, screams passed our car. I barely flinch. More bikes join the thunder. Riding them, Clay's men and the Butcher brothers break away from us.

The three motorbikes howl up the narrow road like bats out of hell. The only light comes from the eyes of each headlight.

They vanish into the fog's thick depths.

The car is still and silent again.

I look down at my curled fingers—still clutching, clutching at nothing, at everything, at his shirt, at reality, the past and the present—as they vibrate violently. "Make them stop curling," I whisper, staring at my hands. "They won't stop."

The car slows down. Clay reaches over the seat, unbuckles me, and hauls me across the console to kneel either side of his body. My hands look *strange.*

"We need to get away from the campsite, sweet girl. Listen to me." He cups my cheeks with firm authority, forcing me to look at him and focus on his intent blue gaze. His actions offer me a sense of affection, while the hollow depth within his stare forces chills up my spine.

He's the boss right now. Not Sir or Clay. "This is the adrenaline," he continues methodically. "All you need to do is breathe. That is all your body needs. Can you do that for me, little deer?"

I nod with his hands cradling my face. "Yes."

"Good girl."

He grips my waist, slides me to my seat, and buckles me in before setting off down the road again. Then a hole of normality appears ahead, a break in the forest tunnel, the twinkling of city lights, the end of it...

The smoke holds us to the scene a moment longer, drawing it out, with a large demonic reach until we break through, the grey clouds separating over the bonnet, ripping us from the forest's grasping fingers.

The clear air circles us, and we're out.

And I don't know how to feel.

CHAPTER TWENTY-SIX

JUST BREATHE.

He has my eyes.

Rather, I have his.

Just breathe.

Breathing—definitely breathing—I stare out the tinted window of the Chrysler. The national park, the bodies, the fast-forwarded world, a distant orange landscape in the rear-view mirror. But... *Dustin Nerrock's* eyes came into the clear with me, reflect at me in the glass.

My dad's eyes.

I can't ignore that the man killed tonight shared my blood—not with those eyes. Entirely a different colour to my blue and green, but the position, the shape... I can't pretend he was merely a stranger.

I want to care more about him...

Guilt bleeds through my clearing confusion.

Guilt that I'm not grieving him.

Guilt that I want to.

Guilt that I defied Clay.

And guilt that I'd do it again.

As Clay navigates the streets of Connolly, his icy mien has not wavered or relented. Is he rolling the word *betrayal* over in his mind? From me. From Max. Even from Xander.

"Sir?" I think I say aloud.

But maybe I didn't, as silence is his answer. Loud breath shudders from me.

We drive between the white gates to the estate, and the vision of a pregnant blonde girl standing at the intercom only months earlier comes to me unbidden. She worries her bottom lip. Twists her hair around her finger. And imagines what that man might look like... Now she knows.

I wish I cared more...

I gaze down at the black ash and soot stains covering my jeans, experiencing my body normally. My limbs and heart move at the same time as the outside world. I'm grounded in the present, but it's bleak.

Frowning, I poke the tip of my finger through a small hole in the fabric. The rocks and twigs must have made it when I was dragged beneath Clay. Sadness is circling relief, and exhaustion is just so overwhelming they both seem muted.

But for the guilt...

The mansion comes into view, lit up by rows of external wall lights. I blink at the figure at the top of the steps. Aurora waits for us with an entourage of soldiers and maids.

When I step from the car, she sighs her relief so hard that even from the foot of the steps I can see her chest fall. "*Madonna Mia.*" She rushes to me.

Her long arms pull me in, and I wrap mine around her. I think she is my family. For reasons I can't explain, tears that are not for Dustin or me, not for anyone, fall softly against her shoulder. Tears of leaking exhaustion, of the word betrayal, of guilt, of the *still* that I am not ready to join.

She strokes my hair down my head. "It is over now."

Clay's presence behind me sends heat through my spine, and I lift my head to gaze at the lovely dark liquor-coloured eyes of his wife. "I met my father," I say to her and to myself, reaching for that *grief,* a moment of mourning him.

Like I should.

Shouldn't I?

"I know." She nods at something in the distance. "Look at the size of your moon, sweet Fawn. It's so close tonight."

My lip twitches with a smile, but one doesn't quite form. She told me that she never looks at the moon.

Gazing at the large glowing orb, I inhale the air. Inhale the grass. The scent of flowers. Inhale the *still.*

I exhale the fire.

Rushes of light play along the plane of the moon tonight when my back meets Clay's torso.

I press further into the hard, formidable wall of his body; the lingering smell of smoke and charred wood doesn't mask the masculine scent that is all his own. He still smells like him. Even if his armour is blocking out his heart tonight. It's still him.

Sadness and exhaustion deflate me as I realise it is over, the night is over, the fight, the revenge, and I fall further into him as my legs lose a little strength.

He stoops to scoop me up, and I sigh against him, feeling that fatigue hood my eyes. My arms flop around his neck, my lashes slowly batting in front of the moon.

Aurora touches Clay's cheek. "Is everyone safe? Xander? Bronson?" She pauses. "Max? Cassidy called a few minutes ago. They arrived home safely, but he's hurt. Your father left to check on him. Was he burnt and shot? Is it serious?"

"He still managed to trek back to his car," he says, contempt tightly coiled around each word. "I will call Cassidy after Fawn is in bed."

Is Clay still angry with Max?

He took a bullet for me.

Her hand slides from his cheek. "Clay... *I* will call Cassidy and check in. You need to rest. You're no good to anyone if you don't... And I worry."

"What a waste of your time," he says to her, his tone cold, closed off. "And that is simply not possible. The men need to be debriefed. A cleaning crew needs to remove evidence and stage an accident."

"I am more than capable of contacting our cleaner and having him troll the campsite. He knows what to do. I need just approve it," she insists.

I add, "Let Aurora do it, Sir. *Please*. Stay with me."

He hums, his gaze falls to my face briefly, the corner of his mouth twitching. "Very well," he accepts tightly, and his detached, guarded timbre stirs me.

He strides away, and Aurora heads down the steps to meet the convoy of cars that are now arriving. Distant conversations relay events. And I watch from over Clay's shoulder as Aurora stands in her element, and the men, they nod respectfully for her.

Clay carries me through the house and although I can walk, I'm exhausted enough to appreciate it.

I blink up at Clay. "Are you angry with Max, Sir?" I ask him as we approach our bedroom. "It was my idea."

"Not now, sweet girl."

"Max took a bullet for me—"

"That changes nothing!" he spits out before schooling himself again. "I would take a bullet for his fucking dog, but I would never undermine his decisions relating to Cassidy. I would never take her."

"You undermined his *concerns* when it came to Xander... though, Sir." *Fuck.* I actually said that. I swallow over the lump forming around those words, wishing them back down as the powerful muscles holding me bunch.

I don't push him further.

Not right now.

In the bathroom, Clay runs the shower. The seclusion of this space, the soft splashing sound, and the strange stillness after such intensity make pin pricks hit the back of my eyes.

Alone now.

Weak. Suddenly so weak I barely want to stand, weighed down by the sorrow of all those lives, the horror, the heat, and how quickly I picked Clay and his family over my own blood. It all splinters me. Creates thin cracks in my soul.

And I picked *Clay* even as Dustin's eyes blinked in a kindred way to mine, shifted the same...

I roll the events in my mind, list and sort them. The night I met my dad, he was murdered. That happened. And I stood by. But it wasn't a murder... A murder is vile, uncalled for. This was revenge. This was an execution.

Thinking about my dad's eyes, I barely notice when Clay removes our clothes. Stepping from my knickers absently, I wonder whether Dustin had the same ears as me too. Or the same mannerisms.

In the shower, the warm spray falls around my shoulders while Clay stands outside of its warmth. Allowing me all its attention.

He lifts me and sets me on the ledge; our eyes are level. And he starts to wash the ash and dirt from my shoulders and across my chest.

I think I lose focus, staring through the stacks of muscles at his chest and the coils down his forearms, staring at the tattoos he refused to explain the last time I asked him. At the large scar that etches from his shoulder to the dip of his neck. The one he hides with a vine. *How many more does he have after tonight? How many do they all have?*

Suddenly, he lifts my hand and places it over the scar, having obviously noticed my distant gaze. My eyes jump up to meet the intense blue glowing in his. "You asked me once what this was. Would you like to know, sweet girl? Would you like to know the kind of man I really am?"

I know what kind of man you are, Sir.

A dangerous man.

I simply nod, my lips thin, my heart shuddering to scream I don't care. I accept you. "Yes."

He uses his big hands to caress soap from my fingers over his collarbone down the length of my arm. "No one quite understands, sweet girl, that just like you believed in the moon, I believed in the *Cosa Nostra*. It is—*was*—my entire life.

"It was what I was born to do. Me. The heir. I had pride in that. I accepted long ago that this was my future... Just this. I wanted it. Was seduced by it. And when you don't have a choice, your decisions become remarkably clear. Life becomes black and white."

He continues to wash me as he speaks. "When I was

your age, I was just out of boarding school, and for the first time in my entire adolescence, I was staying in the family home. As part of my initiation, I was ordered to kill a girl. Jimmy and your father told me it was an honour of mine to finish this job for my family. They were proud when I accepted. I had presumed, as I always did, that by *family*, they meant my father and my brothers and the *Cosa Nostra*."

His brows draw in. "*She* was the daughter of a man who knew too much. So, *she* knew too much. That is all they told me, and that was enough for me then. I didn't question it. I accepted their words and orders. Your father went with me that day. She was young. Nine or so. And I put a pillow over her head, and I held it down." He pauses, and my throat tightens. "And I killed her. For them. That is the man I am."

Tears stream down my cheeks, meeting the water from the showerhead as they slide together down my trembling lips.

He presses his hand over mine, applying pressure to the scar, holding it, protecting it, as if we can heal it together.

His eyes level on me with an intensity and honesty I have never seen in him before. Not like this. "She fought back, little deer." He almost smiles. "She sliced me with some kind of ornament she had hidden under her pillow. And left me with this scar to remember her by... I should have asked questions. I should have spoken up. I never did."

An ache moves through my chest for him... not her. *What kind of person does that make me?*

It's the truth in his blue eyes, the gravelly aftershock to his timbre, that hurts my heart. A heart only whole and healed, trusting and strong, because he loves it. I can't see this man as *bad* when he is my number one good thing. So, I accept, he's the villain in that girl's story, but he'll never be the villain in mine. "You were following orders. You—"

"You cannot make excuses for this, little deer," he grounds, wanting my disdain, my shock and horror. "I was exactly your age when I blindly followed that order. I was not a child. Why do you think I told you this? Why now?"

"I don't know."

"You defied me tonight."

"I didn't want—"

"You left," he cuts me off. "You made your own decisions. You knew what the plan was. You heard what I said. Heard my orders. And you put yourself in danger. Why?"

"Because of Xander."

"Yes. But I told everyone that I was taking care of it. Try again," he challenges. "Say the words."

I breathe out hard, pushing the truth through my lips. "I thought you were making a mistake, Sir."

"Good girl," he praises. "You did." He nods slowly as his face tightens in regret. "But, little deer, you also decided that I wasn't reasonable enough to listen to your concerns. You didn't even try to convince me. You just left me. Tell me the truth now."

My lips won't stop vibrating as I admit, "*Yes.* I didn't think you would listen to me. I thought you'd lock me away."

A deep sigh leaves him, and he curses before saying, "*Christ.* I've failed you."

I shake my head. "*No.* It's not—"

"Yes." He cups my cheeks and presses his lips to mine, talking against the water and tears glazing them. "You didn't come to me." His voice sounds strange. Strained. As though he is fighting a battle in his throat. "I don't want you to feel as though you must take orders from me blindly. *Dammit*, Fawn. Question me." He kisses me and presses his forehead to mine, rolling it hard as he says, "Use your voice, sweet girl. And I will listen to your concerns. I will listen to you, Fawn. Every damn word that comes out of your pretty mouth, I will listen, but I swear to God, if you ever leave me like that again without at least giving me a goddamn chance to—"

"I won't." I grip the back of his neck, his shoulders are large ridges coiled with taut muscles, and I pull his mouth to mine again. Our kiss is tight, a wince of emotion thinning both of our mouths. "I'm sorry," I say against his lips. "I'm so *so* sorry."

"Swear it to me, sweet girl."

"I will never leave you again."

One of his hands slides back and fists my hair, using his grip to curve my neck so he can drag his lips down the column. I swallow over a lump of nerves, and he ardently licks along the rolling of my throat.

As his fingers twist in my blonde strands, my hair bites at the scalp. I whimper, feeling his darkness fill the room.

His breathing gets heavy and fierce, and his teeth now scrape along my skin. "I will kill the next person who tries to take you from me." He spreads my thighs and tugs me to the edge of the ledge, swiping two fingers through my slit before forcing me to take his cock in one brutal movement.

A yelp falls from me.

Impaled beautifully in a gasp.

He growls, and I dig my nails into the muscle cording his neck and shoulders. Then he starts to fuck me, powered by the confusion, the vulnerability, the confessions, and the honesty.

"I *would* have locked you up," he admits darkly, gripping my arse and thigh with one hand and using my pelvis to meet his hard drives. "I would have thrown away the damn key. You're right. I wouldn't have seen reason. I wouldn't have taken a chance. Not with your life." Deep grunts fall from him with each punch of his hips. "Not with you. Never you."

His lips slide up to my mouth and I gasp into them. He fucks my mouth with his tongue as he ruthlessly thrusts into me. Fucking the truth from himself, the hatred, blame, stoicism, and control.

Breaking off from our bruising kiss, he smothers my small body to his formidable, packed muscles, my head to his chest, held there by his fingers wrapped around my wet blonde strands. His hips never relent, battering me hard, rutting into me without caution.

My arms envelop his waist. I hold on as his powerful muscles roll and tighten beneath my clutching hands.

"I worship you, Fawn," he goes on roughly. "I fucking worship you, and I won't always be reasonable, but give me the damn chance to be! I'll learn. Give me the damn chance."

He batters the end of me. I cry out as he opens up to me with his words and his hard inward thrusts that have me accepting him and then missing him so quickly one sensation overlaps with the other.

I can't keep up.

Holding on.

He groans, his cock thickening inside me. "You'll have to stop me one day. You'll have to make me see reason when I'm about to tear the world through the middle for you. If you leave me, I'll do it. I will bleed the streets. Kill them all. Nothing could hurt me more than existing without you."

The ecstasy of being full of him, of his words, of his raw lovemaking that is a trembling and desperate chase to a climax, fills my chest.

Vulnerable. Utterly open. He clings to my body, hand in my hair, fearful of any distance. He doesn't just love me. I'm his *everything*. Like he is mine.

Tears continue to stream down my face as we break through mountains and crumbling walls. As we strip off his cool façade that was no choice of his to create. Armour that protected him from questioning the evil around him. A veil that separated him from the innocent girl that affects him still.

He fucks it all out.

His pristine mannerisms.

His unreadable affections.

All the real fear, pain, and regret shine from him and it is beautiful and chaotic and devastating. And he gifts it all to me as he builds towards his orgasm in such a way that makes me feel like his home, his safe space. My body, his sanctuary. A place of redemption.

My dangerous man.

My Clay Butcher.

My number one.

CHAPTER TWENTY-SEVEN

FRESHLY WASHED, fucked, and clinging to the seams of consciousness, we sit on the sofa in our master suite. Inside here, we are alone to be us. Even as the city through the window is a vast landscape of flickering lights and dashing orange lines that beckon him. Want a piece of him.

But not tonight.

I straddle his lap, my bare body on his, as I hold an ice pack to the bruising starting to colour the side of his cheekbone. He was struck during the fight at the camp-site. I didn't see it happen—but otherwise, we are both nearly unscathed. It's a miracle, really. Magic, maybe. No one was going to take away my number one good thing.

He enjoys a cigar while I tend to him. Wolf or lion, the king of this damn District jungle, a wound is a wound, and it has no mistress.

He leans back in a powerful pose. One arm hanging over the top of the sofa, the other by his side, fingers playing with the ends of my hair. Sort of like I do...

The cigar balances between his lips as he draws in

and out, stoking the glowing ember to flare and then darken. His clear, blue gaze watches me quietly. It's as intimate a moment as any other.

The image of my father's eyes and the creases between his eyebrows tumble into my mind. I inhale hard.

"I don't want to think about him," I say. "He didn't really look like me. Not really. But his eyes..."

"Yes, sweet girl. You may feel however you need about tonight. I will not stop you. If you want to grieve that man—"

"I don't." I shake my head. "I don't want to grieve him. I want to forget him. I want to forget that I have his eyes."

He gazes at me for a moment, a frown tightening his forehead. "You know, my brothers hold resentment towards my mother. The fact she favours me is not a secret. The other reasons, I wasn't around to know or understand. But... I have her features," he says to me. "I'm the only one with her bone structure. Cheekbones. Sharper than my brothers. I've always wondered whether the likeness bothered them."

I take him in. "I think you look like Luca."

"I do. But I also look like her. Take your time with this. You don't need to decide how you feel." His eyes are hooded in the dim light of the room. "Just let it happen, sweet girl."

"It's so raw right now, though."

"Would you like me to make you forget?"

A flush of heat paints my skin in a pink hue as his eyes drink me in, roaming my body in an intense way that presses in on me, presses down on me, forcing his intent.

"Yes." I open my mouth to breathe, trying to concentrate on his bruised cheekbone, on the ice that is melting from the pack, when his hand leaves my hair and slides around my naked waist. Following the curve of my backside down to my arse, he circles the rim between my cheeks. I pucker against him, wanting the experience of being full, stretched in that exquisite way.

I dart my gaze to meet smouldering pits of dark intentions and promises. His eyes flare, pupils large, orbed with a glowing ring of sky-blue.

A grin that is pure sex plays in the corner of his mouth. "I want this tonight," he purrs, poking through the tight muscles, and holding the tip of his thick pad inside me.

I whimper but push back to aid him in inserting his forefinger. My pussy ripples, the penetration only inches away like a phantom sensation inside those muscles, pushing in, and if I sit back, maybe I'll feel—

"Stop, sweet girl," he orders in a gravelly, deep timbre that curls my toes. He drops his arm from the top of the sofa and grips my hip hard to still me. "Not without lubrication."

My head swims when I look down at his cock expanding between us, reaching up to his navel. Huge. And veined.

"I like the way you gaze at my cock," he purrs. "With *yearning*. You nearly salivate, little deer. It's the prettiest thing."

Licking my lips, I agree with a nod. The taste of him does things to me.

He smiles at my eagerness. "Be a good girl. Go to my top drawer and bring me the bottle. I'll make you forget tonight."

I climb to my feet, and while I retrieve the bottle, he puts his cigar out in the ashtray on the table.

His powerful physique is leaning back when I approach him again; muscles protrude down the plane of his abdomen with finely cut valleys around each. And down his long arms they create ridges and bulk. His formidability—how quickly he could attack, snap a person in two using those muscles, stokes me into a fever. He is a lion in wait.

I want him. Crawling quickly back on to the lap of this dangerous man, I spread my thighs wide over him. Grinding my hips on the length of him, I slide my pussy up and down, stroking my clit over him, revelling in the simmering pleasure.

He groans his approval but focuses on his task and the bottle in his hand, covering his fingers in clear gel.

I put on a show.

Watching him closely, I rub myself to a wet, primed state.

I should be more anxious. I'm not sure what to expect; I've had a plug in my arse for hours—surely, I can handle the throbbing of his cock inside me.

I flop my arms over his shoulders as he positions me forward. I can feel his hands lathering the length of him behind my spine, hear the rumble of his satisfaction as he jerks himself a few times.

Then he stops and my nose meets his, our eyes inches apart. "Breathe deeply," he purrs, exhaling hard, smoky cigar-scented air hitting my face.

Bracing me at the top of his cock, hovering me over his lap, he pushes one hand flat to my lower spine, arching me. My backside tilting. His other hand grips my hip, rolling me slightly as the bulbous crown of his erection pops through the tight muscles.

My eyes widen, and his darken.

"*Fuck*," we both say.

"Good girl," he whispers hoarsely. "Very, very good. Your first time will be overwhelming. Keep your eyes open so I can see you." He levers my hips as the thick length of him slides excruciatingly slowly inside me. "I don't want you anywhere else when I'm inside you."

I fist his hair when it gets too much, my nails grating his skin. A constant burn around his penetration blazes, the muscles fighting back against the invasion, the sensation of pain growing. Moving up. Into me—

"Stop, stop, stop." I pant, the stretch of those muscles all-consuming, each nerve channelled down there. My body bursts with the need to recoil. To stop the sting. My ears and neck are hot, and my throat tight.

He studies my face, and I glance away evasively, disappointed in myself for stopping him. Other girls do this. Why can't I? I want to do it. I want to feel it...

He pulls himself out of me, and I almost cry at the relief when my arse closes and the burning stops. "I'm sor—"

"Don't you dare use that word. You know what it will get you. Never be *sorry* for recognising your limits."

I blink at him. "How far in were you?"

His brows draw in. "Barely at all, sweet girl."

"What if you don't fit?"

He smiles smoothly and sweeps a rogue hair over my shoulder. "I will, little deer."

"But, how do you know? You're not a girl. What if it really hurts, and you don't know because no one has ever told you. I'm scared it is going to hurt."

"I would never hurt any part of you." He stares at me with intensity playing through a dark thought. "Come with me, sweet girl."

He nods for me to climb from him, and I do as I am 'nodded to do.'

He stands, grabs a perfect diamond-shaped pillow, and walks into the dressing room with it grasped in his fist.

The length of his body a long form, muscles curving and flexing in a smooth predatory way. This man is every bit as formidable and powerful when he's naked as at any other time. More so in a smooth, unaffected fashion, as though he could just as easily kill a man in this state.

His suited form, muscles visible beneath layers of expensive fabric, is not what gives this powerful man his intimidating presence. It is in his very being.

He places the pillow on the ottoman and nods towards it, and I blush, remembering when I touched myself there. "Lay down, mount my pillow, and twist your face towards the mirror. I want you to watch."

Heat creeps up my neck, the warmth of excitement blooming across my skin, and when I crawl on the ottoman and look at myself, my skin is slowly pinkening.

Steadily, I lay flat; the ottoman is long enough to accommodate my entire length. I watch as the deadliest man in the city, naked, all trim lines and tattoos, places a knee on either side of my body. He repositions me and the pillow until it is between my legs and under my pelvis.

His eyes are hooded as he gazes at me—my backside arched up, my pussy instantly grinding on the pillow, yearning for that blissful pressure.

I am swimming in ecstasy as I stare at his reflection. He looks so much larger than me in the mirror. A formidable six-foot-five physique hovering over a smaller frame, barely the same species we are so utterly opposite.

That is what we are. What we look like all the time. The orphan and the Mafia Don.

He uses the bottle in his hand to lubricate his palms. I swallow, my white skin now glowing deep hues of rouge.

I moan as his hands work my muscles down to my backside, attentive and warm. My body is lax and opening. He begins to massage the cheeks at my bum, and I gaze down to watch his cock strain against his navel. Thick like my forearm. Covered in perfect blue veins that pulse.

I roll my bottom lip against the upper to the sight of him, his massaging movements sway his body, his cock heavy, moving with him. It's an erotic view.

"Sir." His name tumbles from my lips when firm palms massage up my back and down again, my entire body loosening under his skilled kneading.

Then his finger touches the rim between my cheeks, but I don't clench around it. I watch him instead. His eyes are glued to his masterful workings. He rims me leisurely, dipping in and then out. Something like a moan but far too guttural to be one, fills my throat. I love the sensation. I begin to press back again, and he stills his finger. "That's my good little deer."

Swimming in heat and thick air, I rock my hips back and forth, rubbing my pussy on the pillow and then taking his finger in slow stretching inches.

"*Christ*," he says through a heavy exhale. "You're simply the prettiest thing I have ever seen. That's very good. Your body loves being full of me. All your pretty holes available and open. You are just nervous, sweet girl. Watch me enjoy your lovely little arse."

I squeeze my eyes shut as he slowly drags his finger from inside me, all my internal muscles rippling, and my body shuddering at the last pop.

He presses the crown of his cock to my puckering rosette, and my eyes fly open to watch him. With his brows tight, his mouth open and panting, he inches inside me.

His cock stretches the tight, defiant rim, sliding through the muscle, forcing my pelvis harder into the pillow. "This is my little arse. My sweet, supple body. I will never hurt it—*Christ*, you feel good," he groans as he continues to penetrate me.

My head spins.

My arousal coats the pillow.

I clench to his choppy breaths.

"Fuck," he bites out. "I want you like this. Laying over my ottoman when I get home. Humping your pillow. Panting. Wanting for my cock to fill your arsehole."

I am riveted to the way this large man takes my body, each inch of his thick erection disappearing within me. I open my mouth to gasp, my tongue flat to the bottom of my jaw, seeking air. I take him. It's all I can do.

My pussy spasms.

As he impales me, he lowers himself to his elbows, and the change of position sends a forewarning thrill of sensation through my backside. There is more.

It screams there is more.

The hand that was playing with my arse before grips the cushioning of the ottoman, squeezing, while his other hand wraps around my jaw and mouth. "Suck on my fingers like a good girl, little deer."

Dipping his index finger and his forefinger between

my lips, he soothes me. I suck them as he starts to fuck me.

Fuck... me...

My pulse is like a perpetual cymbal between my temples. Eyes glued to the prowess of his movements. To his muscles as they contract and tense, his body rolling in a controlled, effortless wave, down to sink inside me and up to draw out. I am so overwhelmed—

By the sight of him using my body.

The sound of his near-violent groans.

The feel of him thrusting through my taut rim, sinking in deep against the contracting, his hard body meeting mine and then lifting again. He is a beautiful machine.

I suck his fingers harder.

"I'm in so deep, sweet girl." He groans, stilling and panting. "Look how well you did. Look at how lovely your body takes my cock. Such a good girl for me."

I gaze at his reflection as he thrusts, working his cock in me, using his hips in a rhythm that rubs my pussy on the pillow, a grin that is carnal ticking to a large menacing curve.

Pleasure builds between my thighs, and my orgasm builds to his rocking motion, perfectly timed with his hips, the pillow stimulating my pulsing flesh while his cock presses against my pussy walls.

Somehow, I can feel him in both deep sensual places.

It's dizzying. Stars burst around my vision. I lose track. Of... Of which sensation is where— My entire pelvis humming with brutal vibrations that play on the cusp of pain, that dance on warning, that flood with euphoria.

I begin to moan.

And I don't stop.

Wanton, and crazed, and sucking his fingers as though I'm starved for the salty taste of them, I come apart.

He throws his head back as I balance on consciousness, his hips taking on a rougher beat, the coils of veins laced up his arms protruding, his powerful physique tensing and bunching as he comes inside me.

"*Madonna Mia.*" He freezes. So deep. His forehead meets my neck, his lips press to my spine, and sweat drips from him to my skin. He begins to speak in another language—*praise*—I can tell he is praising me, but his mind is so wrapped in pleasure he doesn't realise he's not speaking in English.

His fingers slide from my lips.

Long moments pass with him pulsing within me, mounted on my back, braced above me so his weight doesn't crush me. Then he lifts his head.

He collects me into his arms. "I'm so proud of my little deer for taking me so beautifully." I wrap loose, tried limbs around him. Standing, his cock slides from inside me, and the sensation of being emptied drags a cry from my throat. His cum drips from inside me, forcing a blush to creep up my neck and along my cheeks. It is an uncomfortably sensual sensation that is so very primal.

We wash up in the bathroom, and he fingers me *there* to help clean me. My legs near collapse with how much I'm enjoying that stimulation now. I stroke his length as he does, massaging soap into his cock with two hands.

We dry each other.

"Lay down, sweet girl. I'll be back shortly."

I sit on the bed, hug my knees, and stare at the door, already anticipating *shortly* is a lie. The phantom sensation of his fingers and cock inside me still flush arousal through my body as I wait.

Within a minute, he's back with my kitten in hand, and I'm bouncing a little with excitement to see her.

Beaming, I reach for the fluffy animal and instantly fall backwards with her pawing my chest and fumbling in my grip.

Her squeaky meows mix with my voice as I say, "You're going to let her sleep in the bed?"

It surprises me. Yet, I don't know why. I suppose a man who has pillows staged in perfect diamonds and uncomfortable wrought-iron tables placed in prime lounging areas, doesn't strike me as the kind of man who allows white fur over his black sheets or takes kindly to early morning kitten licks to the nose and cheeks.

Sliding onto the mattress, he positions himself on one elbow to watch me and her play. I run the tips of my fingers down her little fur legs, and she pulls them from me like, *'I gotta use those leggies, Mummy.'* I laugh a little at my own inner monologue.

"She can sleep in the bed for now," he answers. A smile that is smooth, devilish charm taps the corner of his lips, making him look younger but no less intimidating.

My heart grows. "For tonight?"

"At least tonight."

I study him, meeting unwavering eyes that are always assessing and watching. He's radiating heat; his muscles are still on fire from the meticulous way he fucked me. I didn't do anything. I never do *much...*

"Did I do okay?" I ask him, tucking a piece of his dark hair behind his ear, rewarded with the easiest of chuckles —the deepest and most contented and just... *Clay.*

"Such a sweet question."

"I didn't—I don't really ever do much." I shrug. "Is that okay?" I stroke my kitten as she meows, falling off my chest into the small gap between Clay and me. "I feel like I just—"

"*Take me* so well. Look so pretty. Flush for me. Open for me. You sound so endearing when you come apart around my cock, and you enjoy the way I control your body. You enjoy being manhandled, little deer. Don't feel ashamed. You're safe with me, sweet girl. Safe to be you."

"Am I enough?" I swallow thickly. "Like that?"

"You are more than enough, little deer," he admits. "My strong, brave, bratty, sweet girl. I don't think you understand what you mean to me. I am changing for you, not the other way around. You wanted comfort; I filled my home with pillows and lounges. Hung a dreamcatcher above my bed. Replaced my books with softer stories. You wanted to be spoilt; I make sure you have every kind of sweet thing available to you. You wanted a purpose, responsibility, so I gave you the kitten. You wanted attention; I'll offer you every moment I have to give.

"And"—his eyes darken— "you wanted to be disciplined, to be held accountable, so I will damn well punish you when you misbehave. You wanted a dangerous man, little deer, and I will threaten the lives of every fucker you meet. *And...*" He pauses, and I'm riveted by his every word. "You want pleasure, so I will give you every kind you desire. Because *you* are not *enough*. You are more. So, I will make the world around you more too."

My heart expands. When I peer up at the dreamcatcher above my head, my smile grows *too*—everything growing, swelling, making room for the future. Thinking about all the love and affection I now have. Friendships. Him. His family. My kitten.

Clay Butcher.

The Don of the *Cosa Nostra,* who hangs dreamcatchers over his bed, sleeps with a nameless white kitten... A man who understands intimately who I am, through my skin and bone to my soul, to my slowly building self-confidence. Who understands what I have been through. Who turns the immaculate world he lives in around to fit my brand of rumpled and eccentric personality, to meet *my* needs.

For a moment, inside my mind, I see a smoke-filled forest and eyes so like mine staring back at me through the fog. As I focus on those brown eyes, my kitten prods me with her little needles. I sigh. I don't need a man with my likeness; I don't need a father or a mother or a sibling or uncle, not when I have *him* as all-consuming and impressive as all those roles combined.

He is my everything.

CHAPTER TWENTY-EIGHT

LUNA.

Luna Butcher.

She pads around in the diamond gap of my legs, occasionally stopping to lick milk from my cereal bowl. The television flashes with the morning news, and I get my first glimpse of Clay since we fell asleep last night.

He was gone this morning.

But there he is, wearing his smooth, charismatic armour, fitted to perfection within a flawless charcoal suit. I know what is under that armour now. And it's volatile. Deep. Vulnerable. Angry. So full of passion and possession it makes me want to weep with joy that a man so *alive* lives beneath that veil.

A familiar-looking red-headed woman interviews him in front of a burnt trunk and, behind them, in the far, far distance, a helicopter circles the glowing forest.

The orange headlining banner scrolling the bottom of the screen reads: *Eight members of the outlaw Stockyard Motorcycle Group and well-known businessman Dustin*

Nerrock have died after becoming trapped in the bushfire due to taking a shortcut back to their motorcycle headquarters.

Clay goes on to say, "I flew back from Dubai the moment I received the regrettable news. The city and all its members send their condolences to the families of the fallen Stockyard Motorcycle community. It is truly a tragedy. We will be hosting a memorial ride through the District on Thursday."

He's a clever man.

"Don't let her eat from your bowl," HJ says, capturing my attention, appearing in the lounge room wearing his all-black suit and tie. "They have worms, Miss Harlow."

I curl up my nose. "Luna does not have worms. They put the little drops on her fur to kill the worms."

He stops staunchly in front of me, his hands hanging down by his sides.

Exhaling hard, I ready myself for another day of being followed, being politely responded to, being treated like a ward. It is what it is.

"You know," he begins, "I'm lucky to still have a job. I'm lucky to still be alive. A month ago, Mr Butcher would have fired me for letting you slip away. Well, at least that would have been the story for why I wasn't around."

Gazing up at him, regret for him but not for my actions plays across my face. "I'm so sorry. I had to."

He nods stiffly. "I know." A rough sigh leaves him. "I need you to remember that it's my job to keep you safe. At the very least, you should have requested I go with you."

I laugh at him. "You wouldn't have let me go."

"No," he admits, "because Mr Butcher is my boss. *And...* your safety is important to me as well."

Luna crawls out from my diamond leg pen and stumbles over to his freshly polished black shoe, rubbing her

face on the reflective surface, smearing it with her drib-
ble. Then she tumbles to the side, her paws going up,
swatting at the black laces.

"So..." I peer up at my henchman/butler/rat, who I am
very fond of even though he is a pain in my arse. "I had no
choice. I'm glad you're not dead, by the way. Even though
you're a rat."

He ignores Luna as she attacks his shoe. "Rats are the
new cats. I read it in a Cosmopolitan."

I laugh, surprised he managed a joke given our new
less-friendly arrangement. "You know, I heard that
people change on death row. I didn't realise it would
happen so quickly, so profoundly. Your sense of humour
has finally returned."

He looks lighter as he says, "Which leads me to the
next thing I have to say to you, Miss Harlow—"

"Wait... Is this about your sense of humour or your
epic experience on death row? I'm fragile, after all."

"You are not fragile. I think that ship has sailed. No,
this is about my job," he advises, amusement in his voice.
A sound I have missed. "Mr Butcher has changed my
contract."

I deadpan. *No.* I don't want a new butler/rat. I like *my*
butler/rat. "Oh. Is he taking you away from me?"

"No." He smiles. "He's giving me to you. I'm officially
under your orders from now on."

I squint at him. "*Wait...*" As I try to understand what
that means, I pause and watch Luna try to crawl up his
leg. "What does that mean?"

Looking down at the kitten as she makes her way
towards his crotch, he tries to gently shake her off his leg.
She doesn't budge. So, he pries her from his thigh and

sets her on the ground again. She makes a squeaky call of annoyance.

"I'll do what you ask of me," he says, pulling my focus back to the knowing sparkle in his eyes.

Happiness plays along my mouth as the meaning behind that gesture registers. "He trusts you with me—"

"He trusts *you*, Miss Harlow."

My breath catches. "Woah." A little flicker of control, of place, identity, and acceptance rolls around inside me. I beam. "I have an employee. Can I request that you call me Fawn?"

He grins. "Yes, Boss."

I crack up laughing, finding the word '*boss*' exciting as all hell, now understanding why Clay Butcher looks and smells like power... Because that's what he is—walking, talking, smelling perfect power. And I have a little borrowed power of my own now, too.

I get an idea.

Now that the threat of my dad is... over, I take a big breath. "Can I leave the house?"

"You may." He holds his hand out for me to take, and I do, standing with his assistance. "Where would you like to go?"

"To Max and Cassidy's house. Then to see Xander," I say immediately, brushing the short white hairs from my jeans and flowy pink crop top. I got a little head spin from jumping up fast but rattle the fuzz around until it releases its hold.

His brows draw in. "Of all the places you could go, you want to head straight towards drama again?"

"Yes. I want to make sure he's okay. He took a bullet for me. And he's pissed Clay off. And Cassidy must be so upset. Fuck, maybe with *me*..." I fumble on the unwelcome thought, remembering the last time I saw her and Shoshanna, I avoided them. Avoided the accusation in their sorrowful eyes. "Damn." I cringe at the memory. "Yeah. I have to go. And I have to see Xander too. It's my fault he was taken. And he's... *my friend*."

"And you should eat more before we go," he insists. "Don't think for a second I didn't just see you nearly faint—"

"I didn't *nearly faint*. Don't be dramatic." After putting Luna back in her pen, I walk towards the kitchen. He trails me, his dubious expression like a hand tapping me on the shoulder.

"You went whiter than you are naturally."

"No, I didn't," I dismiss, grabbing a muffin from the basket of goods Maggie fills with freshly baked pastries and cakes. "See." I wave the orange and poppyseed muffin at him.

Wandering towards the front door, I take a bite because he isn't wrong. I've eaten. I had cereal. But when I stood up, I did get a little wave of dark coasting across my vision, a moment of weakness, heavy headiness, but I'm set on seeing Clay's brothers and Cassidy.

My direction—towards the front doors— spikes my pulse as though any minute now I will get tackled to the ground for trying to escape.

I open the left one and slowly step out into the spacious air, utterly free, standing at the top of the stairs in the far-reaching daylight. It is a beautiful estate. The hedges roll into the distance towards those looming white fences.

At the foot of the front steps, shiny black vehicles line the side parking lot with one standing out like a sore thumb—it's red. Henchman Jeeves is suddenly at my side, and the out of place car flashes ahead. The sound of it unlocking resonates like independence.

"That's your vehicle, Fawn. And they"—he points to the four men now climbing into another car nearby— "will be following us. They work for Clay."

Of course.

"I knew he couldn't relinquish complete control." I jog down the steps and rush over to the car, eager to touch it. I run my fingers across the metallic red paint—no, orange, no, gold... Depending on the angle, the car flashes with various analogous colours. I smile. "It's a nice offer though. Isn't it?"

"It is." He rounds the vehicle and steps into the driver's side with one foot, staring at me over the sparkling red/orange roof. "Jump in, and I'll take you to see Mr Butcher."

I grin over the roof, then wiggle my eyebrows with mischief dancing around on them. "Do you think he'll teach me to drive it one day?"

"I doubt it. Anyway, you have me."

"Hmm. I'll work on him."

IT TAKES twenty minutes to get to Max and Cassidy's neighbourhood. The houses are mostly two storeys, a bit smaller than the ones in Connolly, but the appearance of wealth is still in the cleanliness, the perfect green lawns.

All those cultivated roses.

Being from the other side of Stormy River, I've only ever seen poverty. Rusty bikes and motor vehicles abandoned on lawns. Couches in strange outdoor positions. The kind I'd never sit on. Not for a million dollars. Then, a few months ago, I experienced the culture shock of Clay's level of abundant prosperity.

We slow at the base of a small hill. There are no parking spots, so we leave the car on the street. Closely behind us, the car with Clay's soldiers brakes and parks a few lengths away.

Henchman Jeeves opens the passenger door for me, and I make my way up the pretty pebbly walkway to the house.

Ahead of me now, standing on top of the hill, is a home with two levels and low white fencing around a veranda.

The beautiful construction looks like Cassidy and the absolute opposite of Max. It looks friendly. Charming. Not overly big but clearly built with wealth.

Butterflies awaken inside me.

I can do this.

Nodding to myself, I approach the door and knock, instantly met by barking and canine grumbles.

I beam and widen my legs to brace myself for the large Bernese Mountain dog's attention. She can effortlessly bowl my feet out from under me.

Cassidy answers the door with Clara—the noisy canine—peering around her waist to get a good look at me.

"Hi," I breathe the word, suddenly hit with nervousness that fills my chest, creating an airy kind of sensation. "You might not want to see me after everything. It was my fault that Max got hurt and—"

"Look," she says straightaway, ushering Clara away with a little pat. "I am overprotective of my Max. I didn't like what happened. I didn't like not knowing. It really hurt. I care about no one as much as him. He's mine. *My Max.*"

I suck a breath in. "I know. It was my fault—"

"But no, Fawn." Opening the door and stepping to the side for me, she adds, "It was Dustin's fault that Max got hurt. Not yours. It was Max's fault that he did this without telling me. But from what I've heard, if you didn't go with him, Xander might be dead." Her eyes well up. "I'll always be selfish when it comes to Max. I'll always want to keep him safe above anything or anyone else. I don't apologise for that. I can't. But you were so brave, Fawn, to go to him and to think of Xander. You risked your life for Xander's."

I exhale with relief but shake my head at her praise. "I didn't feel brave at all. It was what had to happen."

"Honestly, I didn't see that side of you before this," she admits. "The protective side. The selfless side. Everything has been a little... *"about Fawn-ish"*. I'm sorry for that. It's just how it has seemed from the outside. Clay put you on this pedestal. Don't scare Fawn. Don't upset her. Make sure she eats.

"And these boys are special. And I liked you. I like most people, but now that I look at our interactions, I can see that I didn't really take the time to get to *know* you." She sighs, a little regret tumbling down the sound. "I didn't see you ever risking your life for one of the boys."

I shrug. "It isn't a big deal. You don't owe me anything. I mean, I came the whole way here to avenge a boy who had no fucking respe— Oh. *Shit."* I lower my voice, remembering her daughter, Kelly, could be close by. "Is Kels here? I probably shouldn't swear around her, hey?"

"She's at kindergarten. And it's okay. Max still swears

around her and she says, 'say *frick* daddy.'" Cassidy
giggles once, then says, "finish your story."

I sigh. "Well, he didn't give a shit about me, and I
would have done anything to protect him. So, of course, I
would do anything to protect Xander. He was my first
friend here. He was the one out of everyone who treated
me like an equal."

"And that means a lot to you, doesn't it?" she asks
sadly. "For someone to just treat you with basic human
kindness and interest? Enough for you to risk your life to
save that person." Her throat rolls with emotion. "I knew
you had a hard past, but I can actually see it in your
actions now."

"The damage," I joke, and she smiles a little.

Walking into her beautiful home, I take it all in. It's
large, open plan, and warm with oak-coloured flooring.

"You impressed Max," she states as though that is the
highest of regards. "And he is *not* an easy man to impress.
I guess that means you're a Butcher Girl now." Then the
curve of her mouth dances with amusement as she says,
"You know, it's a lot of responsibility being a Butcher Girl.
We have a secret clubhouse, meetings, bake sales—"

I wrap my arms around her in the doorway, the
gesture shocking her equally as much as it shocks me. I
turn my face into her hair and say, "Thank you."

She returns my hug. "Don't thank me. Didn't I just tell
you about all the responsibilities?"

I laugh gently and step back from her. "I'll do a bake
sale any damn day." Then I take a big breath in and say,
"Can I see Max? Is he badly hurt?"

"Of course. He's in pain, but he's pretending he's not.
You know how that is... They're all outside." She waves a
little, saying, "Follow me."

We walk down the long corridor, well-lit by the windows and glass sliding door at the end. The natural light floods the space, highlighting the family photos lining the white walls. I gaze at pictures as I pass them.

Smiling, I see a lot of Kelly, and Max and Cassidy. Clara too. Then there are some of Bronson and Xander at parties. And finally, wedding photos with the entire family.

A whole collage of photos at a tropical location halts me. My feet unable to move. There is... *Clay and Aurora,* looking very married. *Coupley.* Her wedding dress is like nothing I have ever seen before.

Get over it, Fawn.

I am his everything.

I rub my chest. It still hurts to see another woman experience something with him that I never will. I want all his experiences, all of *him.* I may be selfish, needy, but the sting is real, and it flares in the face of their smiling images.

I stare it down. Wish it away. Focus on all the details like a detective might. Faces directed towards the camera. The position of their hands clasped together. The shape of their smiles. Wanting to see a message, a clue, that even then, on that wonderful day, they were only friends. I don't see it.

I see love.

I find myself glaring at it.

"I had no idea it was an arranged marriage," Cassidy says, stopping beside me, also looking at the picture, and I try for a smile, but I've never been particularly good at feigning them. "So, you can imagine I was shocked, well, by you. But Clay is like a robot. He's hard to read, and he has this trained charm that he turns on for everyone around him. He is always... I dunno, *performing*, ya know? Shoshanna says he's been like that for as long as she has known him."

I scoff with derision.

She touches my shoulder with hers, a little bump of sorts. "And she told me of a time when she was in high school. Clay picked her up from her house. On the drive, he told her that he would not marry for love. That his love story with Aurora was not real. But he wanted love for his brothers, and he would protect them... He's not in love with her, Fawn. And he never was, but he knew what it looked like. He saw it in Shoshanna and Bronson when they were just children. He knew it was worth having. Worth protecting. He just sacrificed his own chance at it for them. Until you."

I sulk. "He looks in love."

"*Little deer.*" His voice nearly throws me over with the deep power in the commanding tone.

I twist to see Clay stepping through Max and Cassidy's front door. His body a formidable machine now sauntering towards me in an expertly tailored navy suit.

My pulse begins to race, just like it always does. My belly swarms with butterflies, vibrating and reminding me he's still the master of my nerves. How is it that I am not used to this man yet?

He stops close, his essence radiating warmth towards me, and I peer up at him through my blonde lashes. Yep. Out of all the atoms in the world, in the universe, the ones that make up Clay Butcher are far more superior than any others.

"I'm staring at the camera, sweet girl," he says pointedly. His finger touches my chin, lifting it. "Since the moment I laid my eyes on you, they have not wanted to be anywhere else. *Remember?*"

"*Naww.*" Cassidy swoons, gazing puppy-eyed at us, and Clay doesn't even flinch, no visual disdain with her cooing over his statement. He is above it. Above embarrassment. "I'll go," she adds quietly. "See you two outside. Everyone is out there."

She wanders away, and I melt into his attention. "I'm glad you're here, Sir. But now you can go make up with your brother."

He steps backward to rake his heated stare over my appearance, his eyes travelling over my flowy shirt and high-waisted jeans. There is a slither of skin between the denim and the shirt, and his eyes stop on it. "You look adorable. *Young.* You make me feel like a dirty old man, sweet girl."

I smile, liking the way his eyes drag along my skin.

He reaches for my hand, threading our fingers together, pressing his palm to mine so every part of his touches every part of mine. "Follow me, then I may take you outside."

May take me? God, he's bossy.

The heat between our bodies rises as we walk in the opposite direction to where Cassidy disappeared. My conditioned response to his intent stirs inside me, a ball of hot need swelling in my core, inducing wetness, igniting an animal instinct. Overly aroused, I try to ignore the pictures of sweet Cassidy dancing in her studio, ballet accolades, and a few of Max boxing that follow me down the corridor.

I am panting by the time we stop outside a closed door, my pulse having picked up pace, now a little trot in my throat. "Here? I'm not exactly quiet—"

"You nearly fainted, little deer."

Unreadable, he reaches for the door and opens it, ushering me inside a—I bump into the ceramic bowl—a toilet?

He shuts the door, pressing his back to it. I turn to look up at his serious expression as he reaches into his pocket and pulls out a small plastic wrapped straw-shaped package. "I need you to remove the cap, urinate on the end of this—"

"*Oh. My. God!*" I exclaim, before spitting out, "That's why you're here! Dobber. Rat. Pain in my arse. I thought he worked for me now. I'm firing him." I call out to the closed door, knowing HJ probably isn't even inside the house, "Hear that? You're fired, Henchman Jeeves—"

Clay takes a firm hold of my jaw, my voice muffled and then silenced completely. "Quiet, sweet girl. Your bratty side will get you fucked." The intensity in his fingers as they dip into my skin snatches my breath; he's deadly serious right now. His eyes change—large ominous pupils expand like black dye until the clear-blue within is merely a thin ring. "I won't wait a moment on this." His voice deepens. "I need to know why you nearly fainted. Now. Sit. Do as I say."

He lowers his mouth to my ear, blanketing me in hot breath, danger, possessiveness, a warning in his radiating heat. "Then I'll tend to that weeping little pussy with my fingers before we go outside."

Releasing his hold on my jaw, his fingertips tend to the divots they left, massaging my cheeks a few times before falling away.

He straightens and nods to the bowl. "I won't leave you needy, sweet girl. Don't leave me concerned."

My pulse upgrades from a trot to a full-blown gallop

in my throat as I take the small plastic package from him. I know what this is. I've done this once before.

And it was positive.

I slide my jeans and knickers down my thighs, sit on the toilet, and hold the tube between my thighs in the bowl. I should be embarrassed with having his eyes so intently glued to me, but being alone in any capacity feels infinitely more uncomfortable than being in his company. I don't know when that happened. When my skin became more perfectly moulded, more contently warm, just in the mere proximity of this powerful man.

I look down at the stick. Holding my breath, I pee on the end. It's a bit mechanical. A bit dutiful, but... something else, too, like—*Significant*. I think. Aurora has his ring, his name, but I— I'll share his children...

It's still not real yet.

Just a possibility.

Does he really want this?

Oh God, don't start panicking.

Swallowing, I place the cylinder on the floor with shaky hands. I don't pull my underwear up in case I have to pee on it again, or it needs more pee, or—I can't think. Can't move.

I glare at the tube as though, by damn will alone, I can make that second strip appear. A pretty, positive test, that will make me *significant*, and him... a dad.

Don't panic.

My eyes widen in my contemplations. He leans down and picks it up, and I follow it. The column is wet, a tiny bit of my pee is on the plastic. He doesn't care.

Clay doesn't stare at the cylinder. Instead, his intense blue eyes spear me, the silence stretching under his attention.

I can hear my breathing but not his. Can hear my heart beating in my ears. Feel it a pounding drum in my neck and face. Why aren't we talking? Why aren't I talking?

Will he be disappointed if I'm not pregnant?

Disappointed in my body?

I've lost a child before.

What if I lose this one?

I always thought I wasn't made of the right stuff—

"You are better than those thoughts, sweet girl. No matter the result, I will love you. I will keep all my promises to you, and I will fuck you until you are."

My throat tightens, tears rising.

I anchor myself in his eyes, fighting the pull of the column in his fist, fighting the need to drag my gaze to it. "What if I can't anymore? That's a thing, right? Sometimes the stuff inside just stops working, after trauma, after..."

He holds my stare effortlessly. "We will make it happen, little deer. I will fill you every night for the rest of your life."

"What if I lose him, like I lost the last one." Panic wins out, rising my voice, "You'll hate me and find someone—"

"I will do no such thing."

I fight the pull. "Will you find someone else?"

"I do not want children, little deer."

My breath hitches. "What?"

"I want children with *you*."

I can't hold it anymore. I have to look at it, have to know the results. My eyes drop to the testing panel while his stay on mine, and there is— There is—

There *are* two lines.

I gasp, the choppy sound falling out as the waves of emotions rise like a flood, bursting out of my eyes under the pressure. I'm too full with—

With happiness.

Fear.

Happiness.

Fear.

Rivulets of tears clog my vision, but I can still see the moment Clay Butcher finally looks at the cylinder.

His brows pinch.

And I can't. I cover my face, unable to handle the throes of what all this means, the gravity and responsibility, the excitement and belonging, of growing his—*HIS*—fucking Clay Butcher's baby inside *my* womb.

I can't.

What if I lose it.

Oh God.

I'm having his baby.

Clay Butcher's baby—

Clay.

Butcher's.

Baby.

He is on his knees in front of me now. Warm hands pull mine from smothering my face. "Do not cover your face for any man. Do not cover your face for *anyone*. You are my queen. Chin high, sweet girl." Holding my trembling hands in his, he stares at me. Inches from me. On the floor of this toilet. His eyes are shiny, intense, reaching inside my gaze to find my soul and hold it with authority and care. "Thank you for giving me this gift, sweet girl," he says in a meaningful, deep timbre that is raw with severity. "I am going to devote my life to the children you make for me."

I slowly shake my head, staring at my small hands protected in his large ones. Blinking at them, the tears rolling out with each bat of my lashes, I remember the first time I saw his hands. Remember how I considered all the men he had probably killed with them... Now, today, I visualise the way they will look so big, gently cradling a little baby.

"What if they ruin your life, Sir?" I peer up from his hands and meet the most striking clear-blue eyes. "What if you hate being a dad?"

"Impossible." He lifts my chin. "You are my air, little deer. So any part of you is the reason I breathe."

And I have my second good thing.

Clay Butcher: number one.

His heir: Number two

CHAPTER TWENTY-NINE

THERE HAVE BEEN many memorable moments in my life, events that changed the very fibres of me. That constructed Clay Butcher. The reasons I act. Behave. Work. My first kill and my mother's reaction to it... changed me—hardened me.

And now this...

My little heirs.

This will forever mould me. Soften me. I can already feel it. I won't be the man I was yesterday, as now I have more to lose, more to die for, more to smile for.

I stare at stunned, emotion-ridden, dual-coloured eyes as beads of tears blink through blonde lashes. She is my everything. Love happened quietly for me, and like most emotions, it brewed against my will. There is—was—no place for sentiment in my life... but I feel it anyway. A building upsurge, then just like a wave, it crashes. Now, I'm below the emotion of it all, surrounded by it as its current controls my every muscle, my every thought and motivation.

It is all her.

I didn't look at the positive test until after I saw her eyes gloss over, until she had experienced the moment herself. This time, her pregnancy will be *hers* first.

I slide the test into my pocket and say, "Stand, sweet girl." She wobbles to her feet, and I slide her underwear and tight denim up her thighs, buttoning the jeans at her navel. I lean in and rub my nose along the little slit between her shirt and jeans, breathing her in. She'll be full and round here. My cock twitches, thinking about her swelling, her smooth flesh stretching, making me an heir. I'll keep her pregnant if I can. It's a state I want her in. "You smell like you need my mouth on you, sweet girl. Let me take you home and spoil your pussy."

She touches my jaw, and I straighten to my full height in front of her. "No," she says. "I want you to make up with Max. Please. I want—"

"As you wish," I say, opening the door for her, then watching her precede me from the bathroom and down the corridor. She is a few metres away from me, but today, the distance grates like razor blades under my skin.

It's too much.

I can't touch her.

Her arse fills out her jeans. I watch the denim stretch around each perfect globe, imagining her belly round, stretching the fabric of her shirts as a feral kind of possessiveness cloaks me, consuming me.

My heart suddenly thrashes in my chest. My fingers dig into my palms, wanting to grip her arse. Feel the weight. Wanting to sink my cock between each cheek, work myself inside her puckering rim.

The need to fuck her, knowing she's pregnant, spurs violent desire through my muscles, a course of adrenaline in my veins. To know I'm inside her in every way.

Walking behind her, I palm my cock and breathe hard, fighting with that need.

It wins.

Reaching forward, I slide my hand around her throat. A gasp rattles in my palm as I pull her backwards. Her lower back connects with my erection, and I grind against her. I growl by her ear, wildly territorial. Over her. The baby. The scent. She's mine forever, and I don't want to share her with them right now. I cup her pussy with my other hand and lessen some of my ache by dry fucking her lower back. "I need you to calm me down, sweet girl. Can't think straight."

Her throat rolls against my palm, and she tries to turn, but I don't let her. I reach for the spare room door and guide her through it. I lock it.

Little feet rise to tippytoes to shuffle in front of me, trying to mind my gait, until we are at the side of the bed.

I bend her over it.

Releasing her throat and pussy, I push her flat. Her arse arches up like a good girl, presenting herself to me. I pull out my cock, all but panting when I fist the throbbing length and jerk myself a few times. The ache. Blood boils and expands inside my erection, the need to come a painful building urge. The veins coiling my cock pulse back in my palm. My heart beats inside them.

Heat hits my ears.

Letting go of my cock, the long hard length throbbing, I tug her jeans down to her ankles, using the material to limit her movements. Then I rip her underwear to the side, baring a tight, young pussy.

Can't wait. I slide into her, bucking her forward when I hit her depths, abruptly taking her from empty to stuffed with my pulsating thick length. She cries out. Just once. *Good girl.*

I still. Release a long deep groan, I see black, the darkness of my shredding resolve taking hold, at just the clenching of her slick strong walls enveloping me. She clings. Pulses. Wanting. More. "*Shh.* Sweet girl. Don't do that. Let me calm down first."

"I want you like this," she moans, her voice strained, muffled, her fingers digging into the sheets by her head.

"No. You don't. I can't lose control with you anymore."

"Who else will you lose control with then, Sir?"

"*Christ,*" I growl when her pussy massages me. *Damn her.* "Fist the sheets harder, sweet girl. Hold tight." I press my hand to the seam of her arse, slide my thumb to play with her pretty arsehole, and watch myself fuck her wanton little channel.

The lips of her pussy hug the root of my cock. So stretched. So pink. Then I draw out quickly against all her muscles working around me for control. I slam back in, beat another cry from her, and study the way she swallows my cock again. "Fuck. So responsive around me."

I drop my knees to either side of her, cover her soft spine with my torso, buck my hips, and fuck her fast, each thrust taking me deeper. Taking her like a fucking feral dog, I grunt to the beat of my hips. Feeding my hand between her abdomen and the mattress, I cradle her womb. She is growing my children. "You're pregnant, sweet girl. You're mine in every way now. My little body to fill and use."

That's it. A violent groan sounds from my throat, losing my load in her early, faster than I've ever done before. Uncontrolled. I pump in hard, spurting hotly, tremors racketing through convulsing pelvic muscles.

I pull out before I've even finished and shove my fingers into her swollen wet depths, pushing my cum in further, knowing she was close, intent on making her come. My cock still drips as I work her writhing little body until she's trembling and squirming. Coming on my hand and to my penetration.

She gasps, "*Sir*," worming slowly on the mattress.

A few moments pass by with the steady twisting of my fingers in her warm pussy. The peak of her pleasure slowly levels, her trembling muscles falling lax to the mattress. "God. *Sir*. You can always lose control with me... but you know,"—I can hear her cheeky grin as she says— "I love you works too."

I smile through the corner of my mouth. "I love you, little deer."

CHAPTER THIRTY

A TWINGE between my thighs plays out in my slow, sultry walk as I stride in time with Clay's confident steps towards the outside area. The entire west wall of the house is glass panelling. Through the span of window-panes, a smaller building is set a few metres from the grassed lawn. A granny flat or a gym. I don't know which, but it's lavish.

The abundant lawn stretches for many metres, rolling over a small hill and down. A trampoline—one of those with a protective net—is set up under a large tree thick with foliage. I've never been on a trampoline. I hope our children have one of those, too.

In an alfresco of sorts, I spot Max sitting on an outside lounger. Across from him, Cassidy natters sweetly, her strawberry-blonde hair is in a high ponytail, bouncing behind her as she talks.

I can't hear voices through the glass, but I can see Xander and Bronson both standing over them, their eyes trained on Max. Conversation passes, causing smiles and chuckles. The Butcher brothers are more casual—ordinary— than I'm used to since being with Clay. They are in jeans and tee-shirts, looking every bit young Australian men.

Bronson is painted from his neck to the tips of his fingers in colourful tattoos, and I'm not sure I ever notice just how many there are... And Max has muscles bigger than my head bulging from his upper arms... And Xander looks so perfectly cut, he may have no body fat at all. All the boys blue eyed, dark haired, confident, pinch-your-self-kind-of-gorgeous. So, really, they couldn't be 'ordinary' if they tried.

Despite that, my feet take me impatiently towards them, until I am slightly ahead of Clay, pulling the sliding door open, earning myself the attention of all three Butcher boys and Cassidy.

I rush to Xander when his baby blues land on me and throw my arms around him, warmth from his embrace suffusing me. He's my friend. I'd do it again. "You're okay."

"Hey, girlie." He holds me to him for a quick moment before pushing me out in front of him. "Now. You listen to me. Don't ever put yourself in danger for me again. *I* fucked up. I went out on my own. You are not to blame for what happened. I am, ya hear me?"

Sighing, I nod because he's right. He did fuck up. "You did fuck up. Don't do that again."

He laughs with that-boy-next-door ease, cool and charismatic. The sound bounces around the alfresco in a welcoming way. "Yes, Boss."

Feeling eyes on me, I look at Max. His left leg propped up on the cushioning, bandages wrapped with care around his thigh, angry red flesh peeking out above and below the white fabric. I swallow and shake my head. "Are you in pain?"

A smirk builds across his face. "Never been better."

I laugh a little. "You said that like you really meant it."

He looks at Cassidy, meaning and affection in his grey eyes. "I did." Then his gaze shifts over my shoulder to Clay, his smirk dropping and his brows weaving. "You here to give me a hard time?"

"I'm here to check on my brothers." Clay strides over to Xander, cupping his bruised cheeks and checking him over for a moment before kissing both sides. It is a very European gesture. One I have only seen him do a few times. "Are you well?"

Xander nods with his big brother's palms bracketing his cheeks. "You did the right thing, Clay. You know—"

Clay pulls him to his chest, a firm hold that silences more words between them. "That's enough. There was no decision without pain." He releases Xander and focuses his attention on Max. "I won't take what you did lightly." Warning wraps around each word. "One day soon, when you're healed and strong, we will beat that night out of each other in the ring."

I can't think of anything worse than seeing the Butcher brothers fight. But Max stares straight at Clay, his eyes meeting the challenge, the warning, in an accepting way. He leans back further into the lounge but stifles a wince that forces Cassidy to inhale a shaky breath as though she was struck with pain at the exact same moment. "You should be in bed, *Max*—"

"I'm not living in a damn bed for the next two months, little one." He reaches out and strokes her cheek. "Don't press this. That's not me."

"Let's play the betrayed brother game another time,"

Bronson states coolly but in a way that suggests he's not going to allow a rebuttal. "Maxipad is being skinned at the moment. I know burns, and that's gotta feel like he's losing a layer. Also, I'm hungry. Those two points are not related..." He ponders. "I don't think."

Cassidy curls her nose up, her hazel freckles collecting along the bridge. "Gross, Bronson."

"I know Butch has visited." Clay keeps his eyes on Max but walks me over to a spare chair, nodding for me to sit down on it. I do as I'm *nodded-to-do.*

"Yes. Twice," Cassidy says, pridefully.

Clay stands behind me, resting his hands on my shoulders, his fingers circling the nape of my neck slowly. "Has mother been to visit you?"

Quickly they flick their gazes around the room, bouncing a look of significance between them. It's deeply personal. Painful too. I can see it hidden in their eyes. Clay notices it; his fingers on my neck have stilled, uncertainty in their frozen tips.

"Why would she visit?" Cassidy asks. Clay's younger brothers somehow grow larger when she speaks. A visual display of cloaking themselves, averse to the topic.

"I know there are some issues here," Clay begins smoothly, an aura of authority to his delivery. "She's made mistakes, boys, but she is your mother."

"Mistakes?" Cassidy whispers. The anxious way she said that chills my skin.

"Little one, don't," Max says deeply.

Clay's fingers still haven't moved, haven't continued in a contented, relaxed way across my skin. Stiff like needles now.

His voice is deep and raspy behind me as he says, "I'm

going to need you three to finally explain what the hell the woman who brought you into this world did that is so beyond redemption all three of you despise her. Her life was not easy either. She was taken from England, from her family, dropped in the District and made to raise you three while Butch fucked around. I know she's cold. But after all she has been through—"

"I don't despise her! She despises *us*." Xander's words howl around the three brothers like a ghost exorcised from a soul. Goosebumps rush along my arms, raising my little blonde hairs. "She tried to kill us."

Clay's fingers twitch. "What do you mean?"

Max's eyes fall to Cassidy's paling face. "Go inside, little one. I don't want you here for—"

"Don't you dare, Max Butcher." She shakes her head defiantly. "Don't you dare. I'm not leaving your side."

Xander continues, "She smacked us around."

Oh, God, what is happening...

Smacked them around?

"*—been through with that cunt Victoria.*" Shoshanna's words leak back into my mind, and my cheeks fall cold.

"She *disciplined* you," Clay corrects, and I hate his tone in this moment. Seeing Xander wince, Bronson turn to stone, and Max growl at Clay's blatant dismissal, I hold my stomach protectively. Something bad has happened to them. Something that they have never shared with Clay. It's clear in the way that sentence affects them deeply; their reactions all mimic and bar as though they can't escape the influence.

"Fuck you, Clay. She tried to drown Bronson." Xander's face twists in anguish as he points to Max. "She left him in a bathtub until he was so cold his heart was barely beating. She left me in a closet for two weeks and told everyone I was staying at a friend's house. That's not even the half of it! She isn't going to check on Max, Clay. She doesn't care."

My hands shake on my abdomen. *Clay didn't know...* Then I remember Max's outburst from a few days ago... *"What about when we were just children? Dammit! We needed our big brother! What about then?"*

It is as though Clay hears those words as I do, his breathing becoming rough and defensive.

Sadness spreads through my veins like acid. "Clay didn't know," I mutter aloud, and they look at me as though I've spouted another head. "Why didn't you tell him?"

"He didn't want to know," Max spits out.

"That is not true!" Clay curses through gritted teeth. "What were the circumstances of this? What did you do to—"

"Is there a situation"—Xander steps closer— "that would make locking me in a closet for two weeks a suitable punishment from a mother to a child?"

"No." Clay drops his hands from my shoulders altogether, balling them into tight, white-knuckled fists. "I only mean that—"

"Would it be a suitable punishment to drown your child if they broke something?" Xander challenges.

"No."

"Would it be excusable if she was drunk, not in her right mind?"

"Of course not!"

Xander's eyes fill with tears. "Then why do you need the circumstances and reasons for why this happened—"

"Because that is how I handle things, goddamn it!" Clay shouts, and I jump to my feet.

Turning to touch his shoulder for support, I feel the powerful muscles that are hot, pulsing, and ready. Clay Butcher, a man whose control is unparalleled, sounds and feels as though he may be breaking down.

Clay glances over his shoulder at me, his eyes dropping to my abdomen. "*Your brothers will only get in your way*," he utters, and it's a sentence lost in a memory that sparks through his gaze like wildfire. His eyes shift to Xander again. "You didn't tell me."

"The bruises didn't give it away?" Xander asks, his voice low and broken, forcing my heart to squeeze.

I picture her talking to me by the pool, interrogating me. Needing to please, like always, I thought she was like Clay. Just guarded. Unreadable. Maybe slightly bitter due to her hardships. No.

I was wrong.

I touch my lower belly.

I don't want her anywhere near you, sweet baby.

"I presumed you'd been in fights," Clay says angrily, his tone laced with confusion and regret. Then he bites out, "*Fuck,*" to himself.

Bronson nods once as he says, "So did everyone else."

"And you didn't fight back," Clay states to himself more than to his brothers. "You let her hurt you?"

Bronson hums. "What would you have us do, beautiful brother? Hit our pretty mother back?"

"Butch doesn't know," Max says curtly. "We keep it that way. No one knows. No one needs to know."

Clay nods stiffly and reaches for Xander, who is losing his battle to stifle his anguish. The honesty rips through him. The truth bleeds out as they embrace.

Xander buries his head. "I wanted to tell you so many times. I wanted to go to you so many times."

Clay holds his little brother, and it. All. Comes. Out. A flood of sentiment, the captive feeling he masks so well, the need to remain strong, to make them strong, all flowing from him.

"I wasn't there for you." Clay's voice is strained. "I know. I'll make it up to you... If you'll let me."

Both men shake slightly as the moment passes between them. A significant moment that binds their pasts, the fork that divided them slowly being bridged. I thought they had him on a pedestal, and maybe they did, but more than that, Clay's brothers thought he was unreachable, unreasonable, uncaring, maybe... Maybe he was... until now.

Bronson moves over to their shoulders. "I'm getting jelly," he mocks, hiding his raw response within humour, but Clay doesn't have his armour up anymore. He isn't suited and smooth. He's confused, and I bet confusion in a man like Clay Butcher stokes intensity. He cares, showing this by dragging Bronson into the huddle.

"I'm proud of you," he says to him. "You were the better big brother." He chokes on the words. "You were the right one."

Tears fall from my eyes, watching them unleash the decades-old lies. They always loved each other, but they were torn apart by the actions of a woman who didn't love any of them.

Clay pulls from their huddle and rounds the chair, heading straight for Max.

"Don't do that," Max warns.

Clay ignores him, kneeling at his brother's side. Max stiffens at the closeness, and my breaths become shallow as my lungs war with whether to breathe relief or surge from my body with panic.

So when Clay presses his forehead to Max's and squeezes his eyes shut with words and pain moving them below his eyelids, I nearly whimper at the rawness.

Max lifts his arms to shove him away—*No.*

He doesn't.

Instead, he tenses on the act of defensiveness but... *stops* himself. *God.* My spine steels, and I sense everyone in the alfresco—Bronson, Xander, Cassidy—collectively freeze in case the smallest change in energy, the beat of a butterfly's wings, jolts Max from accepting this moment.

Max lets Clay stay close. Still stiff and looking like a dog cornered. A pained groan leaves Max's throat as his big brother holds their foreheads together.

A sob breaks from my lips.

"I understand, brother." Clay's strong timbre is guttural and angry and sorrowful—a raw symphony of all those sounds combined. "I understand."

My heart is exhausted, overthrown by too many emotions, experiencing all of Clay's as plainly as I feel my own.

I stare at Bronson and Xander, watching them smile at Clay and Max, at Cassidy, who sobs silent tears with her hand over her mouth. There is so much love here. Even when it is stretched thin, under extreme pressure, through tests and betrayals, they never give up on family. I hold my stomach, thinking about never leaving her/him alone in a caravan...

Thinking about the kind of love displayed in front of me between the most powerful men in the city. Thinking about irrefutable loyalties, not giving up on one another

—*family*. And I realise my fairy-tale—an orphan's fairy-tale—is coming true.

And there it is; my third good thing.

Clay Butcher: Number one.

His heir: Number two.

Family: Number three.

CHAPTER THIRTY-ONE

HE HASN'T SAID a word to me since we left Max and Cassidy's house. He gazes at our joined hands in his lap, at his thumb as it trails over my knuckles so softly it's barely a feather touching the wind.

He's disappeared into his eyes, and my heart drops under the weight of all the truth set free today.

The energy in the car is thick, smothering me with his melancholy and regret. It's not his fault. Or... did he suspect all along? I wonder whether he knew—deep down, whether he saw the signs that his mother used to abuse his younger brothers but just like with the little girl in the hospital, he didn't ask questions.

The Cosa Nostra was infallible.

The Cosa Nostra was his moon.

And his mother is a part of that.

"Can I take you somewhere, Sir?" I turn my body to face his and pull our connected hands to my thighs. His arm is heavy and lifeless until he refocuses and lifts his gaze to meet mine.

"*Hey*," I say softly, seeing him dark, consumed, lost

within his own blue eyes. "Can I take you somewhere, Sir?" I lean towards him and touch his warm cheek; his jawline is coarse with the start of new hairs. As I hold his face, he closes his eyes and sighs roughly, forcing my heart to twist.

"It's okay, Sir."

Desperate to be closer, I twist to unbuckle my belt, needing to crawl onto his lap, hold him, and tell him it's not his fault, he couldn't have known, but he stops me by covering my hand with his.

"No." He shakes his head once and lightly squeezes my fingers over the buckle. "Your belt stays on, sweet girl."

I blink at him as he turns to face forward, the backs of my eyes burning. He is dealing with his thoughts in isolation.

"How far away is Stormy River Junction from here?" I ask.

"Twenty minutes or so, little deer," he responds absently, but pulls our hands to his lap, authoritarian and dominant, and continues to stroke my skin with the pad of his thumb. That is it; his way of letting me in, and I can accept it. From a man like Clay Butcher, even the glimmer of vulnerabilities should be cherished, noticed, and appreciated.

I relax my hand in his. "Can I show you something? Can I take you somewhere, Sir?"

"Of course."

LOOKING through the clean tinted windows at the slums of Stormy River, it seems like a million years have passed since I lived in this neighbourhood.

Housing flats shadow the road on both sides. The lawns have stories to tell—secrets in the blades. Like every patch, every dried circle of dirt and roots, tells of a party or a stripped vehicle or a tent from an evictee. The poverty and boredom echo, the grass never having time to recover.

That's poverty.

Patches of grass.

"Here." I point, and the vehicle pulls up beside a brown-brick block of flats with a dozen men—older than me but younger than Clay—sitting on the steps.

They rise to their feet, eyeing the sparkling Chrysler like a prize as we park. Behind us, our convoy lines the street, including one shiny red beauty—my car driven by my *butler/rat.*

Clay steps out in that suave effortless confidence I adore. That everyone is drawn to, envious of, that speaks of danger and warning without the need to scream or demand it. It's implicit. Infallible.

From inside the vehicle, I watch him take his time, smooth down his tie, and calmly assess the neighbourhood, the park across from us, and the flats to our side.

He rounds the black bonnet and opens my door for me. The air is stale and lacking as it enters the car. Everything in Connolly smells like something: flowers, lawn clipping, cigars, roses, but here, there is little to settle on.

Nothing and too much all at once.

I climb out, and my nerves spike, butterflies taking flight, seeing the world I no longer belong to reflected at me in the stares of the men now swaggering slowly towards us.

Clay faces them, his expression as impassive as the Devil's might be staring at angry stray dogs. Unimpressed. Unaffected.

Our driver appears beside Clay, halts by the car, and sweeps the sides of his black jacket back when he grips each hip. Guns on both sides flash in the sun.

The gang of men freezes on a patch of dried lawn. A new memory collects there. The day Clay Butcher came to town. The men converse quietly and then return to their spot on the steps, deciding not to cause trouble.

Staring across the street at the open park with the old tombstones, I take a big breath and thread my fingers through Clay's. I lead him across the street and into the cemetery. It was the cheapest one in the District at the time.

I only had the money from the sale of the caravan to use, and it all went on this plot. "Cremation is cheaper," they had told me. But how would she become a butterfly if they burned her body? It was an unbearable question.

It still is.

It represents my innocence.

It instils my ideals.

The parts of me that are 'her.'

My eyes start to scorch, hot pokers of sorrow sliding in while tears are wanting out. I don't know why. I don't know why I'm suddenly affected by this place, by her. I just wanted to introduce Clay to my mum. Thought he might talk about his if he knew more about mine.

We get to the spot—at least, I think. I use my sandals to move the overgrown grass on the metal plates until I find her. Then I sit down on the grass, folding my legs below my backside.

I read the plate. "Ashlee Harlow... my *mum*." I pause and look up at Clay. His dark brows are pinched together, a thick worry line protruding between them. I like his frown. All his emotions, really.

Every. Single. One.

"Mum, this is Clay Butcher."

Smiling sadly, I look back at her name. It cost extra for more letters. So, I only put her name. Not 'beloved mum or friend or... whatever.' Just her name.

"I know it's been a while." I pull my hair over my shoulder and play with the ends at my waist. "But then, we spent so little time together when you were alive; it doesn't seem that strange. I didn't really miss you—" I'm suddenly choked on that redundant lie as it moves to the back of my throat, forcing me to swallow around it. "I do miss you," I admit aloud and to myself. "It's just easier to miss you now because I missed you so fucking much when you were alive. I miss you *less* now because I don't expect you... but I *do* still miss you."

Suddenly, Clay sits down behind me. He pulls me back to rest my spine on his hard, packed torso, with his long muscular legs bracketing mine. He's processing today, and I understand. He's still present, though, and he's making sure I know it.

"I'm pregnant," I say to the plate and the patchy grass, and Clay's heart thumps faster behind me. "The happy kind, though, Mum. Not the mistake kind."

I lean further into him, rolling my head along his hard chest. "Sir?" I muse, and he hums in response. "*I think*... you didn't know your mum very well"—I twirl my hair around my finger— "and I can relate. But we shouldn't lie anymore. I miss my mum. I missed her when she was alive, and I miss her now. And I think that you should ask questions this time. That you should find the truth and not let the lies keep everyone apart."

He hums. "Are you taking care of me now, sweet girl?"

I smile at that. "Yes, because you're letting me, Sir."

"*This* truth is dangerous, little deer. There is no good that can come from—"

"*I think* your brothers need you to do this. I think, they need you to be their protector now. It's not too late."

"What would you suggest?"

I swallow and whisper, "Make her liable. I wish I could make mine see what she did, understand it. She killed herself and left me to the system. She *was* never liable for me, alive or not. And now she *will* never be liable for me. Make sure your mum is."

"I have my father to consider."

"It will destroy your brothers if you ignore what happened today."

"I don't plan on ignoring it, sweet girl."

"End the secrets, Sir. If they have to continue to live with this secret. They may look like big, strong men now, but inside they are still letting her hurt them."

"They're still protecting her."

"Yeah, but who is protecting them?"

He exhales hard.

As he contemplates, moments move between us with the breeze and the stale Stormy River air.

Finally, Clay says, "My pretty little queen." He leans down and runs his nose against the curve of my neck, breathing me in hard. "Strong and confident and full of opinions. Using her voice."

Beaming at my mother's grave, accepting her ideals

and my own inner strength, at peace with *me*, I cuddle my middle, cradling my stomach. "Because of *your* baby in my belly, Sir."

"No, sweet girl." His arms sweep over mine to mirror my position. My heart expands in my ribcage, hope streams through my veins, and our future grows in my womb. "*Your* power has nothing to do with me, little deer."

CHAPTER THIRTY-TWO

STARING at her through the glass French doors, I'm tense with the small distance between us. Knowing the profound things taking part inside of her, knowing what *I* put inside her, my responsibility, draws me to her like gravity. My pretty little queen. My child.

Mine.

I loved her first.

And I'll worship what she gives me.

Everything my father said to me is true; missing her swell, becoming a mother, raising our children, would be the worst kind of suffering.

And her mother missed everything. Her whole young life. She left her alone. To survive.

I won't do that—can't even bear the thought of her alone and huddled in our bed with a swollen stomach.

And dammit, I won't share those moments either, outsource them, have others protect her, dote on her, so I can work in the city. Unacceptable. I refuse to miss a moment, refuse to have her live a similar life to her younger self, alone and wanting her mother—I will be present.

Liable.

Madonna Mia.

I'm going to resign as mayor.

I draw my cigar in, the ember eating at the paper, and watch my young pregnant girl play with her white kitten. My little deer is so many things. At first glance, she's fragile and delicate, playing on the floor with a creature she matches. Yet, two days ago, she was trekking through a burnt forest to protect my brother. This morning, she was taking my feral thrusts to calm and settle the volatility inside me. And mere hours ago, she was counselling me with wisdom far beyond her age... How the world put her together so flawlessly, it's hard to fathom such a perfect creature.

She is made for me.

Innocence.

Resilience.

Determination.

Sexual submission.

And she's so fucking fertile, it makes me frenzied. I'll keep her pregnant, and it'll be easy. She'll carry my heirs. She'll make me a better man... *Christ.* I've seen it. She'll keep me grounded. Open for my family. Empathetic and mindful of my brothers when in the past I wasn't—

My awareness drifts to their confessions, to the reasons Max closed off, Bronson lost his mind, and Xander hides his.

Butch failed them.

I failed them!

My focus on the *Cosa Nostra*, on Jimmy Storm, on

being the heir, is my downfall as a brother. It laid the path that kept us divided. I regret my father's ignorance, but I can't blame him for his passion. Not now that I understand it.

Dual-coloured eyes flash at me through the window, and I drop the half-smoked cigar to the ground, preferring her scent to that of my long-term addiction.

The ember smudges the pavers as I step on it and walk inside, twitching to be closer to my reason to breathe. She is my reality now. After the truths from my brothers, the concept of my present, of my past, being riddled with these secrets, she is the constant. The thing I use to ground myself.

She smiles at me, her long blonde hair cascading down her shoulders like a golden stream, and I drop to my knees in front of her, pressing my forehead to her chest.

She holds me to her, and I sigh. "Tell me, sweet girl. Does what my brothers told us today make you uneasy?"

"Of course."

I hum, displeasure in my very veins over that. "Does it scare you? Does her presence scare you, little deer?"

"I don't want her anywhere near us," she says quietly, and her honesty stokes the displeasure to a burn.

I don't like that. "You need to go to bed, sweet girl," I state, my voice rough in that order.

She cups the back of my neck, and I roll my face against her little breasts. The supple flesh moulds around me, earning her a groan for her perfection. I'm so damn enamoured, so utterly raw with her, so unnaturally protective, it aches and bleeds. It cuts in through layers and spills violent thoughts.

Love is— *Christ.* It is heart thrashing, fists clenching, muscles taut and ready. It is fight mode.

"Go to bed," I state curtly, knowing what I must do now. "Stay in bed. I'm going to have a whiskey with my mother tonight."

"I could come with—"

"Absolutely not. Believe me, the last thing I want is to be even an inch away from you. If I could, sweet girl, I would exist only when with you,"—I slide my palms up her slim legs and thighs and cover her abdomen from hip to hip with protective hands— "And him. One day, I will exist only for you and what you make for me... but I have to ask—"

"Questions."

"*Yes.*" I close my eyes, holding them pressed together with my forehead against her chest. Her nipples pebble beneath her shirt, and my cock responds. I mouth them softly, and her fingers tighten in my hair as she moans. "For my little deer who told me to do so," I say against her flesh. "And for my brothers." I continue to roll my face against her. "And I won't bring you into any stressful situations. Nothing but comfort for you, little deer." Imagining her defying me again, escaping, picturing her rushing across the parking lot with my baby inside her, her nervousness about being around my mother, I growl. *Fuck.* "Don't push me now. You will do as you're told or drive me to the edge of insanity. I won't handle you defying me. I won't— Do. As. You're. Told."

"Yes, Sir."

I open my eyes and lift my head to meet a vibrant green and a cloudy blue iris staring at me. Uncertain but not afraid.

She sees me.

Raising one hand, I stroke downward from her brows, forcing her eyes closed with my fingertips, needing to touch her enchanting gaze. "I worship you," I say, still on my knees for her; it's almost a goddamn prayer position.

As I rise to my full height, she cranes her neck to keep eye contact, a hint of worry coasting across her pretty face. It stirs me further. Knowing she's uncomfortable, awakening evil that reaps for her. Her alone. Fixing things.

I lean down to take her lips, forcing moans of enjoyment through them that I claim as my own, suck into my mouth. She gasps for air around my tongue.

Breaking our kiss, I nod at the stairs, then watch intensely as her beautiful body turns and climbs them—

Fuck.

I have to move us to the first floor.

She disappears, and I clench my teeth within a smooth smile when I no longer have my eyes on her. The volatility is there, simmering.

Flattening my tie, I walk towards the cigar lounge on the far side of the house, paging Que to bring my mother to me as I go.

WITHIN A FEW MOMENTS, her voice precedes her high heels. "Well, what a lovely invitation to receive."

I lean back, nursing my liquor, watching her approach in a white blouse and navy satin pants.

This room is dim, intimate, and perfect for deemed privacy. I've not used it since Jimmy died. He used to have gatherings between these walls. The kind that ended in lust-filled exhibitionism. I liked it then. Now, I want nothing more than to watch my little deer in any capacity.

Through the sliding doors to my left, an outhouse with a sauna stands and I've taken my fair share of women in that space, even under the eye of Jimmy's strategically placed surveillance.

I make a note to take Fawn there, have her spread her pretty, white thighs, sweat and come while I watch.

Returning my gaze to my mother, I say, "You have been asking me for a drink for months now. I've been busy. So, I am making time for you." Nodding to the opposite sofa chair, I order her to sit.

Que heads towards the raised corner bar, readying himself to be at my disposal for beverages with *a twist*.

Across from me, another whiskey waits, and within the brown pool is a concoction consisting of a few things, namely sodium pentothal—otherwise known as truth serum.

I've used it in the past in interrogations; the *Cosa Nostra* has used it throughout history.

Its street name is a lie. It is not a magical serum that forces the user to spout the truth through fighting lips. It is, however, a sedative that relaxes the brain and inhibits clever thinking. It fogs. The facts are easy to recall, whereas it's far harder to construct a lie when under the influence.

She slides onto the ruby-hued sofa and reaches for the short glass, eager to start drinking. *Good girl.* "What has brought this on, Clay?"

"I wasn't pleased with the way you spoke in the

meeting a few days ago," I reprimand with a hint of distaste. "I wasn't happy with the way you *appeared* either. Is my father treating you well?"

"He does his thing." She stares into the translucent dark liquor, thrilled by it. Her old friend. "I do mine. Clay, you have far more important things to concern yourself with."

I deadpan. "I concern myself with whatever I choose, Mother. And right now, that is you."

"Well, I thought you wanted me to lay off the alcohol. Always so concerned about me. What has caused this sudden change in your disposition?"

She isn't a fool.

Remember who she is.

"I do not like you drinking. I do... find myself often protective over you... But Fawn is pregnant," I offer as a way to explain my change of heart, my desire to discuss my future, discuss *motherhood.* "I'm making an exception tonight while I find myself in a position I never thought I would be in. And perhaps, you are the only person to understand my predicament. I never wanted children," I say, lifting my ankle to rest on my knee. "I was contented with my brothers producing heirs for the *Cosa Nostra.*"

She folds one thigh over the other, sipping her whiskey. Her eyes rest on my face easily. "I'm pleased you put the girl to use, Clay."

I clench my jaw; she is not worthy to have an opinion on Fawn. My lips slice into a smile that is entirely lethal. "She is not like you," I say, bearing the acid on my tongue as that was phrased as a compliment.

"I'm like you." She rocks her top leg over her other. She's comfortable in a man's space. She knows it. She's stared at the misogyny in our business with venom pursing her red-painted lips. It must have bred hatred in her. "I should have been born a man."

"I don't enjoy children."

"Neither do I," she says matter-of-factly. "You were barely a child to me. Raised by the *Cosa Nostra*. It was only your brothers who were children to me. But you won't be stuck with your children, Clay. She will. You won't have to concern yourself with them. Just make them. You can come and go as you please and fuck whomever you want. That is your right."

I sip my whiskey, wishing for a cigar, but I won't smoke inside anymore. Reaching up I rub my jaw, contemplating her words. They are full of bitterness. Her tone, masking a true motivation. I let the time, her contentment, and her deemed status as my equal pass between us as she drinks.

Finally, I say, "That's not what you want me to do."

"Yes. I do," she presses, with a smile that is anything but wholesome, curved in a way that suggests she cares little about Fawn; only what Fawn can give us. "I'm glad you're not falling all over her like your brothers' do for their women. It makes me so disappointed. I'm glad you're more like me."

"Not like my father?" I pry, watching her liberally enjoy the liquor. "He was never around either. You want me to be like him and—"

"No, Clay. Your father is soft. Your father was never around because he spent most of his life grovelling over —" She smiles wryly, and I glance at her half-empty whiskey. "Never mind. You, you have always been more like me. Not soft for anyone. We're the same."

"I have always felt so."

"You are nothing like your brothers." She smiles approvingly, and I dislike that. "Bronson was such a wimp when he was a baby. He would cry so much. And at everything. I couldn't stand it. You won't have to worry about that. Only make sure she doesn't coddle them. Make them hard. Discipline them hard. Or you'll end up with weaklings."

I force myself to relax, resting my fist below my chin, casual as I assess her every expression. "I would have drowned him," I say without mirth.

"I nearly did," she admits unbidden. And my veins set ablaze, but outwardly I merely chuckle. She discloses it so easily, so seamlessly. She continues, "I was alone in the house. It wasn't my fault. I was struggling. And he would scream and scream. My mother was in England. My husband—" She sneers, derision and contempt dripping from her lips. "Off chasing another woman, of course. I was all alone to deal with them. *You* won't have to do that."

I zero in on her eyes, filled with accusations, bubbling with memories. Men and women enjoy nothing more than connecting over their dislikes, their hate. Toxic discussions are addictive, so I use them. Use her isolation, her self-pity, and ask, "What other woman?"

"*Clay*,"—she waves her empty glass of whiskey, making a large gesture with it— "your half-brother's mother. It is not a secret anymore. Luca has told you."

A woman scorned...

"*Larger gestures after relaxed ones indicate a spike in passion.*" I hear my deceased Don's words. Jimmy Storm was the master of reading body language, every pantomime, every tic, he was a fucking hound, and he taught me about tells.

I nod at Que, and he dutifully offers her a refill of the dastardly concoction. As is her way, she accepts without offering him her attention. An elitist with her every glance.

"Konnor's mother," I confirm.

"Yes. *Madeline.*" Her name falls from my mother's mouth like poison. "She had all the men in the District pawing after her. I couldn't stand the little mouse. And now, your father is set on healing this memory. He talks about her with the bastard. He brings him around our house." She stares at me expectantly, yearning for my sympathy, for my outrage. I tighten my brows. Let her vent. "Can you imagine what that is like for me?"

The bastard...

My children will be bastards.

Lifting my whiskey glass, I silently order Que to top it up, making it seem as though I am drinking generously also. "This is why you have looked so unwell?" I say smoothly.

"At least *you have* noticed." Her spine hits the sofa seat behind her, her position slumping. Her arms are seemingly heavier than before, but she doesn't notice, keenly fighting the weight to finish her second glass. "It was her death anniversary a few days ago, or whatever people call it. And he had the boy around to mourn her, to wallow. I can't stand to be in that house with that flaunted in front of me."

I set my glass down on the table, lean back further, and ram down the regret swarming through me. She hates them... *everyone.* "I don't like that."

"I know you don't." Her head hits the back of the chair, her neck now too loose to control. She is slipping from reason. Her eyes begin to daze and her speech comes out slurred. "You have always looked at me as though you wanted to protect me from this entire world. Even when you were young. I am the only woman you have ever looked at like that. Not Aurora. Not that Fawn, girl. You care about your mother."

She goes on, "But your father, well, he turned out to be a disappointment, simpering after that Australian tart, risking alliances with Nerrock and the entire *Cosa Nostra* to do so. Well—" She releases an unruly chuckle. "I put a stop to that years ago."

A wave of unease rises through my chest, lifting the stakes of this conversation as I ask, "How did you put a stop to it, Mother?"

She tries to smile, but the curve of her lips won't settle, her mouth becoming hard to control. "I tried to *help* him, Clay. Lessen the hold she had on him," she drawls. "It was brutal to see him so *pathetic*. I tried to make Luca's life easier when I saw how much she tormented him. I had to do something."

I nod.

"I had to help end it."

I nod again, using my silence to encourage her to fill the space with carefree words and thought.

"I went to Dustin," she states, and I hiss through my teeth, closing my eyes to her deadly confession. "I cared enough to tell him the boy wasn't his. That Luca and Madeline were having an affair. I did it for him. For your dad. And for you. You deserved better, Clay. So, I got rid of the temptation of that child and that woman."

Christ.

"But they kept him alive, didn't they?" She shakes her face on an *exaggerated* sigh. "Kept him alive, and here we are. I would have killed him myself if I was Dustin. That would have been easier for everyone" She points her long slender finger at me, drowning in the laced whiskey's depths. "That is what *you* should do. As Boss. Finish it. You should dispose of him for me."

I am dangerously still.

Christ.

Did you just ask me to kill my half-brother?

What have you just done, Mother.

The heat from agony clings to my throat as I lean towards her, elbows meeting my knees, eyes drilling holes through her. Stunning woman. Cold as ice. She can't see much right now. Her eyes are glassy, lost in the memory, in her dark truths, in her uncaring recall.

Loyalty is black and white.

My brows pinch at the sight of the woman who birthed me. A blunt pain hits my chest like a fist thrusting through my ribs to seize my beating heart—for not seeing her true colours before, not questioning her. She betrayed my father, hurt my brothers, and set the entire feud between Nerrock and Butcher into action. All the bad blood stems from her. A catalyst.

How much of my brothers' trauma is because she couldn't love them?

My mother sips her spiked whiskey sloppily, spilling some on her blouse, hardly noticing when the liquor seeps in, spreading through the white fabric like her lies.

"Did you enjoy hurting your sons?" I finally break the stillness; my voice is deeper and coarse, as though the whiskey was mixed with gravel. It's the anguish. My hand forced. "Did you enjoy it or are you ashamed?"

"Ashamed?" She slurs. "I was disciplining them as best I could. They were wild. Horrible to me. It-it- was all on me..." She trails off, and then bounces back in.

"They-they were *bad* seeds. Bad kids. Their father is *bad* too—"

I nod at Que, and he leaves the room while she continues to talk and moan. I stare at her in her mumbling, slack state, disappearing for a moment into darkness.

As I consider her closely, panning my gaze over the expensive *Cosa Nostra* bought jewellery and the flawlessly applied makeup, she slips further into a mindless place. When her body slumps to the side, her spine slides down awkwardly.

I want to excuse you, Mother.

Dammit, she is my blood—a Butcher.

I want to pardon her...

The thing about loyalty is that it is black and white. You are either loyal or you are not.

I rise to my full height.

Rounding the table in front of us, I approach her. I grip the sofa on either side of her body, hovering close. She's asleep. Soundless. Peaceful. And for a moment she looks harmless, and I despise her even more for her spite in this condition than when she is spitting hatred. Despise her stunning features that always confused me, that once made me hopeful that deep down beneath the layers, she may be vulnerable.

I understand, Mother.

I sweep a blonde hair from her face. *You're a woman trapped in a man's world, overlooked, and undervalued, choked by the neglect of misogyny, and left to decay. Your sense of the Cosa Nostra, of loyalty, of love, has decayed with you, Mother.*

There is no coming back.

I can't trust you.

That is the bottom line.

"DOES HER PRESENCE SCARE YOU, *little deer?"*

"I don't want her anywhere near us."

WITH THAT RECALL, I lift her feet to gently rest on the sofa, positioning her comfortably as though she were merely asleep. Not drugged by her son. Not drunk.

Then I retrieve the black pillow set perfectly into a diamond by her head and place it over her face, pressing down hard. No retaliation. No twitching. No response. The drugs have snatched all the fight from her limbs.

Staring emptily at the dark fabric over her face, I find myself transported back to that hospital room from more than a decade ago. Feel darkness take over. Sense hot tears spill down my face. Hate them.

"Butchers don't cry."

I press down on the pillow.

"Bronson was such a wimp."

I know the truth.

"You have always looked at me as though you wanted to protect me from this entire world."

I asked the questions.

"You should dispose of him for me."

And I am making her liable.

"Make the tough calls."

Baring my teeth, crunching them together until they ache within my jaw, I apply more of my weight to the back of the pillow, smothering my mother as the clock ticks slowly, over and over, dragging the seconds into minutes until her lifeless essence and bitter memory is all that remains.

"*WHAT YOU DID today was only the start*," she says, *and I listen to her. I always listen. "You are not like everyone else. You are better. One day, it will be your job to weed out betrayals. To finalise loose ends. To make the tough calls."*

CHAPTER THIRTY-THREE

"I NEED YOU, little deer. Open your mouth."

I'm woken by his fingers sliding down the slit between my lips and the dangerous need in his voice. I'm on my side. My head is by the edge of the bed. I can tell it is late by the humming of the air conditioner as it breaks through the quiet.

With my eyes still closed, a moan slips from me as I part my lips for him, accepting his finger between my teeth.

He dips two long forefingers down the length of my tongue, provoking my mouth to salivate around the salty digits. He's slow. Tense. His breaths are heavy but controlled.

I don't gag, instead undulating my tongue up and against them, showing off my skills, wanting his praise.

"That's my good little girl," he growls, his voice sounding deeper, harder, cold. The way he said it didn't sound the same as before. It sounded disconnected. "Keep your eyes closed. Don't defy me tonight."

Something feels wrong.

His fingers leave my mouth wanting when he slides his hand back to take a firm hold of the nape of my neck. At the feel of his cock rubbing wetly against my lips, I force them wider to accept his entire smooth crown.

Chills rush along my spine.

The flavours of his skin, a salty, male musk that causes my mouth to water, fills me with arousal that seeps down to my toes. I curl them as he slowly deepens his penetration. But he is too controlled. Too slow. My arousal is suddenly mixed with the twitching of nerves as dark, formidable energy circles me and him, and—

I nearly gag, so I concentrate. My throat closing around the crown, and my breathing becoming hard and strained through my nose. He's dark tonight. An aura to him that has my thighs clenching, my skin flushing with a fever, and my heart galloping between my ears.

I don't dare open my eyes, don't risk a glance, focusing on the slow penetration in the depth of my throat. I lift my hands to brace myself on his thighs by my face—

"No!" he snaps hoarsely, and my heart stalls before it quickens. "Hands down. Don't touch me."

I would have preferred a slap to the face. My strength and self-confidence are squashed at the bite in his timbre. I cower slightly but fight my innate response to pull away, ask what's going on and beg him to let me in this time.

Tell me he loves me. That it's okay, sweet girl. I love you. I'm just angry... Something happened...

Always about me. I'm not a fucking Harlow. Weak and needy, chasing after boys that don't want me, desperate for the crumbs. I'm more than that, and I need to rise above my own self-doubt, ignore the way his tone shrinks me, and stifle the insecurities that wrestle to consume me.

I have to fight my old self.

Be the woman he believes me to be, the one he needs, because Clay Butcher won't forever live alone with the darkness inside him. I will cradle him and his evil.

My tongue pulses below a thick vein, trailing it as he slides in and out slowly. The pace is killing me. Hurting. It is so methodical. Lifeless.

I squeeze my eyes, fighting to keep them closed when I'm desperate to open them. To see his face. See the pain I hear in his voice flash within his eyes, the hurt that is plain in his distance.

I whimper my sadness but accept the way he's using my mouth; accept the way he *is*...

He groans. "Oh. Fuck."

I ball my hands into fists by my chest.

Needing more, needing more passion, so I start to suck and mouth him. His teeth clench in response, the sound of them grinding loud even through my drumming pulse.

He doesn't deny me the pace I desire, groaning, "Very well, little deer. Make me come."

I work my neck and head, taking him deep, drawing out, the smooth, plush head flopping and bobbing. I dive down again, my movements desperate and needy while his tight grip on my neck is unyielding and distant.

Tears squeeze out of my closed eyes, quickly streaming down my face, wetting me and his cock.

"You think you can handle my evil, sweet girl?" he taunts, and it hurts, but his anger isn't for me. His need is. *I know it, I know it*, I chant.

Oh. God.

What has happened tonight, Sir?

Where are you?

Frightened by his remoteness, by his cruel, provocative air, I use my mouth to prove I can handle any part of him, all of him, even as my heart aches and my tears fall. I can handle his evil. I can.

His breath suddenly jerks, his hips buck, and he squeezes my nape until I whimper under the pressure. He holds my mouth wide around his root, the length of him down my throat, his cum pulsing out hard and fast.

"Suck it all out of me, little deer," he hisses. "You want it. Swallow all my fucking evil like a good girl."

The first sign of passion between all his stony detachment comes out as his body shakes, his teeth snap on a growl, and I swallow around the deep penetration, accepting him and his evil, drinking both in.

Barely finished; he stills.

I fight to breathe.

Keep my hands in fists.

Obediently squeeze my eyes.

Silently, he backs away, his cock sliding from the depths of my throat, leaving me gasping.

I sit up with a start, drawing in air and allowing myself to sob, unable to restrain it. I blink the tears. It's dim in the room, but I cover my face anyway, peeking through the gaps in my fingers, and seeing his blurry silhouette walk from the bedroom through the pools of my tears.

CHAPTER THIRTY-FOUR

"SHE DID IT," he utters, sensing me or hearing me as I press my shoulder to the bedroom wall, having searched the entire mansion for him after he left and now finding him in a strange room that smells of perfume. "She did everything they accused her of doing and *more*."

Wariness ripples through me.

As he moves around the all-white and grey bedroom, his gait is slow—meaningful. Two walls have 3D embossing—geometric patterns in the white plaster. No room in this house is boring and flat. They all have dimensions.

He scans the lavish space, looking at nothing and everything as though for the first and last time. I came to tell him he hurt me, but find him suffering more pain than I'm in.

He stops by the closet door and runs his palm down the red material of a dress hanging on the door. It's *her* dress. I can tell by the fabric, the column style.

I try to keep my breaths shallow, concerned my

panting will stir, awaken, or spook whatever dark entity is circling him. "What happened tonight?"

"She confessed," he hisses out, stopping to touch a bottle on the bedside drawer. His touch is stiff. "To beating my brothers," he continues. "To despising them." He winces. "*Christ.* She hated them. How did I not see that before?"

Past tense—hated. "Hated?"

I hardly have the will for words, feeling his testimony on his tongue, hearing it in his deadly timbre, seeing it before me as he touches things, his fingertips collecting memories.

"She was the informant, sweet girl. She told Nerrock —your father—that his son wasn't his."

Rounding the bed now, he stops. He sits on the edge, facing the door and stares at me frozen in the jamb. I straighten under his gaze.

Where is she?

Clay makes a pyramid with his hands, resting his fingers on his lower lip. His gaze is vacant.

A swamp of darkness moves across his eyes, growing the pupils until nothing but thin rings of blue remain.

Where is she?

This is where she was staying, but it's after midnight and the house is quiet. Even the halls were empty of house staff. I blink at him.

My heart tells me to go to him, cradle him, kiss him, use my voice, but something stops me.

He eyes me. "She... was responsible for it all. She was the reason Konnor was locked away. The reason Dustin loathed us... but she was still my mother, little deer. Just like Jimmy, I had affection for her."

I swallow over the lump in my throat. *Past tense—was.* "*Was* your mother?"

"*Yes*," he says, a chilling utterance that slithers inside my ears and delivers the answer without further words.

Yes—was.

"She asked me to dispose of Konnor," he states adamantly. "She wants the *bastard* gone."

"*Oh my God*," I gasp. Wrestling with my feet, I will them to move towards him. They do. Taking me closer, steady and slow, and I feel the way he tracks my movements.

He is too still now that I am closer, as though he is unsure whether it is safe for him to move. "She told me to make my sons hard," he mentions, emotionless.

No. "*No,*" I say, taking another small step, my eyes unwavering from him. "Don't do that."

Heat radiates from him, hitting me from across the room as he says, "I killed her."

I stop mid-stride, my tippytoe on the floor, my heel raised, my pulse screaming through my veins to use that foot to run away. "*Clay.*"

"I killed her," he says again, each word punching the air. He starts to vibrate with rage, his eyes locked on mine, his anger brewing. "I made the tough call," he preaches—chants—a line from a book or story, and not his own natural words. "I weeded out betrayals. I made her liable. I protected my brothers. I—"

I cover my mouth, gaping at him over my hands. He shoots to his feet, lunging for the bottle by the bedside, hurling it at the wall, the pieces shattering, the crash echoing down the hall.

I jump back.

He doesn't stop. He reaches for another, pelting it at

the dress he fondly touched earlier, breaking the canister open, spilling its contents all over the fabric.

He finds another.

Then another.

Another.

And as he breaks the room apart, he breaks apart with it. Glass shards everywhere. His body shakes. Exploding bottles. He growls through clenched teeth.

But I'd walk through glass and fire and smoke for him. Through debris and ash. I have. I will again. I take a step towards him.

He freezes for a moment. The destruction stops. He clenches his fist so tight his shoulder muscles bunch and bulge. Grow. Demonically. The strength in them protrudes from his suit. "Fuck!"

It hurts. *God.* "Clay," I reach forward, but he raises his hand to stop me. It hurts to see him so volatile and yet— I can handle his evil. I said I could. Tears find their ways into my eyes for him—not her—always for him.

And I know I should keep my distance, but I'm not afraid of my everything even as his evil spills across the room.

I walk towards him. He stays in one place, holding himself together, eyeing me from the side, panting like an animal barely restrained from a carnal urge.

I reach for him, dragging his thick defiant arm down so he can't block me with it. He twitches when I place my hand softly on his chest, his eyes snapping to me, pinning me in place with a warning. I gasp on a breath but stay close to him.

I can be what he needs. "I can handle your evil, Sir."

His jaw works. "No. I don't want that. Leave."

"I can share it with you."

"Stop."

"You don't have to make the tough calls alone anymore." On my tippytoes now, I lean up and touch his jaw. The muscles beneath pulse angrily, pressing back at my palm, pushing me away. "You are not alone."

"Stop it," he growls, staring sideways at me. "I did this. I planned Jimmy's execution. I ordered Dustin's. I may not always thrust the knife, but I damn well make the call. I'm— I'm fucking... losing it." His neck is tight, ridged down the column.

I stay slow and tender, contradictory to his stiff and burning hot. "You're not alone, *Clay*." I use his name, articulate it, make sure he hears me. *Clay*.

He smiles bitterly, shaking his head. "A leader is always alone, Fawn."

My name... I try to smile at him because he's so beautiful and I am so proud of the man he is for his family. He is breathtaking even when he's breaking down the centre, even as he loses all his classic control. And just like the rose needs the thorns—pretty things need ugly defences. The thorns need the rose to reproduce, to keep existing, to spread their roots and ground them. "We can lead together."

He closes his eyes on a sigh. "Impossible."

"Why?" I ask, and his gaze finds mine, settling in deep. "The thorns need the rose too. I can raise your children," I state. "I can love them. I can love you too. And your brothers. I'll be here for them, and we can heal this family together. Don't you believe in me, Sir?"

As I stroke upward towards his chiselled jaw, he snatches my wrist. I gasp but refuse to break eye contact with him, even as he bands the small limb.

He glares at me through his lashes, his chin high, his lips a straight cut across his face. "I killed my mother."

I nod—small. "I know."

"I drugged her. Suffocated her," he bites out, provoking. "Que will find her in the morning. Stage everything. Clean this room. It'll be an overdose. I'll get away with it. Like all the hundreds of others. *Hundreds* of deaths." He squeezes my wrist. "At my hands. And my brothers can never know the truth. This is my evil. Do you understand? *Mine.* Do you understand what this life is with me, sweet girl?"

My lungs strain. "*My* life."

He frowns. "You think you can handle that?"

I look at his hand cuffing my wrist. "I can."

"Don't be what I need right now," he says, releasing my wrist as though I burn his palms, scorch through his muscles with my resilience, overpowering his brutal hold. "Not after what I just did—"

"I'm not hurt by that anymore," I admit, understanding him and the moment, understanding his bite, his need to taunt me with the evil inside him. He was taunting himself.

"That was careless. Selfish—"

"No. It was honest. Real. And you want me to be appalled by it. Shocked. You're pushing me away even though you would never let me leave. What you don't realise is... I can handle your evil, Clay."

Lifting to the tips of my toes again, I place my palms on either side of his neck and kiss him gently. His lips are tight, ready to hiss. But I find a groan in his mouth and when he accepts my tenderness, I fill his clenched kiss with a moan of my own.

I break away from our kiss, leading my lips down his

throat. Nervous, never having done this before. His hands come to my hair, gripping me hard, with meaning and acceptance.

With need.

The harsh skin on his jaw chafes my lips in the most amazing, painful, and violent way. It matches his energy, and the way I am willing to suffer it for the taste of him.

"You needed me," I say against his skin. "You said so yourself. I can be what you need, whenever you need it. I can be the right woman for you, Clay Butcher. I can be your pretty little queen. Let me."

He pushes me from his neck, ripping my lips away and bracketing my face for his harsh perusal. He stares down at me. "But you'll still be my sweet girl."

I pant below his deadly blue gaze. "Yes."

He bristles. "You won't become cold."

"No."

"*A statue*," he mutters, and then bites out, "Dammit, Fawn. You'll play with your kitten! Blush when you touch yourself. Suck my cock to sleep. Look at the goddamn moon, and hang a dreamcatcher over our son's bed!"

I feel the tears rising, finally attuned with why he doesn't want me to *handle* his evil. Why he keeps me at arm's length when he's consumed by dark dealings. He doesn't want me to change. I am already the right woman for him. "Did you think I'd just change all of a sudden?"

"Evil can change the very fibres of us, little deer."

"But we know evil, Sir. We know pain. Trauma. For people like us, only love can change our fibres," I counter, holding his powerful blue gaze with my own. A smaller body in front of him. But a strong heart, a gentle touch, a submissive and a brat and his little deer. "*And so much more, little deer.*"

I continue, "We didn't grow up in the cotton-wool love other children had. We didn't have love coming and going from people who filter in and out. We didn't have unconditional love from a mother." I hold his pained gaze. "Our love is like a *cocoon*, Sir. It only happens once, and the effect is irreversible."

Months ago, I came in search of a dangerous man. I found the Devil's prototype in a flawless dark suit. With clear-blue eyes and dark hair, an aura larger than life and a kaleidoscope of colours—*I can see it today, Mum.*

A man who kills brutally, fucks territorially, and hides his emotions deep within layers of smooth control. He is the Don of the *Cosa Nostra.* Evil. Beautiful. Ruthless.

But he's not the villain of my story.

He is my everything.

CHAPTER THIRTY-FIVE

"THE POLICE ARE HERE, BOSS," Que mentions through the closed bedroom door, and I slide my gaze across to where my sweet girl, my powerful little deer, sleepily rolls from one shoulder to the other at the sound of his interruption.

She stirs further. Her tiny white kitten—Luna—paws around the bed, swatting at the rippling sheets.

I sigh, watching Fawn's lashes feather her cheeks, her eyes batting open in slow, sleepy waves. No creature alive has ever been more perfect for a man like me.

Resilience. Survival. Strength. Innocence, wrapped into a sweet, trim, flawless figure that reminds me that pretty things can survive even in dark worlds.

Que continues through the door, and I consider firing him for waking her. I won't. Not today, at least. "And the press is outside. Lorna is talking to Mrs Butcher."

Mrs Butcher.

My wife.

I look back at my reflection, blue eyes like my mother's drilling holes through me. The eyes of blue stone from a marble statue that is unpleasant to embrace.

Sweeping the black tie around my neck, I feed it down the collar of my black shirt—I suit myself in the clothes of a grieving son. A grieving family man.

"Kudos, Satan."

I twist to see my little deer standing, naked but for her long pearly-blonde hair that curtains parts of her pert breasts but fails to cover her pebbled nipples that thrust through the strands. I lick my lips. Her pussy, a delta between her thighs, lightly coated in pretty blonde hairs. I like her natural.

She walks into the dressing room, approaching me with a sway of confidence that resonates in my cock.

She glances quietly at the ottoman and a flush of pink creeps up the slim column of her neck.

After last night, after swallowing my evil, matching my resolve, and holding her own, I can't imagine existing without her close to handle my evil. To blush for me. To open for me. To hold me accountable to my brothers and to her.

"What did you just say, sweet girl?"

She stops beside me and cranes her neck up, her tiny five-foot-five frame shadowed by my six-foot-five form. Her blonde brows furrow at the height difference. She glares at the length of me and makes a small humph sound. Then she walks away, returning quickly with a step.

A grin ticks the corner of my mouth.

She sets the step down and climbs onto it, only a few inches shorter than me now, but petite, nonetheless. The new height makes her no less fragile from my perspective, but she lifts her chin for me to see how confident she is at my level.

My sweet girl reaches across and adjusts my tie, a slight smile active on her lips. "I said, Kudos, Satan."

She fusses with my tie, and I let her draw it out, my chest warm from the sweet curve on her lips. Smoothing it down for me—like I usually do—she nods resolutely. I know what I have to do for this beautiful girl who gifts me so much.

I kneel before her. "I won't be like your mother, and you won't be like mine." With the aid of the stool, my head meets her abdomen and I cradle our unborn baby. My large hands cover her entire trim stomach. "I am going to resign today. Take my leave. My mother's death... seems a reasonable time to hand in my notice."

"But what—"

"I refuse to miss a moment of your life, sweet girl. I want all your time, all your firsts. All your experiences. I won't settle for anything less."

Her hands fall to the back of my head, her delicate fingers combing the strands soothingly. I expect her to beam, bounce, to accept my offering, but she counters it. "And you're going to divorce Aurora. You wanted a list of what I want. I have one for you now."

I stifle a grin against her abdomen. "Go on."

She takes an exaggerated breath, strength hiding hints of sweet hesitation. I adore this girl's coy strength, her tiny voice and her big one. "This is the list. I want you to marry me. Happily ever after for *Fawn Butcher,* and I won't settle for anything less," she repeats my words. "Cassidy, Shoshanna, and Jasmine will be my bridesmaids. Aurora will be my maid of honour. I am going to find my accomplishments in being a good mother and wife. And you're going to let me handle all the moments you struggle to handle alone. You will let me handle your evil."

Amused and impressed, I stand, her arms lifting, her hands settling either side of my neck. I lock eyes with her, deadly serious as I say, "Anything else?"

"Yes," she says through a short chuckle. "I want you to teach me to drive— *Oh*! And I want to go back to Dubai. I want to see the entire city, every inch of it."

I fight that damn grin. "Is that all?"

She thinks, chewing her lower lip. "For now."

I muse, before saying, "And I promised to give you everything you want. Didn't I, sweet girl?"

"Yes, Sir." She holds my stare. "You did."

Drinking in her dual-coloured eyes—one cloudy blue, the other, green—I nod an order to her. She raises her chin at my silent command, and I finally lose to the smirk building across my lips. "And you know what my evil looks like now, little deer?"

She turns to gaze at me in the mirror, panning my body, measuring me intimately, while my eyes stay on her, not wanting to be anywhere else. Beside me, at my level, she is naked, exposed, inviting, and utterly glowing with certainty. With sweet, humble confidence that sparks a hue of crimson beneath her pretty white cheeks.

"It looks like *everything* I ever wanted, Sir."

"Good girl."

THE END

their broken legend
- book six

Agitation gathers in my forehead, so I rub my temples. I'm dying for a wank or a fight or a fight, then a wank— *Focus, Xander.*

"I know this is a bad time, Mr Butcher." Anderson squirms in his chair. "But I have no one else to turn to." Across the desk from us, my brother Clay stares Anderson down. Most men shrink a few feet in Clay's presence. He's the Don of the *Cosa Nostra* in a Mafia-ruled city, so when speaking with him, it's best to take it seriously. "My daughter has been getting some unwanted attention from..." Anderson tugs at his collar.

"From?" I press, and he looks over at me for a moment before braving Clay's line of sight again.

Spit it out, Anderson.

My brother can be reasonable. On occasions, such an opportunity has presented itself, but Anderson is fucking right—this is a bullshit evening to be asking for favours. Our mother's wake continues in the adjacent room.

We have an open house for the evening; most of the District worth knowing is here, including the owner of a popular tavern who sits across from us now— That's the only reason he's been granted an audience with my brother.

He goes on, "The son of Daniel Young. The banker. His younger son, Grayson, has been harassing my daughter. Taking pictures—"

I lean back in my chair when I hear that name. Grayson *Young*... My headache flares as the image of a red-headed man with a face like a bucket of smashed crabs comes to mind. *Dipshit.* I crack my knuckles as tension builds within them.

Daniel Young has two sons: Grayson, who I have heard is a princess with a cock, and *Charles.* Charles Young, better known in the boxing circuit as the Young Chuck Norris, is a seasoned boxer. And he's been chomping at the bit to fight me, but he's midweight, so he fucking can't.

Desperate to be taken seriously, Anderson spits out, "She's underage! She's only twelve, Mr Butcher. He's twenty-five. It's not right. What he's doing. I tried— He laughed at me when I spoke to him. He said he's above the law."

"And?" I press, knowing Clay needs to hear the exact request leave Anderson's lips.

I want this over with. The funeral was enough. I'm not in the mood to play this role after that, my skin crawling over my muscles, muscles twitching over bone. I'm on fire. Get me to the gym. Get me something hard. Fast. Real. So, I can box this bullshit day from me.

Box the lies out.

Feel *something*.

Pain and pleasure.

I need something *real*. There are secrets surrounding last week when my mother overdosed, but I must trust in the infallible nature of the *Cosa Nostra*, of Clay Butcher— the Don. What was done, needed to be so.

Accept.

Just trust...

Like Max and Bronson do.

Unlike me, my brothers bear no ache from her suspicious passing as they shared no affection for her—she was a narcissist. I know this.

But I feel I'm to blame...

Clearing my throat, I remind myself that my mother was an alcoholic who abused many drugs, and under these great loves, she eventually suffocated.

Just accept.

Impatient, I grow restless.

Patiently, Clay smiles.

My brother's smile has always awed and annoyed me. It reminds me of how different we are. How a perfect one can form effortlessly on his lips amid the worst events. And, well, all my emotions are far more honest. Jarringly, so. Just like pain, pleasure, blood, and cum—*honest.*

My favourite things.

"And what would you like me to do about it?" Clay asks, drawing me away from that simulated smile, chilling to view on a grieving son's face.

As Anderson mumbles his answer, I look down at my fists, the skin of my knuckles ripped and raw from boxing. My gaze moves to the empty whiskey glass I poured when we entered this room ten minutes ago, then to

Clay's glass which spins on the desk in his fingers, nearly untouched.

My big brother is 'on.'

Always on.

Not me.

"Speak up, Anderson," I state. "I won't ask you again."

"Well..." Anderson begins shakily, "you know."

"No. I don't," Clay states, an effortless warning carrying his words across the desk. "Do I look like the kind of man who asks questions not expecting an answer?"

Anderson pales further. "No, Mr Butcher."

"Then"—Clay raises his hand from the desk— "give me my answer, *se*?"

"I want someone to speak with him," Anderson finally admits. "Scare him. Threaten him. Whatever it takes for him to leave her alone."

There we go.

You can't ask for favours without asking.

And my brother loves to watch them squirm.

The clock ticks.

Time stretches between us. Clay stares contemplatively at the man across from him. Anderson's neck gathers beads of sweat, and I watch the red fear on his face rise like water filling a glass cup.

Minutes after silence, Clay rises to his feet, smoothing down his black tie. "I accept."

Anderson looks startled, his mouth flapping with words that don't quite form.

Clay continues, "Xander will get the details. If you don't mind, I have people to see."

The door to Clay's office opens before he reaches it.

Que, his first assistant, stands on the other side as Clay exits the room.

Now, I'm up.

"Where does he usually take these pictures? At his house? Yours?" I ask Anderson as he runs his sweaty hands down his thighs and breathes hard with relief.

I can't help but smile this time—a real fucking smile because that's me. "Calm down. What did you think would happen? You're in our home. Taking up our time. Just answer my questions so we can both get the hell out of this room. You look like you need a drink."

He nods. As he talks about Grayson's perverted interest in his twelve-year-old child—he follows her to the restroom and corners her at the shopping centre—the discomfort rushing beneath my skin intensifies.

I hum. "But he's never touched her?"

"I don't know," Anderson answers sadly. "She says no, but she's my daughter. She won't tell me."

"Tell me about these pictures?"

Disgust tightens his face as he begins to describe the images he's witnessed—some taken down her jeans, others up her skirt, and a few simply of her blushing.

It's not my job to enforce. I'm supposed to get the details and organise our soldiers to complete the job.

In fact, Clay would hate it if I left this sham wake and went straight over to Grayson Young's house to complete this job, but I can't imagine anything more therapeutic than using Chuck's sick little brother's face to beat some candour into my day—yeah, Clay would fucking hate it.

My smile widens.

"That's enough," I state, cutting him off mid-sentence. "You'll have a visitor tomorrow to collect fifteen thousand dollars in cash, and Grayson will stop bothering your daughter."

"Fifteen. Just to talk to him—"

"Yes. That's a lot cheaper than my big bro would have asked for, mate. Trust me. The Youngs aren't just any normal District residents. They are wealthy, influential, and well known, which means high risk." I lean in and lower my voice, done with him. "And they could offer us double what I'm charging you and not bat an eye. Just take the deal."

He looks at his hands. "Okay."

"It'll be alright, mate. Go home," I say, standing up.

I see him out the front door, and despite wanting to escape, I dutifully walk back inside. As I head into Clay's hall, I'm met with sober expressions. To be expected. After all, I'm her youngest. Brightest.

"I'm really sorry, Xander," a lady says to me, her name a mystery, but she smells like my mum—Armani and blame.

I nod stiffly but don't pause to chat, my stride remaining steady all the way to the bar. My mother's favourite place. It eventually became her. And now she is dead, in a coffin, looking beautiful as always and no colder than when alive.

After I pour myself a drink, I stand behind the wooden counter and watch the spectacle. That is what this is, after all.

My heart beats hard.

My brother Max sits in the corner, his usual mask of displeasure suited to the occasion—he may even pass for a grieving son. Beside him, his wife and daughter talk politely with guests.

I rub at my chest, feeling restricted.

Across the other side of the room, Bronson hides his madness well for the event; his psychotic alter ego, though, screams in the vivid tattoos that lick up from beneath his black collar and stretch the length of each finger. His skin is a complete canvas. A manifestation of his madness.

He eyes the party like a hound, always watching us, studying Max and then Clay and then—me.

Lifting my chin at him, I acknowledge his green-blue gaze. His dark brows raise with a question—he knows I'm uncomfortable, offering me company in that simple gesture. And he'll be over here any minute to shoulder me, hold me, make a joke, or insist on a bear hug. Basically, he'll do anything I want or need apart from letting me go.

They think they know what's best.

Before he can corner me—as pure as his intentions are—I walk from the room, using what small amount of time I have to jog down the steps to my car, a sense of urgency pulsing through my body.

I have one foot in my Jeep when the front door opens. I freeze. Looking over the hood, I see a sad brunette in all black hovering on the top steps. Elegant as fuck. Curves like a damn cartoon pin-up girl manifested in real life.

My best mate, Stacey, stares at me, tears swimming in her brown eyes. She's not crying for my mother. She's crying for us. For me and my brothers. And she knows what is happening inside me right now and how it won't let me stay.

All I can offer her is a shrug and a careless, "Dunno, Stace, just gotta bolt."

Reluctance weaves her brows, but she accepts with a nod and closes the double doors. The bullshit event is locked inside with her—she has my back. She's had my back since the first year of high school. I don't see her as much these days. I box. She works. But she's family—a constant.

Wishing I could be the type of man to stand with his brothers and wear a sad, practised smile at his mother's wake, I climb into the car.

I can't be that man.

So, I drive over to Grayson Young's house in the Connolly Hills.

his perfect little heirs

For the epilogue lovers, the smut fiends, I give you:
His Perfect Little Heirs.
All the happily ever afters!

A Butcher Brother Novella
Clay & Fawn
Max & Cassidy
Shoshanna & Bronson

Smut. Smut. Smut.
Babies, & spice, & romance, oh, my!

Get it here

Join Harris's Harem of Dark Romance Lovers
Stalk us.

our thing - book one & two

Have you read Max and Cassidy's story?

Blurb:

The city's golden girl falls heart-first into a dark underworld.

I want two things in life: to be the leading ballerina in my academy—

And Max Butcher...

A massive, tattooed boxer, and renowned thug. And my very first crush...

I may be a silly little girl to him, but he's intent on protecting, possessing, and claiming me in every way—his little piece of purity.

But there is more to Max Butcher than the cold, cruel facade he wears like armour. I know; I saw the broken boy inside him one day when we were only children.

So, even as I stand in the shadows with him, as people get hurt...*as people die...* I refuse to let him believe he's nothing more than a piece in his family's corrupt empire.

There is good inside Max Butcher, and I refuse to let him live in the dark forever.

Get book

nicci who?

I'm an Australian chick writing real love stories for dark
souls.
Stalk me.
**Meet other Butcher Boy lovers on Facebook. Join
Harris's Harem of Dark Romance Lovers
Stalk us.**

It's taken three years into my author career to write a
biography because, let's face it, you probably don't care
that I live in Australia, hate owls, am sober, or that my
husband's name is Ed—not Edward or Eddie—Ed... like
who names their son 'just' Ed? (love my in-laws, btw).

Anyway, you probably don't really care that my son's name is Jarrah—not Jarrod or Jason—to compensate for his dad's name *Ed*...

I ramble...

Here's what you really want to know. I'm a contradiction. Contradictory people are my jam. I am an independent woman who has lived her entire life doing things the wrong way, the impulsive way, the risky way... my way. I'm not from a rich family but I've taken wealthy people chances... I'm my own boss. I'm a full-time author, an Amazon best-seller, all despite the amount of people who said I couldn't, shouldn't, wouldn't... I'm that person.

So while I live a feminist kind of life... I write about men who kill, who control, who take their women like it's their last breath, pinning them down and whispering *"good girl"* and *"mine"* and *"you belong to me"* and all the red flag utterances that would have most independent women rolling their eyes so hard they see their brains.

I write about men who protect their women. Men who control them because they are so obsessed, so in love, they are terrified not to... Do I have daddy issues? *Probably.* Did I need to be controlled and protected more as a child and this is my outlet? *Possibly.*

So... if you don't like that... if you don't see the internal strength in my heroines, how they are the emotional rocks for these controlling *alphahole* men... then don't read my books. You won't like them. We can still be friends.

But I want both. I want my cake and to have a six-foot-five, tattooed, alphamale eat it too.

f facebook.com/authornicciharris

a amazon.com/author/nicciharris

BB bookbub.com/authors/nicci-harris

g goodreads.com/nicciharris

○ instagram.com/author.nicciharris

Made in United States
North Haven, CT
31 August 2024

56787468R00228